WHERE THE
CROWS
FLY

WHERE THE CROWS FLY

SHARON FRAME GAY

HAT CREEK

HAT CREEK

An Imprint of Roan & Weatherford Publishing Associates, LLC
Bentonville, Arkansas
www.roanweatherford.com

Library of Congress Cataloging-in-Publication Data
Names: Gay, Sharon Frame, author.
Title: Where the Crows Fly/Sharon Frame Gay
Description: First Edition | Bentonville: Hat Creek, 2025.
Identifiers: LCCN: 2025940074 | ISBN: 979-8-89299-029-5 (trade paperback) | ISBN: 979-8-89299-030-1 (eBook)
Subjects: BISAC: FICTION/Mystery & Detective/Historical, FICTION/Westerns, FICTION/Thrillers / Suspense

LC record available at: https://lccn.loc.gov/ 2025940074

Hat Creek edition June, 2025

Cover Design by Casey W. Cowan
Interior Design by Natalie Brianne
Editing by Dennis Doty & Rachel Santino

This book is dedicated to the three most important women in my life; my grandmother, Irmagard Bovik, my mother, Barbara Wallin, and my daughter, Jennifer Hogan Belding. Like the Queen Anne's Lace by the shores of a lake, we bend in the wind, but never will break.

ACKNOWLEDGMENTS

I am grateful to my family and friends for their support, to Dennis W. Doty at Hat Creek for his endless patience and wisdom, and to everyone at Roan and Weatherford for this opportunity.

PROLOGUE

BREYER, TEXAS, 1883

B REYER, TEXAS, LOOKED LIKE A pile of lumber flung by sulky giants on land that carried a grudge. As old Doc Winters used to say, "Give Breyer a chance, and it will buck you right off, then kick ya in the teeth, just to make sure you learned your lesson."

Smack in the middle of nowhere, it appeared to rise out of a mirage of endless miles of arid land, lined with dust and sagebrush. It was a mystery, really, why the town was built. It wasn't near anything interesting, like a river or high chaparral, although a thin creek with broad ambition trickled down from higher ground, enough to provide water, but not enough to soak your cattle in.

It fulfilled a need, though. Originally an outpost for cattle ranchers, it grew in time to give birth to a main street, complete with three saloons, a dry goods store, and a sheriff's office. Later, it added a few other shops, including a blacksmith shop with a barn that housed everything from horses to mules to dead bodies while they waited for internment.

Later on, the town persuaded a doctor to set up practice. Then the railroad decided it wouldn't be a bad idea to build a station, where it stopped on its way to somewhere better twice a week. The train attracted more people, gamblers and hustlers, to be specific, who slunk into town long enough to fleece its residents of their hard-earned money. Then, they'd climb back on the train and ride to the next town with a pocketful of dollars and a smirk.

Eventually there was a lady's clothing store and a bank to serve Breyer. All these new folks coming to town meant more sinners, so they constructed a church at the far end of town where the hard-packed dirt was a little softer. Behind the church was the town cemetery, a sorry-looking place with a spindly fence around it. The fence kept nothing out, and often a passerby would see a murder of crows hopping around the grounds or resting on top of the crudely made crosses that popped up in the graveyard. Some fool erected a scarecrow to keep out the birds, but that never deterred them. However, it was fairly off-putting to the townspeople to see its vacant, burlap face flapping in the breeze when they walked by.

"Why, it looks like a ghost rose straight out of a coffin and danced around, looking for God knows what," said Miss Emily Augusta. "It's not Christian. It looks like the devil's work, and it needs to go."

Pastor Green agreed, removing the forlorn scarecrow and placing it in Breyer's biggest garden, forged by Mrs. Cora Sanders, who was determined to grow vegetables and flowers amid the bleak countryside.

Breyer was a good place to come from, on your way to a better life. It was the kind of town that people passed through with nary a thought. It infiltrated no one's imagination, and certainly no yearning to return for those fortunate to seek an existence elsewhere. Even the children in Breyer were lackluster. Playing with half an iron hoop or a ragged doll with so much Texas dirt on it, the poor thing looked as though it had been dug up from a grave in the cemetery. The solitary hoop was rusty and broken in two, with one half missing. Several boys took turns dragging it down Main Street.

Ken, the town blacksmith, wrinkled his brow. "One of these days, I swear I'll forge that hoop back into a circle or make a new one. It ain't natural to see that thing drug around like a dead cat." But iron was scarce, and the amount needed to make a proper hoop would shoe plenty a horse instead, so the hoop was left wanting, like everything else in town.

Miss Augusta, on the other hand, was determined to make a silk purse out of a sow's ear. Her lady's store, Buttons and Bows, had a large paned window, chock full of pretty things on display. It seemed out of place in Breyer, but was the siren song of every rancher's wife and town woman from there to El Paso. Business was always good at Buttons and Bows, and the women, though plain as brown paper themselves, cherished the dresses, gloves, and hats that made their way out the door and into their homes.

Of course, no town would be complete without a number of saloons. They were the mainstay of Breyer and probably the biggest reason the dusty town hadn't turned into an abandoned memory of old boards that flapped in the wind.

And no respectable town in Texas was complete without a whorehouse. Women were scarce, easy women even more scarce. The Crow Fly Saloon was an oasis for any lonely cowboy who rode into town on a Saturday night looking for female companionship. The lure of a lady who won't say no drew them in from miles away. And The Crow Fly didn't disappoint.

It was run by a host of women, and they did a brisk business. So brisk, in fact, that the saloon brimmed with good drink, willing women, and a tinny-sounding piano that came all the way from California.

Here in the whiskey-soaked confines of the saloon, a man could try his hand at a game of cards, quench his thirst with a watered-down whiskey, or climb the stairs with a woman for only a handful of dollars.

If there was a vision for the town, it hadn't been found yet. People existed day to day, in a simple way. Nobody had the gumption or the desire to make Breyer any more, or less, than what it was. If a town could suffer from low self-esteem, it was Breyer. But it gamely continued, year after year, and now seemed as much a part of the landscape as the arroyos that circled it like a bracelet of sand.

Breyer looked best in the dark. On any given Saturday night, the population swelled with the voices of cowboys in from the range. It seemed like the whole town woke up when the sun went down, the homely main street lit with lanterns that twinkled in the night, light spilling into the street. Music rang out from all three saloons. The cacophony of sounds, though strident at times, was pleasing to the ear.

The sheriff, Jed Thornton, rested up all week, so he'd be prepared for the chaos on Friday and Saturday night. By Sunday, things calmed down again and he could breathe easy for a while. Every year, it got a little more complicated. He'd had to shoot a man last summer and tossed half a dozen behind bars. There was something about the smell of cheap women and the taste of cheaper whiskey that raised a cowboy's dander. Sometimes Thornton figured humans weren't much different from other animals.

Like stallions, the men sniff up the ladies and try to cut 'em out of the herd, he thought. *Only there ain't enough women to go around, so it becomes a battle of sorts. Why, if I had any brains, I'd import more women to this town, and wouldn't that calm things down a bit?* He smiled at the thought and wondered what his wife Lara would think of him procuring prostitutes for Breyer. It wouldn't work unless he planned on sleeping in the shed forever. And besides, the women of The Crow Fly had a handle on the whoring business, and they weren't about to let go. He reflected on the saloon and its denizens.

Ever since the murder of Big Andy Connor—the proprietor

of The Crow Fly—the saloon fell into the hands of the ladies of the night, and business was booming. Miss Emily Augusta, who owned the dress shop, had begrudgingly agreed to handle the finances of the saloon for the women. She balked at first, but it was good for her own business, and the whores paid her well. In return, she helped shape The Crow Fly into a solid establishment. The whiskey was no longer watery, like it was when Big Andy ran the saloon. As their fortunes increased, the women tidied themselves up with pretty dresses and camisoles from Buttons and Bows.

Just recently, a new girl, Cocheta, had joined the others. Her skin was dark as clay, long black hair flowing down her back like a river at midnight. Old Peg, who took on the role of madam at The Crow Fly after Big Andy died, talked Cocheta out of her deerskin clothes and into a dress. The result was stunning, like the moon and the sun floating in the same sky.

Jed Thornton cleared his throat and decided it was best to think about something else, so he concentrated on polishing his pistols and cleaning up the jail.

Breyer was in constant need of care, it seemed. The endless wind that whipped across the Texas plains lingered long enough to nick the paint off the buildings and stir the dust into devils that peppered one's eyes and mocked any attempt at keeping your clothes clean. The women in town scurried outside every day with brooms, their skirts billowing in the breeze, sweeping back and forth vigorously. But all they did was move the dirt from one place to another. Tumbleweeds were regularly captured and hauled off behind the buildings, only to escape in the wee hours and parade through town again.

Besides the saloons, the biggest entertainment was the train depot. It crouched at the end of Main Street as though poised to thunder down the rails all on its own. It seemed the only thing that held it down was the lonesome cry of the whistle, twice a week, heading east, then west. One train in the morning, one in the afternoon.

It was a matter of great speculation to see who disembarked when the noisy engine slowed, then stopped in front of the broken sign in front of the station. It read *EYER* and more than one passenger got off, then hopped right back on the train, thinking they were in the wrong town. The railroad promised to fix it, but so far, it had been that way for years.

Old Gus Peters ran the depot. It was easy work. He only had to amble down there on Tuesdays and Fridays to sell a ticket or help people off the train. The rest of the time, he sat in his cabin three miles out of town and carved wooden whistles. Then he'd try to sell them to children, but few little ones ever got off the train, so they languished in a wooden bucket on his desk with a handmade sign. *Whistles - 2 Cents.* Next to the bucket was a jar for the money. It was always empty. One day, Gus found an old spider setting up shop in the bottom of the jar. That was the most action the jar had ever seen.

Passengers received a lot of attention. Men hoped to see a young woman alight on the platform, and the few single women in town wished for a prosperous gentleman. Only one man with any sort of wealth got off the train and stayed, and that was Lyle Confort. Within a week, everybody despised him.

A portly man of questionable heritage, he used a cherry walking stick with a silver knob shaped like a snarling lion. From the day he arrived in Breyer, he'd created storm clouds and worry for the folks in town. He fancied a bowler hat and a waistcoat, barely covering his growing belly. A ruddy complexion that spoke of too much drink flushed his cheeks and watered his eyes, which, if you were to describe them, were small and mean as a wild boar. His gaze was proprietary when he walked through Breyer, greedy as a coyote with a fresh kill. Although he tipped his hat at the ladies and nodded to the men, they met his greetings with nothing more than distrust.

The first thing Confort did when he arrived was buy the dry goods mercantile right out from under Thomas Smythe. Smythe said later he barely knew what hit him. The offer was so good, and Breyer was so bad, that he gleefully took the cash fanned out in the hands of Confort and took the next train out of town the following morning before the man might come to his senses and change his mind.

After that, Lyle Confort aimed his vision at other buildings. Fortunately for him, several owners were happy to be relieved of their burden, and sold out. Of course, the first thing Confort did was raise the rent on the businesses in the buildings, which included The Crow Fly Saloon, Buttons and Bows dress shop, and the livery stable.

"This is outrageous!" said Kate Dawson, a lady of the night, as she paced back and forth in front of the bar at The Crow Fly. "How does he think he can get away with this? Why, everybody should just refuse, and go elsewhere with their business!"

"Where would that be, Kate?" Emily Augusta stood at the far end of the bar, one ankle in front of the other in a winsome pose. Even though it was warm inside the saloon, she looked cool and calm in a sunny yellow dress. "Where would The Crow Fly go?"

Kate looked at her in despair. "It's just not fair! This is more than a ten percent raise in rent, and he's just getting started."

Emily nodded. "Yes, I suspect he is. If he runs you gals out of The Crow Fly, why, he can take it over for himself, hire more women, let you all go, and keep the name to boot! There's not a lot you can do but pay up or leave altogether."

Kate stopped wiping the counter with a cloth. Her cheeks were flushed, and her hair clung to her forehead in sweaty tendrils. She peered at Emily.

"What the hell are you going to do, Emily? Close up Buttons and Bows?"

"No. At least not right now. I'm not sure what I'll do eventually, but for now I'll pay his ransom while I figure it out. And that's what I would advise you girls. Pay that evil man, until you have a better idea, or you'll be wandering through the sage looking for your next meal."

"But it's so tempting to leave, to teach him a lesson!"

"The only lesson learned will be yours, Kate. He's holding all the cards."

Ken Pierce, the man who ran the livery stable and blacksmith shop, didn't agree. He took his horses and buggies out of the barn and moved. He owned a piece of land right on the outskirts of Breyer and decided he'd rather spend his money building a barn on it and running the stable from there than deal with Confort.

"Could we do that?" Molly Brewster peered into a cloudy glass of water and twirled a hank of hair around her finger. The youngest of the whores, she had enough fire left in her to rebel. Molly still thought that if life was unfair, you could fix it somehow.

Old Peg looked at her and shook her head. She swiped at her cheek, and left a trail of rouge across her nose, making her look like she had a sunburn.

"Miss Augusta's right. Just hunker down for a while until we see what will happen next. Hell, he could choke on his beef in the hotel tonight. One never knows."

"Wishful thinking again," Emily said. "The fact of the matter is we're all stuck right now, and he knows it. He'll likely raise the rent again and again and yet again. Because he wins either way. He either makes more money off of all of us or simply evicts us, starts his own businesses, and pretty soon he'll take over the whole town."

Peg laughed. "The whole town except the church. It would burn down if he ever tried to enter. He's the Devil himself, and now the Devil's come to Breyer."

"He didn't have far to come, now, did he?" Kate replied.

Besides the church, there was one other building Confort wouldn't pester. A one-room schoolhouse sat behind Main Street on a dusty knoll. Its white clapboard siding housed Breyer's children. Sheriff Thornton's wife, Lara, taught them four days a week. She coaxed them to recite their alphabet, add numbers, and read and write.

Today was a school day. Lara handed her two daughters their lunch buckets, and the three stepped out the door into a hot Texas morning. They trudged down Main Street to the little schoolhouse on the hill. Lara rang the bell hanging by the door. It's sound pealed across town, a grace note in the morning air. Another day in Breyer had begun.

Near the church in the cemetery, the wind blew across Big Andy Connor's grave, a whisper on the breeze. His corpse lay in repose in a pine box under a blanket of dirt. There had been a murder in Breyer two years ago, and the Texas wind was impatient to claim Big Andy's soul so he could rest in peace.

It took four men to dig Big Andy's grave. The earth was stubborn and hard as nails. Each man took his turn with the shovel, sweating and cursing. The deceased's remains rested in a pine coffin under the only shade tree in the cemetery. The fact escaped nobody.

When they grunted and pushed and dragged the departed over to the hole and lowered his casket, the men grinned and whooped. Then they remembered the circumstances and sobered up. After they shoveled all the dirt over the coffin and left the cemetery, Andy was just a memory, and they were more than ready for a drink.

Big Andy owned The Crow Fly Saloon, dead center in the middle of town. It wasn't the biggest bar in Breyer, but it was always popular. Probably because Andy Connor offered whores along with the liquor, so it brought a fair number of cowboys in from the ranches on a Saturday night.

The ladies of the night who worked at The Crow Fly weren't a memorable bunch, but they made up for it with enthusiasm. Some weren't particularly pretty, but nobody was looking at their faces, anyway. So, it all seemed to work to everyone's advantage, and Big Andy made a lot of money over the years.

It was a mystery who killed the saloonkeeper. Besides the whores, there were plenty of people in town who would have liked to see his lights go out. It took two bullets to bring him down. At least, that's what old Doc Winters thought when Andy was found behind the saloon on a Sunday morning.

Miss Emily Augusta cut behind The Crow Fly on her way to church each week. She didn't want to socialize with people on the street while preparing to hear the gospel. A shortcut behind the saloon and past the local mercantile came out right in front of the church. Emily always arrived at church early and chose a pew toward the back, where she'd sit and judge others.

Miss Augusta said later that she almost walked right past him, but truth be known, even sprawled on the ground by the back door, Big Andy was pretty hard to miss. Two crows lifted off his chest, flapping their wings, and the movement caught her eye. She stopped short and dropped her Bible in the dirt. Then she turned and raced back the way she came, dashing out into the middle of the road, where she hollered for help.

Sheriff Jed Thornton was the first to hear her. He had just shaved and slicked back his hair when the piercing cry drew his attention. Jamming his hat on his head, Jed grabbed a rifle and rushed out the door, following the sound.

"Miss Augusta, what's wrong?" he shouted as he ran toward her.

She tearfully pointed toward The Crow Fly. "Big Andy's behind the saloon. It looks like he's either sick or dead. I was afraid to get too close!"

Thornton ran between the buildings, taking the same path the dressmaker had taken. "Go get Doc Winters!" he said over his shoulder.

Emily nodded and fetched the doctor, who was eating his breakfast at the kitchen table, and wasn't too pleased to be interrupted. Shaking, she told him what happened. He grabbed his bag and headed out the door, Emily close on his heels.

When they reached the back of the saloon, the sheriff was standing next to the body.

"Stay back, Miss Emily. This is nothing for a lady to see. I'll check in with you later today or tomorrow to get a statement."

Emily Augusta sensed her job was now over, so she resolutely walked toward the small clapboard church at the end of the street. She wasn't going to say anything at first, but it was far too salacious to keep to herself. Cora Sanders encouraged her to speak, her eyes dancing in anticipation. So, by the time the preacher entered the building from a side door, the entire congregation was talking a blue streak and asking Miss Emily so many questions she thought she'd faint with regret for even mentioning it.

After morning worship, news traveled fast throughout Breyer. By noon the next day, every citizen knew about Big Andy's death. The whole town was afire with questions and gossip.

Sheriff Thornton wanted to talk to Miss Augusta. She sat in his office and went through the entire experience, dabbing at her eyes with a handkerchief. Her story unraveled before him like a skein of yarn, punctuated with sighs and sobs. When she finished, she sat back and shuddered.

"I'll be interviewing several other people," Thornton said. "I will ask you not to discuss this case further with anybody right now." He peered at her across the desk. "Please," he said, and flattened his mouth in disapproval.

Emily squirmed in her seat and nodded her head. This would be the hardest promise to make. The murder was a stunning turn of events in Breyer, and she had firsthand knowledge. Miss Augusta normally kept to herself and didn't engage in gossip. Especially under these types of circumstances. But Emily thought that sharing the experience with others might end up becoming an asset. In one way or another.

The next day was the funeral. The pastor decided not to bother with a church ceremony, as the departed was not a member of the congregation. Better to lay him to rest outside in the graveyard with a few words from the Bible. Only a handful of folks showed up. Those that did were likely just curious, or, as somebody said later, wanted to make sure he was gone for good.

The whores opened The Crow Fly after the burial for free drinks. It was the least they could do to honor Andy, they figured. Besides, he wasn't there to complain or add water to the bottles. Drinks flowed like a river. Half the town was in its cups by nightfall. Folks forgot why they were there, and business hummed. A few fistfights broke out like any other night, and soon the saloon was in full swing. Before long, everyone was in a jolly mood. The painted ladies had a profitable evening. They took the coin the men gave them and kept the money all to themselves.

As the sun came up, the women locked the doors of The Crow Fly and sat wearily at a table to discuss their future.

"What's gonna happen next?" asked Molly Brewster as she stuffed a dollar bill inside her corset. She'd taken her shoes off and massaged her feet. She shook loose her russet hair and patted her neck with a wet cloth. Dawn was breaking, and it was already hot in the saloon. Molly thought of the big copper tub in the kitchen and how nice it would feel to wash the night off and then go to bed.

Kate Dawson looked around the saloon and shrugged. She scratched at a stain on the table with a broken fingernail. A tall woman with deep gray eyes and a pockmarked face, she'd worked for Andy longer than the other two whores.

"Looks like the saloon will be closin' down now that Andy's gone. Guess I'll head up to New Mexico for a while, see if any place might hire me."

The other women nodded.

"Maybe we should rent a wagon and all go together?" Kate asked. She hoped they'd come with her, so it wouldn't seem so lonely.

Old Peg leaned back in her chair and massaged her temples. "Nah, I was about to get out of here, anyway. I'm too old anymore for all that lovemakin' and such. I think I'll head back toward Illinois and see if my cousin Eileen might take me in."

Kate stood and stretched. The first shafts of sunlight drifted under the doors, exposing the saloon in the harsh eye of day. The floor needed a good scrubbing, and the place reeked of male sweat and booze.

"Well, it's a shame none of us can keep this place running," she said. "It's been a pretty damned good business, when you think about it. Better still without Big Andy." She watched a mouse dart under the swinging doors and take refuge behind the piano.

Peg pursed her lips and tapped her fingers against her chin. "It would take money to buy the liquor and somebody to run the saloon. Anybody here have much book learning?"

The women shook their heads.

"I got up to fifth grade," said Molly, the youngest of the women. "I can add numbers a little, and read pretty well. But I don't think that's enough."

Peg piped up. "I'd be happy enough to run the place, as long as I didn't have to whore anymore. I'd be like one of those fancy madams like they have in New York City." She closed her eyes and smiled at the thought. "I'd need to get a silk dress with a feather hat to look the part. A blue one." She stabbed at the air with a warning finger. "I can add numbers and keep books, but I absolutely won't do it. I am not in the least bit interested." She sniffed and straightened her skirt in a resolute way.

Kate frowned, but nodded in agreement. "That makes sense, Peg. We'd each give you a piece of the night's take for doing the job. And the rest of the money we'd get to keep. I bet the bar tabs would pay for the piano player, bartender, rent, and the liquor."

"We could be rich!" said Molly. "Big Andy took most of our money. If we got to keep it instead, just imagine how much we'd make."

There was silence around the table. Each woman thought about her future. One by one, they agreed this might be the best of all answers. Why, they wouldn't have to leave town and start all over again. They had men who favored them. Building a clientele was hard to do.

"I think Rick might stay and play the piano if we asked him," Kate said. "Hell, he probably doesn't want to leave either! Same with Bob, the bartender. And Bob knows where Andy ordered all the liquor and food." Kate took a final sip and slammed her glass down. The last of her whiskey splashed onto the table. She rubbed it off with her sleeve.

"Trouble is," Kate said, "we still need somebody willing to count all the money and help us with the bills and inventory. Molly and I can't add or subtract enough to know if we were cheated or not. And Peg says she won't do it." She glanced around the room and lowered her voice. "I wouldn't trust Bob. I've seen him slip a bottle or two out the back door some nights. We'd have to keep an eye on him to make sure he wasn't stealing. No way should he handle the money."

Molly scratched at her neck and frowned. "I guess it ain't nothing but a dream, then." She rose and started toward the kitchen.

"Well, wait a minute," Kate said. "I've been thinking about it, and have an idea. It may be crazy, but worth a try. Let's all meet here tomorrow morning to talk about it."

Molly and Peg looked at her, then nodded. Wearily, the women went their separate ways. That night The Crow Fly would be closed. They could all get some much-needed rest.

Later that day, Kate stretched out on her bed while she thought. It felt so luxurious to just lay on the mattress without having to satisfy a man. She planned to sleep as late as she wanted, then explore her idea.

A PROPOSITION

EMILY AUGUSTA SHIFTED FROM FOOT to foot, peering over Kate's shoulder to the street, searching for passersby. Her small white cottage sat on the edge of town, away from the hustle-bustle, but there was always somebody wandering up and down the road, and people liked to gossip. The dressmaker appeared repulsed by the woman who knocked at her door. Here it was, ten in the morning, and Kate was still in her saloon clothes. The tight green satin dress she wore had seen better days. Emily shuddered even thinking about it.

Kate pulled herself up straight and proper and smiled. "If you don't mind, Miss Augusta, I sure would like to talk to you about something." Her dirty blonde hair hung about her neck in tendrils, and she smelled of cheap perfume. Rouge stood out on her cheeks like a setting sun.

Emily didn't want to linger outside and talk to the woman for the whole town to see, so she opened the door wider and asked her in.

Kate peered around the small cottage. It was elegant, with beautiful lace curtains on the windows, a soft green velvet sofa, and two pretty chairs in a delicate pink color. Floral wallpaper festooned the walls. *Oh, to live like this.* She imagined entertaining friends at the round oak table in the corner, pouring tea out of a real china teapot, passing a sugar bowl and a plate of cookies.

"What would you like to speak to me about?" Emily asked, taking care not to invite the woman to sit down. Her blue eyes were direct and stern. She looked out of place in her own home. The room was soft as morning while Emily looked flinty and cold.

"I'm Kate Dawson from over at The Crow Fly."

"I know who you are. I've seen you around town."

Kate blushed and twisted her hands together. Her mouth went dry. Maybe this was a stupid idea.

"Now that Big Andy died, there's nobody to come forward and claim the saloon, so we girls thought we might run it ourselves."

Emily's eyes widened. "Were there no heirs? Nobody to take over the business? No will?"

"No, not that we know of. I talked with Jed Thornton and he said Andy was paying rent on the building to a man over in Fort Worth, but the man doesn't want to take over the saloon. Instead, he wants to rent out the building to any business that's interested. That would be us." Kate's voice trailed off.

"So, what does this have to do with me?" Emily crossed her arms and chewed on her lower lip. What could she possibly have to do with such a sordid affair? Perspiration peppered her forehead, and her stomach churned.

"Well, you own the dress shop in town, so we figure you know how to handle money. And we figure you're about the only woman in Breyer who has her own business. We girls need somebody to do the accounting for us. Molly and I don't have enough business knowledge. Old Peg says she doesn't want to fuss with it. We need to find somebody we can trust, and we thought you might be interested?"

Emily was as shocked as if a horse had walked through the kitchen. It took her a moment or two to recover.

"Surely you jest, Miss Dawson! Why would I want to take on the books of The Crow Fly?"

"We thought we'd pay you ten percent of the profits." Kate's eyes brightened as she talked. Clearly, she had given it plenty of thought. "We could all do well if you'd help us."

Emily thought about it. All that was expected of her was to keep the books, the same way she did for Buttons and Bows. The extra money would go a long way toward purchasing more fabric for her shop, and if the saloon profited, the whores might also come to her for new dresses. Why, just last month, she'd helped Mrs. Dwyer at the feedstore whose husband had died. She showed the new widow how to add the figures and work on the inventory. Emily's thin lips flattened in aggravation. All she had gotten out of her efforts was a thank-you from Mrs. Dwyer and a bag of flour. After all her hours of work! She also helped out at the church sometimes, when old Pastor Green had trouble counting the collections and putting things in order with his fading eyesight. The church couldn't afford to pay for her time, and she didn't mind because she saw it as her duty. She had helped others before. Why would this be any different?

Her blue eyes narrowed. "I wouldn't want it known all over town that I did your accounting. I have my reputation to maintain, you know." She took a step away from Kate, hands folded primly in front of her.

Kate agreed. "We understand that. It isn't something we'd brag about to every person who walked through the door. But it's not sinful either. You would just be doing business, like you do with Buttons and Bows. It wouldn't be shameful."

Emily showed Kate to the door. Her voice was crisp and businesslike. "Let me think about it. I'll send a note over tomorrow."

"Thank you kindly. We look forward to hearing from you." Kate stepped into the morning heat and hurried on her way.

After she left, Emily threw open the window to air the house out and poured herself a proper cup of tea, her ankles crossed perfectly as she sat in her lovely chair. There certainly was a lot to ponder.

TWO YEARS LATER

SHERIFF JED THORNTON ENJOYED GOING to church on Sundays. It was the only time he could relax during the weekend. All the cowboys had left the saloons by dawn and made the trek back to the ranches and cattle drives. Seldom were there disorderly men in his jail. If there were one or two surly cow-pokes, Jed usually let them out on Sunday morning to go home before he left for the tiny clapboard church on the knoll next to the cemetery.

Thornton insisted on sitting in the very back pew of the church with his wife, Lara, and their two daughters, Nan and Beth. He told Lara it was to provide security to the congregation, but truth be told, he could stretch out his long legs, peer down at his chest, pretend to be listening to the sermon, and nod off.

He missed all the Bible thumping while he dozed, but figured God saw him show up and pay his respects. After a restful hour under the drone of the preacher's voice, he looked forward to a nice meal at home.

He'd only missed one Sunday supper in years, and that was when Andy Connor was found dead behind The Crow Fly saloon.

Andy had lived in Breyer for several years, building his establishment into a popular watering hole and brothel.

Jed reflected on that Sunday morning and still thought things
didn't make sense. Something was missing, something elusive, yet
right under his nose if he paid attention. The unsolved murder
hung over his conscience like a storm cloud.

Miss Emily Augusta found Andy on her way to church that
morning. Connor had two bullet holes in him and a surprised
look on his face.

Doc Winters guessed the corpse had been dead for several
hours. He turned the body over and examined Andy.

"Probably the bullet that entered his chest was the one that
killed him," he said to Thornton. "The second one in his belly
would've eventually killed Andy too. He was clearly murdered.
Looks like you've got your work cut out for you, Jed."

The sheriff nodded. As he stood above the body, his mind
ticked off the many possibilities as to who would have killed the
saloon owner. Naturally, it might be somebody who knew him,
and most likely it was. But it could also be any gambler or hustler
who visited The Crow Fly and left with bitters in his mouth.
Could have even been a stray Indian drifting through the back
alley in the early morning hours.

The whores at The Crow Fly were a good bet. Old Peg, Kate
Dawson, and Molly Brewster worked for Andy, and none of them
had anything good to say about the man. Then again, nobody in
town was particularly fond of him. He was the kind of man who
disappeared from life when he died, his footprint leaving only
echoes of a person soon forgotten. His grave was already showing
signs of wear and weeds as the earth took back its own. Nobody
tended it. The roughhewn wooden cross with Andy's name on
it leaned to one side over the mound that bore the soul of a man
who likely didn't know God by His first name, or cared.

Truth was, it was hardly worth investing much effort into
finding Andy Connor's killer. There were too many prospects,

and, although Jed would like to bring the murderer to justice, it seemed like a lot of work, possibly arresting somebody who was a far better person than the deceased.

But he doggedly pursued the case. Jed interviewed the whores next after Miss Emily, and all of them seemed to have an iron-clad alibi, that of hustling men up and down the stairs of the saloon and into dingy rooms where they entertained them. The bartender and piano player were busy, too, until the wee hours, when The Crow Fly closed its doors. Then everybody went to bed until all the commotion the morning Big Andy was discovered stirred them.

Main Street on a Saturday night—and particularly The Crow Fly—was so noisy nobody would have heard the shots. Or even if they did, they'd figure a drunk cowboy was shooting his pistol into the air to whoop it up.

There were no telltale marks on the body except for the two bullet holes. It didn't look like Andy put up much of a fight, so Jed figured it was a surprise attack of some sort. An ambush, perhaps. Or somebody shooting him in an unplanned moment of rage. There was nothing different about the clothes he wore, although his boots looked freshly polished. Andy's hair was slicked back with oil and if Jed got close, there was a strange smell on the body. Not an unpleasant smell at all, but something Jed couldn't identify. He tucked it away in a corner of his mind and came back to it again and again over time.

Nobody looked particularly guilty. Most of the town just looked relieved. The women of Breyer hoped The Crow Fly might shut down after the murder and the whores leave town. They clucked and clacked to each other in whispers, lifting their chins into the air if any of the women of The Crow Fly walked past, then following them with judgmental eyes.

It was a bit of a surprise when the ladies of the night announced they were staying and would continue to run The Crow Fly. Kate Dawson hired a bouncer named Shorty to keep them safe, and kept Rick James, the piano player, as well as Bob Campbell, the bartender, employed. The Crow Fly was doing a thriving business and running smooth as glass.

Jed picked at his jacket as he squirmed in the back pew. He wanted to get up and open the door to let fresh air inside, but it was too late. The sermon was in full swing. So, he rubbed the back of his neck and turned his thoughts back to Big Andy. The murder was an ongoing investigation, but he pretty much left it in his back pocket most days, along with a comb that was missing some teeth and a tin of tobacco. Every once in a while, he brought the case out again and peered at it.

A man of conscience, he wouldn't just ignore Andy Connor's death. But as each month went by with no solid leads, hope of finding the killer was fading. However, he doggedly interviewed folks and continued the investigation. He hoped eventually it might smoke the criminal out, knowing that Jed was always watching and wondering. But so far, life in Breyer trudged on, and nobody seemed to miss Big Andy at all.

Thornton jerked as his wife nudged him hard in the ribs.

"Jed, don't you go back to sleep, now," Lara said in a whisper. "You were snoring a while ago."

"Sorry." He stretched his legs and cracked his knuckles, then straightened as he caught the eye of the preacher. He could tell by Pastor Green's hoarse voice that things were winding down, and Jed started thinking about that slab of ham at home and the beans simmering on the stove.

AN HONEST MAN IS HARD TO FIND

JED THORNTON LIKED IT IN Breyer. After leaving the U.S. Cavalry, he wasn't sure where he'd find work. Still a young man when he mustered out, but with several years in the army under his belt, he figured the only job a soldier might find was working as a lawman or for the railroad as a detective.

A tall man with a quick smile that never quite made it to his green eyes, Thornton commanded a presence in town. Some might call him handsome. His wife Lara did. His hair was the color of wheat at the end of summer, and he sported a handle-bar mustache he tweaked from time to time when thinking hard. There was a sense of danger surrounding him. Nobody could put their finger on it. Thornton was simply somebody to avoid if you were prone to cause trouble.

Jed met Lara at Fort Davis. It was his last assignment with the cavalry, and she was the post commander's daughter. Lara was set to go back East to school when they met at a dance. They hit it off right away. After she returned to Boston, she and Jed exchanged letters. The next time she visited Fort Davis, they continued their romance, then married. He mustered out of the cavalry a couple of years later. After that, he was hard-pressed to find work, so he took the offer from Breyer. He figured the best way to do the job was to be as honest and law-abiding as he could, hoping to set an example and win over the trust of the people in town.

Jed followed the letter of the law like a hunting dog. In his mind, the code of life was black or white. A person either committed a crime, or they didn't. A man was good or bad, not in between. He knew his code was harsh, but he prided himself on his own moral convictions, and planned to run as tight a ship as possible in the small, dusty town.

Walking back from church with Lara and the girls, he glanced around and noted the peace and quiet with satisfaction. Lara put her arm through his and smiled up at him. It still confounded Jed why such a beautiful woman agreed to marry him. Wisps of Lara's blonde hair danced in the breeze, threads of gold that reflected the sun. Her blue eyes were deep, like a lake in autumn, and her gentle soul and calm ways were a steady force in Jed's life. Even after two children, her waist was slender and supple. She always welcomed Jed to her bed. He had eyes for no other woman.

The gift from Lara of their two beautiful daughters, Nan and Beth, was a blessing. If Jed ever doubted God, he reminded himself every Sunday to say a prayer of gratitude. He was a man whose life brimmed with such bounty, it often brought tears to his eyes.

Lara never complained, even with dust seeping under their door constantly, and the sky so big it seemed to lurk outside the window, waiting to swallow a person up. The Thorntons carved out a loving life in the hardscrabble town, and brought their two girls into the dusty part of Texas to build a home.

Despite the sinister look of Breyer, it was a fairly quiet town except when a boisterous bunch rode in on a Saturday night. But even that wasn't too harsh. However, lately, it seemed like a new breed of wrangler made their way into Breyer. Jed found it more and more difficult to keep order. For the first time since he took the position as sheriff, he worried about his family, and about his own life sometimes too. He was more determined than ever to keep Breyer peaceful and its citizens safe.

Tonight, after dinner, he would think some more about Big Andy. Then take Lara in his arms and dance with her by the light of the moon as it lit up their bedroom through the window. Tomorrow, he would start investigating all over again.

OLD PEG

JED THORNTON DIDN'T SPEND MUCH time interviewing Peg Rutherford about Big Andy's murder. He knew she'd always be working on the floor of The Crow Fly until it closed its doors each night. Of all the folks there, she'd be the one who wouldn't be able to slip out for long, much less shoot a man. Although it could be possible, he had a feeling in his gut she was innocent.

He sent a note over to The Crow Fly, asking Peg to stop by his office before the saloon opened. She tapped on his door in the early evening, and walked in wearing a fancy blue dress, freshly rouged and ready for the night.

"Sit down, Peg." Jed gestured to the chair across from him. A chair his wife Lara jokingly called the "talking seat." It was well-worn, not very comfortable, and squeaked if you moved a muscle.

Peg plopped herself down and stretched out her legs with a groan. Jed looked her over. She seemed happier since she quit whoring and took the part of a madam at the saloon. He cocked his head and concentrated on her face. She was the oldest of the women, but still handsome. Her green eyes crinkled at the corners in a fetching way, and she wore her blonde hair in an upsweep, sporting a small hat with a feather perched on top. Peg still had a trim figure and a warm smile for everyone, but Jed always thought that some sort of sorrow was etched deep in her soul.

"Is this about Big Andy again?" she asked, taking the time to straighten her skirt as though she were readying herself for more questions. She straightened in her seat, clasped her hands, and raised her shoulders, as though expecting a blow.

Jed leaned back in his chair with his hands behind his neck. "I'm afraid so. I still have to find out who did it, even though two years have gone by. Figure I'd talk to all of you again and see if you remembered anything different about that night."

Peg shrugged. "I can barely remember last night, much less that long ago. I've told you everything I know. I worked until we closed the doors in the morning and then went straight up to bed." She grinned. "My bed's a place I'd rather be right now instead of lookin' down the barrel of another rowdy night."

Jed laughed. "Me too, Peg, me too."

They both had a bit of a chuckle, then Thornton got serious. He leaned forward and tapped on the desk with his thumb in a fast staccato.

"Nothing else to add to that night? Did you notice any strangers that seemed out of place? Did anybody look angry?"

"No more than usual. You know as well as I do that on a Saturday night, a lot of fellas find their way into town and many of them are strangers. Nobody looked any angrier than the usual lot of cowpokes swinging at each other or shooting off their mouths." Peg stopped for a moment. Her eyes went to the top of Jed's head and she pointed.

"Come to think of it, one thing I noticed was how clean and gussied up Big Andy was that night. He had oil in his hair, just like you do now, and wore a clean shirt." She smirked. "I could tell it was clean because he didn't stink as much as usual."

Jed smiled. "Did he get cleaned up very often?"

"Nope. Maybe once a week. On Friday or Saturday nights. I figured he was looking his best for the customers."

Jed's thumb stopped drumming on the desk. "Now, see, that's something new I just learned. Friday or Saturday nights, you say?"

"Well, yeah, he almost always left The Crow Fly on those nights. Usually for a few hours, then he'd come back to close up the place with us."

"So, he'd be gone, would you say, after midnight and then back before dawn?" Thornton twisted his mustache between his fingers.

"Well, yeah. I never paid much attention, except I was always glad when he was gone. We were all happier when he wasn't there."

"Any idea where he went?"

"Nah. Never thought much about it, to tell the truth. Just noticed he'd leave and come back." Peg gazed out the window and watched a young wife scurry by with a baby in her arms. She glanced down, picked at her fingernail and fidgeted in her seat. The chair sang out, and she stilled.

"That's actually pretty helpful. A lead, maybe," Jed said.

Peg straightened in the chair, and it squeaked again. She settled back and planted her feet on the ground.

"Can I leave now? I want to eat something before the night starts."

"Oh, sure, sure. Go ahead. Keep thinking about Big Andy, and let me know if you remember anything else."

Peg rose and walked to the doorway. She turned back toward Jed and shrugged her shoulders.

"Thinking about Big Andy isn't exactly my favorite pastime. But if something comes up, I'll be sure to let you know."

Peg hurried back across the street to The Crow Fly. Funny how she never really thought about Big Andy leaving the saloon during its busiest times. It was odd. She'd have to think about it more. But for now, she wanted to eat her supper before it got cold.

IT WAS A SATURDAY NIGHT, and The Crow Fly Saloon was jumpin'. There'd been a big cattle drive the past two weeks near Breyer, and the cowboys drank enough dust along the way, they swore they spit grit when they talked. The ride into town on payday didn't take nearly as long as the ride back on a Sunday morning. At least twenty horses were tied up outside the saloon that night, and merry music spilled into the street.

The wood floor of The Crow Fly was smeared with dust. Old Peg swept up enough every morning to fill a big hourglass. And that's the way she looked at things lately. As though sand was running through some sort of hourglass, moving faster with every year. Why, it wasn't so long ago when she sashayed around those saloon tables, her perfume wafting a few steps ahead of her.

She thought of her favorite dress back then. It was green, the color of spring, hopeful-looking, with a soft lace edge around the hem. Her waist was tiny. The right sized wrangler could circle it with both hands, with half a thumb left over.

Now, she walked with a limp. Peg's hip hurt, and her feet ached by the end of the evening. She'd had Miss Augusta make a new blue silk dress for her last year, and she wore it with pride. Peg no longer had to pleasure the men. Instead, she took their money and steered them toward some other gal.

Most of the time, she was content, but every once in a while, when Rick played the liveliest tunes, and when new wranglers stepped through the swinging doors, she caught wind of something enticing. She smelled it in the air the way a good hunting dog found birds in the sage. It smelled like excitement. And men. That man-sweat odor she swore she never wanted to smell again, but tonight it carved a longing into her soul that was hard to ignore.

Catching a glimpse of herself in the mirror behind the bar, she grimaced. In this business, a woman at the ripe age of forty-five was considered an old lady. It didn't matter if her blood pumped just the same, or if her thoughts took flight from time to time. Now she was as invisible as the stagnant air that floated to the rafters. It hurt. Tiny cuts and slices of self-esteem found their way out the door each morning with the last of the drunken cowpokes.

Just once. Just one more time, I sure wish some man found me attractive and yearned to spend the night with me.

Even so, Peg knew enough to be thankful for the job she had. The job of madam and the collector of money during the night for the women paid well. Not as well as whoring, but good enough. The girls trusted her. She never stole a single penny from them. She took her percentage and gave the rest to Miss Augusta to count. It had been this way for two years now, and a good two years it was. With the women running The Crow Fly and Big Andy long dead, life wasn't half bad. Better than some other pox-ridden town in the middle of nowhere.

Kate Dawson tipped her chin toward Peg and jutted her thumb slightly toward a tall man standing at the bar. Peg nodded. Kate walked up to the man and started talking. Before long, the man backed away from his empty glass and ambled over to Peg. He towered over her, his blue eyes half shut from drinking too much whiskey. The cowboy wasn't particularly clean, his shirt tattered and stained. An old piece of rawhide held his blond hair back off his face. The man cut an imposing figure, but there was kindness around his mouth. Peg could always tell the nice ones from the mean ones by the way a smile settled on their faces.

"Kate over there said it's three dollars for a poke and I should pay you. That right?"

"Yes, sir, it is. Three dollars for a poke, ten dollars for the whole night. You look like a strapping kind of fella. Sure you don't want to be with Katie till dawn?"

"Nah, just need a poke is all. I gotta get back out there to the herd before morning. Don't need no big event here. Ya want my money or what?"

"Of course. Three dollars, please."

She watched the two climb the stairs, the man's arm around Kate's waist as he whispered in her ear. Kate was tall and willowy, with an elegant way about her. She threw her head back and laughed at something he said, her fingers trailing along the banister.

"Can't be nothing I ain't already heard before." Peg muttered as she walked up to the bar and told Bob to pour her a glass of water. She needed to keep her wits about her. Otherwise, a shot of whiskey tonight would sure smooth out all those wrinkles in her mind. But she'd have to wait until closing time.

The Crow Fly wasn't doing half bad. The new piano in the corner was a source of pride for Rick James, the piano player. Every night before he sat at the bench, he dusted the keys with a clean rag kept in his back pocket. An old feral cat that Molly adopted slept curled up by the bar, oblivious to the noise. The women kept a clean establishment, feminine touches here and there to offset the clumping boots and vulgar talk of the patrons.

Peg thought of moving on when Big Andy died, maybe settle down with a member of her family back East. But the idea of taking a job sewing in a factory or cooking in a hot kitchen just didn't suit her. Now and then, a bit of excitement was welcome.

So, when a fistfight broke out in the corner, and a table fell over, blood danced through her veins. A gambler pulled a pistol from his holster and swung it around like a sword. The man had a mean mouth, Peg thought, and when he opened it, he displayed busted teeth that made him look like a broken picket fence.

The ruckus ended fast, when Shorty, the bouncer, walked over and grabbed the pistol out of the cowpoke's hand and then shoved him. Shorty was so big he barely fit through the swinging doors. Each leg was the size of an oak stump, and his face bore goodwill toward no one. Rumor was he'd killed a man in El Paso. She believed it. He never talked to any of the women. Shorty lined up every Monday morning for his take from the week and showed up right on time every night so he could scowl at the clientele.

Peg always gave Shorty a wide berth. She knew enough about men to figure he was dangerous. The patrons sensed it too. As a result, The Crow Fly was reasonably calm compared to the other saloons in Breyer.

So, it was a big surprise last week when Shorty opened his mouth and said something when she paid him.

"Thanks." He grunted, and tucked the money into his faded red flannel shirt. He looked around the empty bar and hooked his thumb through his belt. "How long did ya say you've worked here, Peg?"

"I didn't say. I came up from Nebraska several years ago. Always meant to leave here, go on to something better, but then when Big Andy died, things changed."

Shorty nodded. "I lived in Nebraska when I was a kid. Been here in Texas most of my life, though. Family still owns land up near Omaha."

He took a deep breath, like he was swallowing back more words. It was a marvel he'd actually talked, and his voice must have sounded loud in his ears. His dark brown eyes looked puzzled, as though he'd somehow surprised himself by being friendly. He turned and walked away without even a goodbye.

Peg walked over to the bartender. "Bob, where the hell does Shorty live, anyway?"

Campbell shrugged. He set down a cloudy glass and swiped at a cheroot that hadn't made its way into the ash can. "I dunno. I think he made camp a few miles out of town. He rides in on an old pinto and ties it out front all night. Then turns around and leaves with nary a word."

Peg and Shorty hadn't exchanged many words since that day, but each Saturday night, Shorty stood in a corner of The Crow Fly, watching over the saloon. Having him was a comfort, and the women were grateful. Peg walked back out on to the floor sipping her water, and pasting a smile on her face.

JOKERS, WILD

EVERYBODY IN BREYER KNEW PEG was the madam at The Crow Fly. It amused her that the men acted a little respectfully around her, as though she could pick who they could be with on a Saturday night. It was up to the gals, pure and simple. Peg had nothing to do with it. All she did was take their money. Generally speaking, Peg and the women were treated kindly.

So, it was unusual when a herd of cowpokes came to town and swaggered through the door like they owned the place, dusting the saloon with easy insults and stubborn behavior. One of them noticed Peg right off and sneered. The man was short, with black curls that stuck straight up on his head as though he'd slept in a windstorm. He wore a filthy blue bandana tied around his neck and his shirt was torn at the shoulder. He stalked over to Peg and looked her up and down.

"Is this the best this joint can supply?" he asked. "Some old heifer prancing around in a blue dress?" He chuckled. "If that's the case, bartender, then load me up on liquor so I can't see near as well as I do now."

The others laughed and nudged her aside on the way to the

bar. She lost her balance and bumped into Rick on the piano bench. Rick glared at the men.

"Rude bastards," he said. "Pay them no mind."

Peg flushed. She peered around the saloon to see who heard. Several men slid their gaze away, avoiding eye contact. They were embarrassed for her, and that made the insult all the worse.

Shorty stood in the corner near the potted plant, watching the newcomers with cold eyes. He picked at his teeth with a fingernail, pushed off from the wall and sauntered over to the bar, but kept quiet. After all, it wasn't his job to teach these men manners. It was his job to teach them a lesson.

The wranglers must have been with the herd for a long time because they kept the women busy all night long. They'd take a girl upstairs, then come back down for another drink or to play cards. Then start all over again.

All the time, Peg wandered around the saloon, smiling and making small talk with the customers, acting as though she wasn't cut to pieces by what that damned cowboy said. And over and over, she took their money and shoved it into the blue beaded purse she kept on a chain over one shoulder.

The night grew rowdier. The more the liquor flowed, the more the men at the bar raised their voices. A few scuffles broke out, which was natural for a night in town. Several men played cards, while others wandered from the bar to the card tables, watching the games, then back again to the bar. Before long, the noise was deafening. The short man who insulted Peg shoved one of his friends into a wall. The friend pushed back, and they wrestled. They laughed and knocked into each other harder, bumping into a table and scattering the cards.

Then the party moved out into Main Street. The troublemakers fired shots into the air. Rowdy revelers mounted their horses and galloped up and down the street, shooting off their mouths as well as their pistols.

The sheriff had his feet up in his office, reading a book about breeding cattle. He'd just been dozing off when the racket started. Jed Thornton jammed his pistol in its holster, grabbed his rifle, and headed for The Crow Fly.

The street was thick with gunsmoke. Men and horses flooded the dusty area in front of the saloon. They made so much ruckus, the patrons of the two other saloons came out to see what was going on. One or two joined in the fun.

Jed fired the rifle in the air, then shot his pistol four times in succession, a rapid set of pops that got everyone's attention.

"That's enough rabble-rousing!" he said. "Stop with the firearms or I'll have to confiscate them. Either go back to camp or back into the saloon, behave yourselves, and quit bothering the folks of Breyer."

Two of the men scowled. One put his hand on his holster, as though he meant to draw his gun, but changed his mind when he saw the look on Thornton's face. Instead, he tethered his horse back on the rail and walked into The Crow Fly. His friend followed him, busting through the doors so hard, they swung back and forth as though a dust devil had come through town.

Peg was still nursing her hurt feelings when the short cowboy approached her again. He sidled close and grinned.

"Well, look here, Jim. I think I've drunk enough whiskey that even this heifer looks good enough to poke!" He wound dirty fingers around Peg's wrist and chortled. "How much will you pay me, Granny, to give you a little ride?"

The men laughed and whooped. Peg blushed clear up to her roots and pushed him away.

"Leave me alone or I'll have to ask you to leave!"

"I ain't leavin' till I want to leave, and I ain't ready yet." He grinned at her through broken teeth, shoved her aside, and stalked over to the bar.

Peg was overwhelmed and upset, but determined nobody was going to see her cry. She swept through the saloon and out the back door.

In the alley where Big Andy was found dead, the ruckus inside The Crow Fly was a little quieter. The night was balmy. Stars poked through the sky, reminding Peg of the diamonds she once saw on a fancy lady in El Paso. Peg sat on the bottom stair and welled up with tears as she straightened her skirt.

I could have been fancy once, she thought. *It doesn't matter who you are, but what turn your fortunes take.*

FOR MARGARET RUTHERFORD, FORTUNES TOOK a bad turn several years ago, somewhere west of Omaha, Nebraska. Her husband, Samuel, never called her Peg. He said she'd always be Margaret to him. Samuel was a kind man. A gentleman. He wasn't rough like the men in Breyer.

They met when Peg was working at her father's general store. Samuel was the local lawyer, always coming through the door in a nicely pressed suit with a pocket watch and a dapper hat. He was ten years older than her. Small wisps of gray hair touched his temples. Peg thought it made him look distinguished. Samuel was a little portly. His waistcoat could use some letting out. It only added to the look of success. When he showed an interest in Peg, she could barely believe that such an educated man might be interested in her, and after a brief courtship, she eagerly agreed to his proposal.

They married in a tiny church on the outskirts of town, old Pastor Anderson performing the ceremony. Peg still had her wedding dress—white with tiny pink flowers embroidered on the bodice, and a deep purple belt around the waist. She never wore it again, but couldn't bear to part with it. Peg carefully packed it in an old, tattered dress box, a memory she could touch.

After three years of marriage, they had a little boy, Jody, who kept Peg so busy she had little time to think about anything else. But Samuel did enough thinking for both of them.

He wanted to move west. Maybe all the way to California.

"There's sure to be a need out there for lawyers," he told Peg one night. He reached across the table and helped himself to another piece of chicken. "After all, the gold miners need somebody to help them with the paperwork for their claims. I figure I'd set up an office up near Placerville and we could live a good life." He settled back in his chair with a satisfied burp. "Lovely dinner, my dear. I'm gonna look into my idea, Margaret."

Peg wasn't so sure. Life was peaceful and comfortable in Illinois. She'd heard stories about hostile Indians and bandits out west. Samuel sent letters to California, and when he got a reply, as far as he was concerned, the decision was made, despite Peg's concerns. He figured she'd get used to the idea. She eventually did, thinking it might be a great adventure for Jody and the chance to live an even better life if Samuel's clients paid him well. Before she knew it, they were moving ahead with plans, and Peg decided it was time to start packing.

"Leave it all here, Margaret," Samuel said, surveying their home. "Just pack our clothes and our important papers and such in a steamer trunk we'll take on the train and later I will commission some furniture and household things from the general store in Placerville." He turned silvery blue eyes to Peg and smiled. "You see, the train won't take us all the way to Placerville. At some point, when the rails run out, we'll need to hire a wagon. So, it's best we travel light." He pecked her on the cheek and gave her arm a squeeze.

Samuel's enthusiasm was contagious and soon Peg became excited and looked forward to the move. Life in Illinois was so quiet you could feel your memories of the day walking right out the door every night. There wasn't much to hang your hat on. Dawn, supper, sunset. Washing clothes. Tending Jody. Maybe this adventure wasn't a half-bad idea. It was hard to leave behind some of her possessions, but Samuel assured her he would replace them.

DARKNESS RIDES
AN IRON HORSE

THE TRAIN OUT OF CHICAGO was crowded with travelers. But soon, passengers disembarked along the way as the train pulled into town after town. Folks trickled in and out at each depot, unfamiliar faces heading for a new land.

Peg remembered the night that changed her life the way a person picks at a scab. It's there, it hurts, but it's just too tempting to not leave it alone. The more she picked at it, the less it healed.

Jody had been fussy the whole day. The train rocked back and forth on spindly rails over rough ground, and the jarring motion made him cry. There were only a few people in the car besides the Rutherfords. An older couple who kept a picnic basket between their feet peered at Peg with curiosity. When Jody cried, they smiled, but Peg could see it was strained. Two men rode alone, one near the front of the car, and one in the middle. Both seemed lost in thought. Jody's behavior might have annoyed one of the men, but he'd kept his eyes down and looked out the window, mouth set in a grim line. It was midafternoon and the day was warming. Dust billowed in from the windows, cloaking the floor with a fine powder.

The sun said farewell before Jody finally fell asleep. He spread himself between Peg and Samuel like a puppy, a small trickle of drool running out of his mouth and on to Samuel's pant leg. Jody's red hair was matted on his forehead, and the few freckles that danced across his nose looked pale in the shadowy car. Outside, the sky lit up in shades of pink and russet, so pretty it took Peg's breath away.

Funny the things you remember, thought Peg as she stared up at the starlit sky. In her dreams at night, she recalled Samuel's pant leg over and over again, thinking how she had to wash it when they'd reach California. She'd wake up and always wonder if she had the chance to clean it, if things would have turned out differently.

The train car was darkening in the coming sunset. A lantern on a hook swung near the front of the car, but the conductor hadn't lit it yet. It was stifling inside, even though the windows were open. A few cinders blew in through the open spaces and nestled on the floor. A man stamped them out with his boot. Peg remembered looking down at her hands and clucking to herself. Her nails were dirty, and her palms were clammy.

For a time, that was the only thing she remembered. Her fingernails. But later, things crept back into her memory. She recalled the sudden grinding of the brakes as the train slowed, then stopped altogether. The sound of footsteps overhead seemed strange. Peg turned to Samuel with questioning eyes. Why was somebody walking on top of the passenger car? Was something wrong with the train?

The door at the back of the car flew open. Fresh air rushed in, and for a moment, Peg welcomed it.

"Everybody sit down and shut up and I won't shoot!" said a male voice behind her. His boots made a scraping noise on the floor as the man approached. Peg stiffened.

"See here! Stop at once!" The man in the middle seat stood up, hands on hips. He threw back his coat, revealing a set of pistols.

A bullet hit him straight between his eyes and he fell like a sapling into the aisle. Somebody screamed. Peg remembered later that it was her.

A calloused hand grabbed her by the elbow, yanked her out of the seat and shoved her onto the floor. Samuel pushed Jody off him and tried to stand. Jody hit the floor and woke up howling. Sobbing, he tried to climb back into his father's lap. A man reached over the seat and hit Samuel on the head with the back of his pistol.

"Shut that kid up!"

Jody looked up from the floor with teary eyes at the bandit, and his mouth opened wide. He shrieked. Peg still remembered the sound of the gun cocking, the sharp report, the way it blew Jody backward, then he slumped along the seat as though he were sleeping.

Another sharp report of the pistol, and Samuel fell forward in his seat, the back of his head coated in blood.

Peg tried to get up, but somebody pushed her down. She hit her head on the floor. As if in a dream, she heard guns popping all around her, the acrid smell of it, mixed with the cinders and filth, blended under her fingernails for the rest of her life.

She struggled to rise once more, then something sharp grazed along her ribs, ripping into her flesh and searing with pain.

I'm dying, and it's okay. I will be with Samuel and Jody.

God had different plans, it seemed. Perhaps He was the kind of God that liked to be cruel because Peg woke up outside on the side of the tracks, with a handful of dirt in her fist. There were voices all around, murmurs and shouts. Her head reeled when she tried to sit up. A woman she didn't recognize rushed over and nudged her back to the ground with a gentle hand.

"Here now, ma'am, rest easy. You took a bullet, but it's gonna be okay. Just pierced your side, it looks like to me. We'll be startin' back on the train just as soon as things get sorted out."

"Where's my husband? Where's my son?" Peg was frantic, as she remembered nothing.

Such a simple question, but one met with silence by the other passengers that cut so deep, Peg thought she'd gone deaf.

In that instant, Peg's life changed. She hardly knew where she was. Barely felt people helping her back on the train. Never cared where they were going or how they got there. The train raced onward into the darkness as Peg slipped in and out of consciousness.

The small whistle-stop on the prairie overflowed with folks when the weary train pulled into the station. Some were gawkers, having heard of the robbery, while others were there to help. Peg found out later that along with Samuel and Jody, the other man in her car was shot and killed by the robbers. The elderly couple fell to the floor and stayed there, clutching each other and praying. They were spared. Two more people a few cars ahead were murdered also. The bandits escaped. But they left a trail of heartache that would never fade away.

Peg buried Samuel and Jody in the small town on a hill overlooking miles of waving grass. The undertaker pounded two rough crosses into their graves. A woman in town painted their names on the wood. She didn't spell the last name right. Peg didn't bother to correct her. The railroad paid for the burials and offered to provide a ticket for Peg to go back to Illinois. She declined. She wasn't about to leave her family in the arms of the wilderness. When she wasn't numb, she was hysterical. She had nowhere to go, and nothing in the world held any future.

The local inn put her up for several days. But eventually Peg had to figure out what to do. Mrs. Sutter, the proprietor, kindly offered that she stay at the inn, in exchange for light work, such as helping her with the cleaning and perhaps a little cooking. Peg agreed. She had no choice. None of it mattered, anyway.

Peg never smiled. She didn't talk much. It was as though a dark veil had been pulled over her head and dimmed her vision and stifled her breath. In Peg's world, the sun never shone. The moon never filled the sky with its dreamy milk. Voices were muted behind a constant ringing in her ears and the distraction of loss.

Eventually, burning anger replaced her vast sorrow. There was nothing left for her. Once in a while, she thought of joining her family buried at the foot of that hill and lying down forever. The sliver of anger smoldered, then bloomed inside her heart. It was the only thing that kept her going. She hated everybody and everything. And most of all, she hated herself. Hated herself for surviving. For breathing. Hated the breeze on her face and the smell of a coming spring. The only love she had was for the ragged crosses in the cemetery.

ONE NIGHT, WHEN THERE WAS little more than a slice of moon in the April sky, Peg threw a shawl over her shoulder and walked through town and up to the graveyard as she did every night. It was almost dark. It wasn't until she was near the crosses that she was aware of footfalls behind her. Startled, she turned and saw the local saloon owner stopping a few feet away. He wore a tall black hat and stroked his graying mustache while mustering up a smile. He nodded at Peg and glanced around the cemetery.

Pulling her shawl tighter, Peg tried to walk around him. He reached out and touched her arm. Peg froze, then rage rose inside her.

"Let me go!" she said and yanked her arm away, taking a step back.

The saloon owner cleared his throat. He took his hat off and stood with legs apart, his eyes glinting in the moonlight. His nose was long and crooked. He looked like a rat when he smiled, teeth sharp and jagged.

"Evening. Sorry if I startled you. I'm Jack Crawford. I own

the Queen of Hearts Saloon. I know your story, Margaret," he said. "Well, hell, I guess the whole town knows what happened to you and your family. I'm just as sorry as I can be for your loss. A fine-looking woman like you... well, here you are in this god-forsaken town. I know you're workin' for room and board over at the inn, and little more. It's a real shame."

He hesitated, scuffed at the ground with his boot, and cleared his throat again. "Looks to me like you could use some money, and we... well, we could sure use another woman at the saloon." His eyes flicked to her blonde hair, then down to her slender waist.

"Doing what?"

"What do you think, Missus Rutherford?"

"Are you asking me to entertain men?" Her anger bloomed into a deep flame. If she'd had a gun, she thought later, she'd have shot him right there in the cemetery. The rage, the sorrow, the loneliness brewed in her soul like a self-destructive poison.

Then it burst as though a volcano blew, or a boil was lanced.

Peg threw her head back and laughed. "Sure, why not?"

She didn't know why she did it. Self-hatred. Deep sorrow. Madness. Probably madness, she figured much later. A reason to self-destruct. A place to go where she had the greatest amount of disgust for herself. Peg, the survivor. Peg, the mother with a child who no longer breathed. She hated the children in town. Hated the mothers. Margaret Rutherford hated everything. So why not hate herself just as much?

That night, Peg climbed the stairs of the Queen of Hearts for the first time, undressed and let a stranger have sex with her. She closed her eyes and drifted far away, back to a little house in Illi-nois and strained to listen to the sound of a redheaded boy in the yard, playing with their old rooster, Hank. The man finished and rose off her. He left without a goodbye. Peg stood up and stared at herself in the mirror. She didn't recognize the woman who stared back with vacant eyes. She shuddered, then got back in her dress and went downstairs.

Peg did it again. And again. So many times, that their faces were a blur, their names meaningless. She wondered if any of them were the robbers. If she ever found out, she'd shoot them with their own pistols when they rolled off her. And in her mind, they were all robbers because they took something from her she would never find again. Her fury and self-hatred fueled her day after day.

But after a while, something else happened. Peg discovered that being held, having sex, rolling in the squat bed in a bare room with a strange man, brought her release. A kind of reprieve from the ghosts that haunted her in the daytime. She knew those ghosts would never walk into this saloon, would never hang above the rafters and look down on her performing these acts.

She enjoyed being a whore. She enjoyed the moment when a man picked her out from the other women and walked her upstairs, unlaced her bodice, and buried his face between her breasts. The hours and minutes when he took her away from herself helped, then he'd leave her on a sea of sorrow when dawn broke.

Three years later, Peg hooked up with a gambler named Jake who decided he wanted to ride to Texas. When he asked her to come along, she said yes. Without even a backward glance at the cemetery on the hill that housed her departed beloveds, she rode off behind him on a spindly buckskin under a shameful moon.

Jake abandoned her in El Paso. Gambling was good, and he was making some decent money. He didn't need Peg around anymore. She was useless now. There were plenty of pretty women to poke in town, and Peg was becoming too much of a burden, with her expressionless face and anger.

Peg didn't care. She mounted the buckskin and rode with no particular place to go. She sang and swore and muttered to herself all the way across the hardscrabble landscape until the old horse gave out and fell to his knees about two miles out of Breyer. Peg left him there in the middle of a windstorm and walked the rest of the way to town and right up to The Crow Fly. Big Andy was more than happy to add another woman to the saloon and Peg was more than happy to begin forgetting again, until the town in Nebraska was nothing more than a mirage, and Samuel and Jody were figments of her imagination.

Over time, she healed. But it was far too late to look for anything else to do. And when Big Andy died, and the whores took over the saloon, it was more than enough for her to decide to stay. She wasn't half lonely here, and although nobody knew the truth about her life, somehow she'd found solace in the smiles of the other women, the tinny sound of the piano, and the smell of men on a Saturday night.

SIGHING, SHE STOOD, SMOOTHED HER blue silk dress and patted her hair. Best to stop ruminating, get back inside and finish out the night, despite the commotion inside. Her memories always exhausted her. She would sleep late tomorrow.

IN THE WAKE
OF MIDNIGHT

WHEN A HAND CLAPPED OVER her mouth and a brawny arm drew her into the shadows, Peg's first thought was *I don't want to die.* Shocked by this admission, she struggled to free herself from her captor. "Look here, Randall, the old granny's got gumption!" The short cowboy with the broken teeth turned her around, hand still clasped over her mouth so she couldn't scream. His other hand snatched at the beaded purse on her shoulder and tossed it to his friend. "Take this and run around front, mount up, and get outta here. I'll meet you near those red rocks an hour down the trail."

He turned his cruel face back to Peg. "But first, let's see what else Granny's got to give me tonight."

He tore her dress straight down the middle, ripping the bodice with a savage yank. Light from the window of the saloon spilled on to Peg's breasts.

"Well, I have to tell ya, that ain't half bad." He smirked and cupped one breast in a filthy hand.

They say your whole life dances before your eyes when you're on your way to meet your Maker. For Peg, she was struck dumb by the notion of wanting to live, something she never would have believed, but there it was, plain as day. And now, once she figured it out, it wouldn't matter because she guessed she was as good as dead, right alongside Big Andy's ghost.

The cowboy must have had his own life dance before his eyes when he died, his neck snapped in Shorty's powerful grip. The dead man fell into Peg as though giving her a loving embrace, then slid down her body and dropped to the ground.

The next thing that surprised Peg was her attempt to cover her bosom, as if the whole saloon hadn't seen it at least once. So startled was she by her responses, she kneeled next to the dead man and covered her face in her hands.

She wailed as she rocked back and forth. "The other man ran off with our money!"

"I know. I dropped him behind the general store. Here's your purse." Shorty set it on the ground next to her.

Peg peered up at him. "Thank you," she said. Only she wasn't just thanking Shorty for saving her or the money. She was thanking God that she no longer wanted to die back there next to the railroad tracks that awful day.

Shorty nodded and turned to walk away. Peg cried then, ugly sobs that only comes when something breaks loose in the heart—good or bad. Shorty stopped, then rushed back, fell to his knees, and cradled her against his massive chest.

"You ain't alone," he said, over and over. "You ain't alone anymore. I'm here."

THE CROW FLY WAS ABUZZ the next day. Why, a robbery took place, right there in back of the saloon where Big Andy died, people said. And some deranged cowpoke tried to hurt Old Peg! But Shorty got him, and got him good, Bob the bartender said. Shorty saved Peg and the money and killed that robber all by himself. That bandit didn't know what hit him. Got the other bastard too. Both men were up at the blacksmith shop now, laying in pine boxes and iced down, waiting for graves to be dug into the reluctant earth.

Where's Old Peg? She went upstairs with Shorty and they still haven't come back down.

It's funny, Peg thought the next morning, as the sun loosened up the day and light spilled into her room. *You never know how you're gonna end up, or why. But in the end, even after all the scars and tears and lonely nights, you're right where you should be. Even if it's upstairs in a room at The Crow Fly in the middle of Breyer, Texas.*

THE SPECKLED PUP

MARIAN HUMPHREY HAD ONE PUPPY left. He was a little speckled guy, smaller than the rest of the litter. There was no royal lineage to the animal. He was a cross between Mrs. Humphrey's spaniel, Sally, and a mysterious lover who rambled through Breyer one night.

White with brown speckles, the puppy had long floppy ears with a smattering of freckles across his face and a heart-shaped spot under his chin. His short tail never stopped wagging, and his tongue often lolled to the side as though he were grinning. As cute as he was, he couldn't seem to find a home. The other puppies were spoken for, and would start their new lives on ranches, or in the arms of children in town. But nobody wanted the speckled pup. There was something different about him.

"I probably should have drowned him when he was born," Mrs. Humphrey said, then shook her head at the terrible idea. She couldn't do something like that. But now, she was stuck with a dog who wasn't quite right. Her husband was not interested in another mouth to feed, even though it was a small one.

They had no children at home. Their son Bill grew up and took a job with the railroad. Sometimes he'd come home to

Breyer on the train and stay for a day or so, but now he lived in Fort Worth.

Looking down at Sally and her remaining pup, Marian couldn't figure out what was so wrong with the little dog. For one thing, he didn't listen. When she'd call the rest of the litter, they'd come running to the doorstep, eager for attention and food. Children came from neighboring houses to play with the dogs every day, filling the yard with laughter and brightening Marian's life. But the speckled pup, although friendly, was always exploring on his own, his tail wagging vigorously as he followed his nose through the brush. Time and again, Marian had to rush out and bring him back so no harm would come to him.

He ate well enough, but was dead last when she put food in the pail. He didn't play with the other puppies very much, entertaining himself by chewing on an old blanket or watching the children when they came to play. More often than not, he'd strike out on his own with an adventurous look in his eyes.

When the puppies were old enough to find a home, they all left on the same day. Folks had picked out their favorite dog weeks before, and one by one, the youngsters headed for their new homes.

All except the speckled pup.

Oh, the little guy was happy enough to see her when he got her in his sights. He'd wag his tail and run into her arms and lick at her face until she laughed. His belly rolled back and forth when he waddled about, and he loved to chase lizards or bark at the crows who flew overhead from their home in the cemetery behind the church.

Nobody was interested in adopting him. And who could blame them? Who wanted a dog that didn't respond? A dog that might take off and run away at a moment's notice? A dog who followed his nose and little else. An independent sort of dog.

Even Sally seemed to lose interest in her offspring. She had weaned the litter weeks ago, and when the speckled pup approached, she'd get up and walk away, leaving him whining and searching for her.

Mr. Humphrey was not happy about the situation.

"You need to find a home for that dog, Marian," he said one night after dinner. He'd pushed back from his chair and drank the last of his coffee. "There's something wrong with that animal and I hardly know what to think about it, but I'm telling you, it ain't right in the head. Probably the best thing to do is put him down."

Marian swallowed. She had thought the same thing not an hour ago, but couldn't bear to bring herself to see him die. He was a sweet little thing, even if he didn't act like a normal dog. Who's to say that a dog, or for that matter, a person, had to act a certain way?

She remembered when she was a child and wanted to dance on the stage. All day long, she made up songs and dances. She didn't want to play dolls with the other girls or throw balls with the boys. She wanted to act. Her daddy tried to whip it out of her, telling her with each belt swipe that only loose women or crazy people cavorted on the stage. Her mother told her to act like a lady, and her older sister teased her relentlessly.

Eventually, she grew out of her dreams. *But isn't that a sad thing*, she thought. To this day, a part of her heart went missing. It wasn't practical. It wasn't proper. But she always wished she'd had a chance to do what she wanted. Even if it made no earthly sense.

Marian winced as she remembered buying a beautiful peach gown from Emily Augusta at Buttons and Bows last year. When she tried it on, she looked like the actress she always wanted to be. It flowed around her ankles like silky water, and the color made her skin look pearly and fresh and enhanced her soft face and deep brown hair. The bow tied around her waist gave the illusion of a slender figure. It was a big expenditure, but she had to have that dress.

The first, and surely last, time she wore it to church, she

sensed she was a laughingstock among the congregation. Some women snickered as she walked to the pew, and she overheard one mutter that she looked as though she were planning to meet the president of the United States. Marian choked back tears all the way home. She wrapped the dress carefully in paper and placed it in a trunk along with her childhood dreams.

In a strange way, she had a kinship with the little pup. She figured the two of them were free spirits. A part of her admired his spunk. She herself was too bashful to do the things she might like to do, but the dog wandered through the days doing exactly what he wanted.

So, the speckled pup stayed on. He had no idea how fragile his future was. He continued to just be himself.

One afternoon, Marian had to return a basket to Emily Augusta. She took the puppy with her. She tied a rope around his neck and trudged down the road to Miss Emily's house at the end of town. The puppy jerked and rolled on the ground, then popped up and galloped in circles around Marian's legs, tripping her. He didn't like the rope at all.

"Come along, now," she said between clenched teeth. Maybe this was a bad idea. "Come on! Here's a treat!" She had a bit of cheese in her hand and when he saw it, he came forward eagerly. Then she tugged on the rope. "Here we go, now."

The dog shook his head back and forth and darted first to one side, then another. He bounded right in front of a wrangler riding down Main Street. The man's horse crow-hopped sideways, almost unseating him.

He pulled on the reins and shouted. "Get out of the way, dammit!"

Marian didn't appreciate being sworn at. She glared at him and gathered the puppy in her arms. She thought of turning back, but was closer to Miss Emily's house than her own, so she carried him the rest of the way. The afternoon heat peppered her forehead, and the warmth of the dog in her arms made the rest of the trip almost unbearable. By the time she reached her destination, her face was red and sweat trickled down her bodice. Exasperated, she tied the puppy to the porch rail and knocked on the door.

Miss Emily answered, her face serene and voice cool as always. She wore a blue gingham frock from her shop and looked fresh as a spring shower. Marian was out of sorts and heavy with perspiration. She swiped at her forehead and struggled to smile.

"Why, Missus Humphrey! What a surprise. Is there something I can help you with?"

"Oh, I have this little basket here for you. If you recall, you left it at the church gathering last week. I noticed it right off and picked it up."

"So that's what happened to it," Emily replied. "I came back but couldn't find it. Wasn't sure exactly where it went." Instead of gratitude, her face puckered with annoyance. She reached for the basket, then took a step back as though to close the door right in Marian's face.

The puppy barked and wagged his tail.

Emily peered at him as he wound himself around her porch railing. "What have we here?"

"This is our last puppy. He's a sweet little dog. But he doesn't act quite right, and none of the children or ranchers wanted him." Marian stopped then. Perhaps she had said too much. Maybe Miss Emily might be interested in adopting the dog. One never knew.

Emily stepped off the porch and gave the pup a pat. Her usually severe face softened. A hint of a smile danced along her lips. Marian thought the woman looked quite pretty when she wasn't so stern.

"Well, he's cute enough, isn't he?" Emily said as she held his face in her hands. The puppy wriggled and pawed at her skirt. "What did you say is wrong with him?"

Marian chose her words carefully. "He just doesn't come when called. Kind of stubborn little soul, I think. He didn't play much with his littermates, and although he loved the children who came to visit the puppies, he always hung back." She smiled at Emily. "However, he sure would make a pleasant companion for somebody."

Emily thought for a moment as she scratched the pup's back. He wriggled with pleasure and licked her hands. "You know, I knew a dog like this when I was growing up. He was different, too, but for a reason."

The speckled pup had turned around and watched a wagon inch its way down the road in front of the house. He wagged his tail and stood on his hind legs, letting out a bark or two.

Emily whispered to Marian. "That's the new family from Dallas. Name's Joseph Hartwell. His wife, Alice, seems nice. They have a little boy. I haven't seen them in church yet. Mister Hartwell will oversee the telegraph office here. They're just settling in by the train depot in that house where the Youngs used to live." Emily was warming to the subject now because she found telling folks something they didn't already know enjoyable. It was obvious from the interested look on Marian's face that she was imparting new and exciting information.

"Well, maybe I'll go visit them soon," Marian said. "Bring them a jar of pickles I made last week. Make them feel welcome."

The speckled pup tugged on the rope, choking himself. Emily picked him up and untied him from the porch.

"So, you said something about a dog you knew as a child?" Marian asked.

Emily turned back from staring at the Hartwell family. "Oh yes, I forgot. Well, you see, that dog didn't act right either. Here, Marian, take the puppy and turn him away from me."

Marian placed the dog toward the street again.

Then Emily let out a whistle so loud that old Mr. Forbes stopped short in the middle of the road on his way to the cemetery, and a horse snorted and tossed his head in a field nearby. Marian flinched in surprise.

The puppy didn't even flick an ear.

"There you have it!" Emily said. "He's deaf! Just like the dog I saw as a kid. Try it!"

Marian stood behind him and clapped her hands. "Here, puppy! Come this way! Puppy! Puppy!"

The speckled pup ignored her.

"Well, I'll be! And all this time, I thought he was stubborn!" Marian laughed, then the full impact of the problem settled on her shoulders.

Whatever would they do with a deaf dog? All the way home, she thought about his fate. Pity flooded her senses and left her in anguish. Once her husband found out, she knew there'd be no keeping him. A deaf dog wouldn't hear wagons or horses or shotguns and could get hurt. He would never come when called nor be able to hunt. A deaf dog was useless in a place like Breyer.

Miss Emily Augusta had already spread the news by the next day that the speckled pup was deaf and needed a home. Perhaps she thought she was doing Marian a service, but it was likely just another tidbit for Emily to toss before her listeners, spreading gossip like a Texas rainstorm and enjoying the look of surprise on their faces.

"You still haven't found a home for that dog yet?" Marian's husband, Charles, asked. He was busy tucking his shirt into his pants and gazing out the window toward the bank where he worked. Marian flicked a piece of lint off his coat and straightened his bow tie.

He pecked Marian on the cheek and jostled past her. "Let's see if we can do something with this dog soon, eh, Marian?" His voice was calm, but Marian knew when he meant business. She still hadn't told him the little guy was deaf. She was hoping for a solution.

Marian kissed him goodbye and watched as he walked down Main Street, then poured herself a cup of coffee. Sally ambled up to her and snuffled her hand with a soft muzzle. The puppy wasn't with her.

"Where's that baby of yours, Sally?"

Worried, Marian stepped out the back door. Their small plot of land was empty. That darned puppy had taken off again. What if he ran into the road? Why, he might get trampled out there! Flustered, she raced around the house to Main Street, but there was no sign of the dog anywhere. She stormed back into the house, grabbed her straw hat, and jammed it on her head.

"Stay," she said, muttering to Sally. "I don't need to lose both of ya." She scurried out the back door again and peered around.

It was already warm and humid. Rain clouds were rolling in from the north. They threatened to douse the prairie.

Out behind their house was a shallow gully that was dry as dirt, but sometimes it would overflow if the sky opened up. She pictured the speckled pup floating downstream, helpless, silent ears dragging in the water. It was a relief to see the gully dry as usual, so she stepped across it and up the other side. Behind the wash was a broad plain. It looked like the only things stirring were artful tumbleweeds dancing across the flat land under a hot wind.

Marian took off her hat and slapped at her dusty skirt. How can you call a dog home when it can't hear? Fear and anger flooded her heart. The poor pup was out there somewhere, oblivious to the hazards of the harsh wilderness.

A sound in the distance stirred her. Coyotes! And more than one. They yipped and howled. Filled with dread, Marian rushed forward. She picked up a large stick from under a cottonwood tree along the way. The howls grew louder as she trotted toward them, her heart pounding until she thought it would leap out of her chest and dance away with the tumbleweeds. It was dangerous out here all by herself. There were predators and snakes and lord knew what else. This was foolish. The act of a foolish woman who could get lost forever.

As she topped the next knoll, Marian saw five coyotes trotting in formation. Walking toward them, nose to the ground as though he hadn't a care in the world, was the speckled pup.

She screamed. "Stop! Stop!" The coyotes turned to look at her. Frantically, she waved the stick back and forth. "Get out of here!" The lead coyote turned away from her and started after the pup, who, in a few more yards, would walk right into him.

The puppy looked up and saw the pack of coyotes. Wagging his silly tail, he bounded forward as though he had found new friends.

Marian shrieked and hollered. She ran harder than she had run in years. She tripped once on her skirt and fell on one knee but got right back up, screaming and yelling the whole way.

Just then, a shot rang out. She turned to see Jed Thornton galloping toward her.

"Stay back, Marian!" he shouted, and drove his horse right toward the pack. They scattered like seeds and hightailed it behind a stand of trees. The pup turned, wagged his tail, then ran toward the sheriff, who scooped him up and brought him safely to Marian.

"I heard your cries clear over in my office," he said. "What on earth happened?"

"Oh, Jed, this poor deaf puppy took off from home, and he was about to be attacked by those horrible coyotes. Thank you so much for your help!" Marian didn't even realize she was crying until she felt the wetness on her cheeks. She slammed her hat back on her head and clung tightly to the speckled pup. "They were going to kill him."

"Yes, I imagine they would." He dismounted and led his horse by the reins. "Come along now. I'll walk you home."

Marian stumbled along beside him, the dog in her arms. When she got home, she placed a rope around his neck and tied him to an old cottonwood tree next to the house. Then she sank down on the porch and regained her breath.

Word was everywhere that afternoon about the speckled pup

and Marian and the pack of coyotes. Tongues wagged. That crazy little dog could have cost them both their lives! Emily Augusta shuddered to think about a pack of hungry animals pouncing on Marian. She pictured the poor woman lying in a heap of gingham, blood pouring out of her into the ground.

The speckled pup had to be dealt with. And soon. Even Marian agreed. She couldn't afford to run from hill to dale after a dog all day long. But his merry brown eyes, his big clumsy feet and eager stub tail had wormed its way into her heart. That night, she tossed and turned like a ship on the ocean, clutching at the covers like a lifeline as she fretted.

The next morning broke warm and sticky. Thunderheads rose from the valley floor beyond Breyer and made their way to town like lazy cowboys on a Friday night. Soon it might rain and then the gully would turn into a torrent.

Marian checked on the speckled pup. He was lying in the shade under the tree and when he saw her, he ran to the end of the rope and flipped backward. He yelped and tucked his tail, but then tried to reach her again. Marian pursed her lips. What on earth should she do with him? It was getting mighty hot outside under that tree. At least Sally had the sense to crawl under a bush to stay cool.

She brought the puppy inside the house and set him down on her newly cleaned floor. He eagerly careened from room to room, stopping only to piddle on the floor, shake her beloved tablecloth between pointed little teeth, and knock over her prize Boston fern, then ate the dirt. Before she could stop him, he'd helped himself to the remnants of Charles's leftover breakfast on the table, then licked the plate clean.

"See here, now," she said, scolding, then realized he couldn't hear her. So, she followed him from room to room while he dashed away, oblivious to the heavy breathing behind him.

In the middle of the chaos, somebody knocked on the front door.

Marian straightened, then glared at the puppy. She smoothed her hair and skirt and grabbed the knob to the bedroom and slammed the door, locking the dog inside. She shuddered to think what he would do in there while she talked to somebody, but it couldn't be helped.

When she opened the door, it surprised Marian to see a young woman she didn't recognize on her porch, holding the hand of a small boy. The boy didn't look to be much past eight years old. Small for his age. He had jet black hair and the brightest eyes Marian had ever seen. They were such a light gray they looked silver.

"Missus Humphrey, I'm Alice Hartwell. This is my little boy, Billy."

Marian smiled. "Nice to meet you, Missus Hartwell. I heard there were newcomers in town and planned to visit you with some homemade pickles. I have a boy named Billy, too, but he's all grown up." She leaned down and patted his head. "How are you, Billy?"

"Fine." The child looked right past her as though surveying the house. He had a sweet smile. One dark lock of hair fell on to his forehead like a question mark.

"Where are my manners? Come in, come in." Marian gestured at the plant on the floor. "I'm sorry about the mess. A little dog knocked it over. Wait! Watch your step, Billy!" The boy walked right through the pile of dirt on the floor. *More of a mess to clean up,* Marian thought, but she smiled at Mrs. Hartwell.

"Actually, we came here to see that pup of yours. We've heard an awful lot about him, and my Billy wanted to meet him."

Marian flushed with excitement. Could they possibly be interested in the little fella?

"Well, he's in the back bedroom. Let me fetch him for you. He's still available if you're interested." Before Mrs. Hartwell could say another word, Marian rushed to the bedroom and opened the door.

The speckled pup shot out the door like his tail was on fire. Around his neck was a pair of Marian's lacy bloomers that had frankly seen better days. His lips were bright red, and Marian realized he must have gotten into her pot of rouge on the dresser. He looked very happy with himself.

The dog took one look at the visitors and ran straight to Billy, knocking him sideways. The two rolled around on the floor together, straight through the dirt from the fallen Boston fern. Billy laughed, throwing his arms around the puppy, who licked his face with joy.

"He seems to like you, Billy," Marian said, turning hopeful eyes toward Mrs. Hartwell.

"I love him! He's exactly everything I always wanted!" Billy said. He captured the dog in his arms and held him close. "Please, Momma, can we keep him?" The puppy squirmed in his arms, but Billy held fast.

Now Marian had a twinge of guilt. She couldn't just shove the dog off on unsuspecting folks. He was a handful and would be for life.

Crossing her arms across her chest as though to fend off any concern, Marian pursed her lips and waggled a finger. "Missus Hartwell, I have to tell you, this little dog has a big problem. Oh, he's the sweetest little thing and bright as a penny. He loves children. But I'm sorry to say, he's stone-deaf. Can't hear a thing. He needs to be watched over every minute or he'll take off and get into mischief." Leaning over, she removed the bloomers from around his neck and hastily hid it behind her skirt.

Mrs. Hartwell smiled. "That's why Billy wanted to meet him."

"Is that so? Why, Billy?"

The boy stood and walked toward Marian. The speckled pup tugged at his sleeve and Billy smiled with such radiance that it was likely why the thunderheads never came up in Breyer that day.

He placed his hand on the dog's head and looked in Marian's direction with those silvery eyes.

"You see, ma'am, I like it that the puppy is deaf. Makes no difference to me. It'll just make me love him more." Billy paused for a moment. "I happen to be blind, myself. I know what it's like to be missin' something, but that don't make it bad. Not bad at all."

The little boy knelt and cradled the dog in his arms. "I can't see and the puppy can't hear. We're broken, in a way. But we're still precious, aren't we, Momma?"

Alice Hartwell smiled at Marian and brushed the lock of hair off his forehead. "That's right, son."

The dog licked Billy's face, and he grinned. "The way I figure it, the two of us may have a piece missing, but together we make a whole. I can listen for things and help the puppy, and he can see for me."

"Are... are you sure, Billy?" Marian looked to Alice Hartwell.

Billy's mother nodded. "There's a small garden behind the house with a fence around it. It's where Billy plays. They'll be safe in there. I keep a good watch over my boy. But it's been so lonely for him since we moved here." She reached out and patted Marian's arms. "We promise to take good care of the puppy. Although, I can't promise you I'll give him any of my bloomers to play with."

Marian stared at her in surprise, then burst out laughing. The two women grinned at each other.

BILLY NAMED HIM FRECKLES BECAUSE his mother told him the puppy was covered in brown speckles. That seemed to suit Freckles just fine. They played together for hours behind the house in the fenced yard, and at night Freckles slept with Billy in his bed. The two soon became inseparable.

Billy's father had the blacksmith make a harness for Freckles. The boy could hold on to it, and the two walked together side by side. Billy taught Freckles to stop when he tapped the dog on the shoulder when he heard a threatening noise, and Freckles led Billy around Breyer just as gentle as a morning in June.

For years, Marian watched Freckles and Billy as they grew up together. Lara Thornton even allowed the dog in the schoolhouse, where Freckles sat next to Billy during his lessons. All the children loved the dog and played with him at recess until he was so tired he'd flop on the floor and sleep the rest of the afternoon.

When Billy left Breyer to go to the School for the Blind in Austin, Freckles went right along with him.

The last Marian Humphrey saw of the two of them was on the train platform with Alice Hartwell. The mighty engine pulled into the station one morning in late August. Billy tapped Freckles's shoulder, and the dog sat, his head leaning on Billy's leg. They waited for the train to stop, then Freckles moved forward, his stub tail wagging as he and Billy boarded. Billy took a window seat. Freckles stuck his head out in the morning breeze, ears flapping and tongue lolling.

The train pulled away, the boy and dog on their way to a new adventure.

Marian waved, even though Billy couldn't see her. She swore Freckles looked right at her and grinned.

"Goodbye, little speckled pup," Marian said, then turned toward home. She knew he'd never hear her, but hoped that somewhere in God's universe, he knew she'd wished him well.

That Sunday, Marian wore the peach gown to church again. She glided proudly down the aisle to the pew right in front of the pulpit, and nobody said a single word.

KATE DAWSON

KATE DAWSON WALKED INTO BUTTONS and Bows clutching a sheaf of papers. The little bell above the door tinkled merrily. Kate smiled. She loved this little dress shop. To her, it was the one nice thing in Breyer. Miss Emily Augusta kept the shop supplied with bolts of fabric, notions, hats, and jewelry. Kate admired how the store had been set up, from the glass counter on one side of the shop housing purses, necklaces, and earrings, to the hats gaily displayed in the window. On the far side of the store were colorful bolts of fabric—a rainbow of delight— filled with promises of a lovely dress or blouse.

Miss Augusta made sure she was up to date on all the latest fashions, even though they could look downright silly on the women living in Breyer. Why, the first time Mrs. Humphrey walked into church wearing a pale peach gown, it kept tongues wagging for days.

"She looks like she's going to meet the president of the United States." Mrs. Donaldson made the proclamation behind her kerchief, sending ladies around her into titters. Heads turned throughout the sermon, irritating Pastor Green and causing Miss Augusta to blush, since she was the one who sold the dress to Marian Humphrey in the first place.

Kate wasn't a churchgoer, but she heard plenty about it on the streets. She looked ruefully down at her own faded pink floral skirt, grimy from crossing the dusty road. It was impossible to keep anything nice here in Breyer, she thought, but she had to keep trying. There was little enough beauty in this town, and she wasn't about to cave in to its dismal whims.

Her gray eyes swept through the shop, noticing a few new things on the tables since the last time she was here. Over in the corner on a hanger was a lovely dress for daytime wear, in the palest lavender. Around the waist was a deeper purple sash. A yellow hat in the window with sprigs of lavender flowers on it would be a lovely accessory. She'd pair it with the beaded handbag on the counter. Her pulse quickened with excitement.

Emily Augusta stepped out from the back of the store and smiled. "Oh, it's you Kate. I thought I heard the bell. What can I do for you today?"

Although Kate was a whore at The Crow Fly, Emily regarded her as a good customer, and therefore kept her sharp tongue to herself. She'd sold Kate several dresses. Her money was as good as anyone else's. Kate was smart. She knew to stay away when other ladies in town were shopping. This afternoon, it was almost closing time. A good time to browse.

Kate took a breath and set the papers on the counter. "I'd like to commission you to make a dress for me, Emily."

"Oh, well, that's lovely, Kate. Would you like to look at my patterns? Or perhaps there's something already made that might suit you?"

"No, thank you. I made my own design."

Kate fanned her drawings out on the countertop. There were several angles of the same dress—front, back, and sides.

"You made these?" Emily asked. They were good, drawn in an elegant hand. Further, they were the latest rage in Paris.

"Yes. I've always loved fashion and dresses, and I wish I could learn to sew better. I buy the fashion magazines from New York and read them cover to cover. I know by the time they make their way clear out here to Texas, they're probably out of date, but this style really caught my eye. So, I drew it up. What would you think about this dress in the deep blue velvet over there on the shelf?"

Emily glanced over at the bolt of fabric. "It would be beautiful, but not too suitable to wear in Breyer." She thought about Mrs. Humphrey and cleared her throat. "Of course, it's up to you, but perhaps this dress you designed would be better in gingham?" She pointed to a row of checked fabrics in several colors.

"Gingham?"

"Well, yes. When you find a pattern that is rather, ah, dressy, you can make it less dressy by using a more modest fabric." Emily walked over to a floral dress draped over a chair and picked it up. "This is what I mean. The fabric is pretty, but it's not something a woman would wear to, say…."

"Meet the president of the United States?" Kate couldn't help it.

Emily blushed and set the dress back on the chair. "Yes, that's what I mean. I made a mistake selling that peach gown to Missus Humphrey. Instead of looking fashionable, she looked rather, well, shall we say, silly?"

Kate nodded. It was true. Perhaps if that dress had been in a nice cotton instead of watered silk, Marian Humphrey would have looked stylish instead of foolish. But Kate dearly wanted the dress she designed to be made in the dark blue velvet.

"I understand, but I think I want the velvet all the same." She giggled. "And I wouldn't be wearing it to church."

Emily hid her smile as she turned toward the blue velvet bolt and took it down from its perch by the window.

"I think there's enough fabric for your dress. Although your design is lovely and well-drawn, I will still have to make a pattern of it so I can sew the dress. I'll also need to take your measurements." She peered up at Kate's face. "This will mean extra time, so it will be more costly than most."

Kate nodded and drew several bills from her bag. "Is this enough to start?"

"Yes. I can begin right away. I should finish it in a week or so. Unless, of course, you needed it sooner?"

"No, take your time. To be honest, I want that dress as a piece of art, in a way. Just for me. Something I can try on and look at, but I likely will never wear it here in Texas."

The two women gazed at each other. Kate never understood quite what Emily was doing out here in the middle of nowhere, although she had a hunch or two. She always felt judged by the woman and it annoyed her. If her money was good enough to buy a dress, why did Miss Augusta treat her so coldly? Emily made it very clear that the women at The Crow Fly weren't to hobnob with the other customers and that they should keep to themselves.

What does it matter? Kate thought. *As long as I get my dress, I'll let things be. But someday, it may not be so easy for Miss Augusta to dismiss me.*

Kate nodded goodbye and turned to leave. This time, when it opened, the tiny bell above the door didn't sound quite so merry. Tears stung her eyes as she stepped off the walk and into the dirty street leading to The Crow Fly. She worked hard for that money, and now felt as though she had been frivolous, and as silly as Mrs. Humphrey. Kate set her chin in a resolute pose and walked across to the saloon.

Emily watched from the window. Kate Dawson was tall. Taller than a lot of men. Her blonde hair and gray eyes were becoming, but her face was pitted with pockmarks, her cheeks rough as a cob, poor thing. She was still young, but her breasts were falling and Emily knew she soon wouldn't be able to extract the good money from the men that she once did if she lost her figure. Why on earth she wanted to waste her pay on a dress she'd never wear was confusing. Emily took the designs and bolt of fabric behind the curtain into the small workroom.

Kate had been the organizer at The Crow Fly when Big Andy

died, Emily reflected. Kate had some sense about her and kept to herself, it seemed. But she had no sense when it came to money. Although Emily was honest with the women at the saloon, she could have worked with them harder to encourage them to invest their money better, but she didn't bother. Kate and Old Peg were the two ringleaders, for certain. Without them, the saloon would probably dry up and blow away, taking them, and Rick the piano player, with it out of town on a lonesome wind.

Emily turned away from the window. All the pretty fabric and hats in the store, no matter how carefully arranged, hid a dark secret that haunted her nights and assured her she could never fully be the lady she yearned to be.

She figured one of these days she'd find the gumption to walk out of this flea-ridden town and make her way back East again. There were plenty of places there, or even farther West, to set up a little dress shop. Her talents were wasted here. But until that day came, she was more than happy to earn money managing The Crow Fly and selling dresses to the local women.

She sniffed. No matter how many years had passed, she still had the stench of her past billowing about her conscience like a petticoat in a windstorm. She worked hard to turn her business into a thriving success, and her home into a beautiful sanctuary, far from the lowlife folks who drifted into The Crow Fly, and the women who worked there. Now, some upstart had the audacity to wander into Buttons and Bows with designs and demands. Kate Dawson had better mind her manners, or she might find herself in trouble.

KATE TOLD PEG SHE HAD a headache that night and stayed in her room. She couldn't bear the thought of entertaining a man after dealing with Miss Emily. She felt filthy under the judgmental eyes of that dratted woman. A flicker of anger crossed her mind. How dare that woman insult her? Who did she think she was, after all? Kate wanted to settle into bed and pull up the covers. She just needed some time. And then one day, she'd find her way out of here. Twisting a strand of hair around her finger, her thoughts drifted back to Kansas and her childhood home.

PRAYERS FOR KATE

WHY KATE RAN AWAY FROM her home in Kansas seemed trivial now. Her mother and father were church-goers in the worst way. They wore their religion like a cape of judgment, woven into tattered slices of criticism. Anybody and everybody in their small town was fodder for the Gatling gun tongue of Fiona Dawson and her prim husband, Jeffrey. Kate looked like her father, with dirty blonde hair and gray eyes. Fiona was dark and swarthy-looking, as though she might be part gypsy. Her mouth was set in a straight line of disapproval as she went about her day. Jeffrey had a quick smile but saved it only for the deeply devoted.

They forced Kate to go to church all day Sunday and on Tuesday evenings, sitting in the hard pew that Fiona staked out every week. It was right in the front, so their presence was known to all. Preacher Galloway invited Fiona to play the piano and asked Jeffrey to pass the basket for offerings. The Dawsons fell upon their duties with enthusiasm. The minister's shaggy brows knotted over eyes filled with fire and brimstone when he preached, intimidating the congregation and sniffing loudly if a family didn't put enough of their hard-earned money into the basket. Fiona and Jeffrey thought he was magnificent as he doled out threats of hell and offering redemption to the God-fearing. Fiona played the hymns with zeal, her music ending in a flourish of fingers as though she were pointing toward heaven before she rose from the bench and glided back to her perch on the pew with Kate and Jeffrey.

The Dawsons appeared well-liked in her little town, but living with such ramrod-straight parents wasn't easy. Fiona found fault with almost everything Kate did. When Kate developed smallpox and picked at her sores, Fiona stood over her, reciting passages from the Bible, begging God to spare her daughter's face. God must not have been listening that day because the constellation of scars stood out on Kate's face as a constant reminder. Somehow, in Fiona's mind, it wasn't God who failed to perform a miracle, but simply because He did not see fit to favor Kate, meaning that Kate had a lot more to learn in order to become a faithful servant of the Lord.

A nice young man wanted to court Kate. James Jurgens was the son of the local doctor. He was kind and good to her. James was tall and gangly, towering over most men in town, but still sported a boyish face. The result was rather shocking when folks looked at him. His black hair and light brown eyes served him well with the girls, and a few had set their cap for him. But the Dawsons found fault in everything he did or said. He was too lanky, Fiona said. Why, he looked like a giraffe. And did you hear his father drinks like a fish? Runs in families, you know. Best that Kate turns her attention to God. Maybe devote her entire life to God, what with that scarred face and all. Maybe the Lord would see fit then to reward her in the afterlife if she led a pious life in this one.

Kate swelled with anger. She liked James. Maybe even loved him. Her heart longed for freedom. Longed for the opportunity to leave her parents behind and explore a new life. Perhaps with

James. She looked forward to seeing him, and encouraged him to stop by as often as he could, despite Fiona's disapproving looks.

James soon learned that Kate liked to leave her strict house and go for long walks by a small creek. He enjoyed them, too, and it was far easier to hold her hand and clasp her under the arm without the prying eyes of the Dawsons. Once or twice, he stole a kiss from Kate. Her soft lips beneath his made his heart surge with desire. She kissed him back too. At night, he dreamed of nothing else.

Kate liked it when James held her hand and when he kissed her. He bent his frame over her and touched her lips with his. The result was electrifying. In Kate's life, this was the only thing that even came close to happiness, and she willingly took part in James's pursuit. When he walked her home after those sessions, she never felt a twinge of shame, just an eagerness for his next visit.

In desperation for happiness, she let James touch her breasts. It sparked feelings in her she didn't know existed. The thrumming in her heart and between her legs were nothing like the hymns pounded out on the stark piano in church, but she felt as though she were close to God in some way. Loving another person was spiritual and exciting. Kate wanted more.

She lost her virginity one night, lying with James under an apple tree, while stars danced in the sky. Kate felt fulfilled. However, James was beside himself later about what they did. He vowed he would not compromise her.

"Kate, I ain't about to shame you in front of the whole town, and our families." He took her by the shoulders and leaned down, looking into her eyes. "We should get married right away."

Kate nodded in agreement. The full impact of what happened made her speechless. What if she had gotten pregnant? Even the thought left her breathless. Breathless with fear. But even more so, breathless with anticipation.

"I'll talk to my father tonight," James said, and gathered her in his arms. Fortified by their betrothal, he mounted her again. Kate did not object. She was happier than she had ever been in her life.

That night, Kate opened her window and stared up at the stars. She hugged herself with joy. Looking around her sparse room, she planned what she would take with her to live with James and carve out a new life. Maybe here in town. Or maybe they would set off on a new adventure altogether. She hardly slept at all, then counted the minutes all day when James would return.

The stricken look on James's face shocked Kate when he came to her door the next evening. Holding his hat in his hand, he stood before her and wiped his brow with his sleeve. The boy looked taller than ever, his rangy frame bending low to speak to Kate.

"Can we talk?"

She nodded and stepped out the door, closing it firmly behind her. She and James walked away from the porch and down toward the creek. He didn't reach out his hand for her, but strode along in silence, his narrow legs leaving a long shadow ahead of him.

"Did you talk to your father?" Kate asked, peering up into his face.

James nodded, his Adam's apple bobbing up and down as though he were holding back the words. He stopped and clasped her hand between his and spread his feet as though he was about to topple over. Taking a breath, he talked fast, words tumbling out of his mouth in a torrent.

"Father was not at all in favor of us marrying, Katie. I'm so sorry. He... he feels like your family is far too religious for us to make a good match. He thinks they're odd, to be truthful. Now, I ain't saying he thinks you're odd, but he thinks your parents are." James placed his hands on her shoulders and squeezed gently. "Father wants me to wait. He said if we married, we couldn't live in his house, and I couldn't train with him to become a doctor." He clutched his hands in fists. "I don't have enough money for us to find a home yet. He knows that. We would have to live with them, or"—he hesitated—"your parents. He said other things too. Things that weren't right to say about folks. Dad had far too much to drink after dinner. We argued. I got mad and threw a punch. Pa hit me in the stomach and told me that if I marry you, he would disown me forever. Forever! Can you believe it?"

Kate's eyes filled with tears. She didn't expect this sort of reaction at all from his parents. "Well, what are you going to do about it, James?"

The boy looked down at his feet. "It kills me to say this, but I think we'll have to wait a while. Maybe a year or two?" His eyes darted everywhere but into her puzzled face. "By then, they might come around, and we could save our money, rent a proper house, and start a life together."

Kate gaped in amazement. All these years, her parents had looked down on everyone in town. Now it was the Dawsons being judged and found to be inadequate. The irony didn't escape her. It hurt and shamed her. Anger set in.

Not only were her parents against her, but James was too, it seemed. What if she was pregnant? What would happen then?

"Then leave, James! Go home to your safe little house with your parents. Leave me with mine. We'll make do. Don't come around again."

James held her hands between his. "Let's try to give this some time! Maybe my family will change their mind. Don't break with me. Please! Maybe we can work something out." He tightened his hold, squeezing her fingers.

Kate wrenched her hands free and rushed up the steps and onto the porch. The boards creaked under her feet as though they were crying along with her.

"Go away, James! Go away!" Kate trembled, overcome with loss and fury.

She tore open the front door and rushed inside. Her parents were kneeling in the sparse parlor, beginning their nightly prayers. Fiona raised her head. She didn't notice Kate's tears.

"Come in. It's time to pray to our Lord."

"Pray? Pray? Pray for what? For my scars to go away? For yours to go away? There is no God! Do you hear me? No God! You're both fools!"

Even as she spoke, Kate knew she had shattered something forever. James. Her parents. God.

Trembling, she crumpled to the floor and sobbed. When she looked up, her father was standing over her. He raised his hand and slapped her hard across the face. She howled.

"Go to your bed, daughter! Do not come back down until you can ask our Lord for forgiveness. And if you cannot, do not darken our doorway again."

Fiona nodded as she stood behind her husband and pointed her finger. "You were always the worst child I could have imagined! There is something dark and sinister inside of you. Something evil and rank. You don't love your God. And you don't love us. Furthermore, you're not a pious girl, and I fear for your soul." Fiona sniffed into her handkerchief and turned away, then leaned against the wall, as though her knees were weak. She covered her eyes with trembling hands. "Go upstairs to your room! I cannot bear to look at you right now."

Jeffrey grabbed at Kate's arm and pulled her up from the floor. He pushed and shoved her toward the stairs. His fingers bit into her arm. In one final push, he aimed Kate toward the steps. She fell, scraping her knees.

"Now!" he said, his voice low and menacing.

As she climbed the stairs, they stood at the bottom, praying for her redemption. They chanted and begged God to deliver them from such evil and to cleanse her filthy soul of all sin.

Kate Dawson packed her few belongings in an old carpetbag and left her home the next morning. Neither of her parents bothered to say goodbye. The only thing Kate could do was turn her back on her home in Kansas, James, her parents, and God. And for years, that's exactly what she did.

A PIG IN A POKE

CORA SANDERS PEERED ACROSS MAIN Street and nudged Marian Humphrey in the ribs with her elbow.

"There she goes again. Miss Emily Augusta. I swear, that woman thinks she's so high and mighty. If she smiled, it would likely crack her face. And did you see her in church last week? Why, her hat was so wide I couldn't see around it. It took up half the pew. Who does she think she is, anyway?"

Marian Humphrey had to agree, although it pained her to gossip. However, some days it was annoying to see Emily Augusta swanning around town as though she were above everybody else. Marian blushed, thinking about a peach-colored gown Miss Emily sold her, and how some ladies in town humiliated her in church one Sunday. All the while, Emily sat in the front pew, cool as ice, knowing darned well that her client looked like a fool.

They watched Miss Emily unlock the door to Buttons and Bows and step inside. A moment later, she turned the sign in the window to *OPEN*. The two women locked arms and walked toward the mercantile. Marian needed headache powders and Cora wanted vegetable seeds and mason jars.

Cora's garden was the talk of the town, or so she liked to think.

Ever since Pastor Green gave her the scarecrow from out of the local cemetery, the garden had flourished. The crows who constantly invaded Breyer and munched on a variety of her tender vegetables had stayed well away from the flapping burlap face. The land, usually so miserly, gifted her with a healthy array of vegetables and flowers. Sunflowers grew in abundance along the fence. Cora loved to watch them follow the sun each day, their faces lifting to the light. In the corner of her yard was a small flower garden, resplendent with sweet peas, black-eyed Susans and bachelor buttons. Morning glories wound their way around a trellis and greeted her each morning in waves of blue. It was a sight to behold, and half the women in Breyer were envious, an emotion that Cora kindled and groomed with her constant bragging.

Cora Sanders's tongue was as sharp as a garden hoe, weeding out all the citizens in town and taking measure of them. So detailed and perfect were her assessments that it struck fear in the hearts of the other ladies in town. In an effort to shield themselves from her judgments and razor-sharp comments, they curried her favor.

Marian was no different. Cora made her head ache, to be honest, but it was always best to err on the side of caution and nod in agreement, and yes, even indulge a bit in the gossip Cora dished out daily. Nobody was safe. And nothing was too personal to escape Cora's wagging tongue.

Today, it was all about the garden again, and its majesty.

"Why, Marian, just last week I had so many beautiful tomatoes I had to bring baskets full of them to the Thorntons and Whites. Lillian said she'd use them in the restaurant. How about that? We all know Lillian uses only the best ingredients for her food." Here, she had to stop and whisper. "If only she would spend as much time on her hair as she does her stews, she might actually look handsome." She tittered behind her hand.

They bumped into Alice Hartwell, one of the new residents of the ever-expanding Breyer, and Cora felt the need to repeat everything she had just said to Marian. And so it went as they flitted from one person to another on their way to the mercantile. By the time they'd reached the store, Marian was fit to be tied. The headache powders were much needed.

Cora gathered the mason jars and seeds into her basket and crooked them under her arm with a flourish. With her other hand, she grabbed Marian's wrist and spun her around.

"Look out yonder, Marian. Lara Thornton looks a little peaked today, wouldn't you say?" She lowered her voice, her breath warm on Marian's face. "I wonder if Jed kept her up too late last night?"

Marian stiffened in protest. "Now, Cora, that's not nice to say. They're a lovely young couple, and if they, well, like to keep each other's company, why...."

"Marian Humphrey! What on earth do you think I meant?" Cora's voice rose until all heads in the store turned her way. "How dare you mistake what I said about the Thorntons! Why, I am appalled, simply appalled."

Marian stared in shock. Her face reddened as she defended herself. "Cora, you said it, not me!"

But by then Cora's swift reproach swept them out the door and into the street. Marian stumbled down the street in a hurry, trying to put as much distance as possible between herself and the maddening Cora Sanders.

The infuriating woman did not miss Marian. Not one bit. Cora found two more women to gossip with. The air was thick with her words as they sliced and pierced the next poor victim. Marian highly suspected it was herself that Cora was now denouncing. She couldn't step back into the calmness of her house fast enough, poured a large amount of headache powder into her glass of water, and swallowed it.

Cora Sanders breathed a sigh of contentment. Today she had commented on so many women and men in Breyer that there were precious few left to attack. She never said much about the women at The Crow Fly. For one thing, she was afraid of them.

One has to be careful dealing with whores. They might carry a pistol. Besides, everybody already knew they were whores and nobody seemed to care much. All the town gossips had their way with those women over the years, enough to make it almost unsporting to volley more words their way.

She hugged the jars closer to her chest as she thought of the cucumbers in the garden, just the right size to make her delicious pickles, the envy of Breyer. Why, women came from far and wide to see her jars, lined up on the windowsill like jewels.

Cora flitted through her front door and set the jars and seeds on the table. Removing her floral bonnet, she replaced it with a wide-brim straw hat and rubbed her hands in anticipation as she launched herself out the back door to the garden.

What she saw was such an abomination that for a moment Cora swiped at her eyes, thinking she was seeing things.

A roving band of wild pigs had taken over her garden! Javelinas. She must have left her gate open. Feral pigs seldom ventured into town. They usually roamed on the fringes of Breyer and kept to themselves. With their sharp tusks curving about their ugly faces, they looked fearsome and ornery. And they were.

Cora felt weak in the knees. Where was her husband when she needed him? Running back through the doorway, she grabbed an old broom and stood on the top step, swishing it back and forth and hollering.

"Hiya! Get out of here! Now! Now!"

The pigs did nothing. They were too busy dining on her cucumbers. One sampled a sunflower and others tore at the delicate morning glories. Another had pulled over the scarecrow and was shredding its burlap face into pieces. Seeing all this set Cora's mind on fire. She no longer thought sensibly. Instead, she stomped off the stairs and approached the fearsome pack of bandits.

She got as far as swatting one of them on its rump, when two or three turned menacingly toward her. One, the largest boar, stamped his feet and lowered his head. He still had a piece of cucumber in his mouth, sticking out like a green cigar.

Frightened, Cora took a step back toward the house. She swung the broom once more, this time at the smallest pig, a baby, and connected. It squealed in pain.

A large sow looked up from the cucumber patch. In one swift motion, she charged at Cora.

The woman scrambled up her stairs, dashed through the house, and ran out the front door to safety. She had forgotten in her haste, however, to close the doors behind her. As she raced off the porch and into the street, she turned around to see the entire herd of pigs rambling through her house. The large boar grabbed her bonnet off the table and knocked the mason jars to the floor. They shattered. Two javelinas relieved themselves on her braided rug before they rummaged through her kitchen. Another got its tusk entangled with her lace curtain and yanked it off the window.

Cora backed away in horror and wailed. "No! No! Help!" Her screams alerted nobody except the angry mother sow. Spotting her enemy through the doorway, the pig grunted and charged again. The animal shouldered its way onto the porch, scrambled down the stairs, and ran at Cora. This seemed to set off a herd reaction. They followed suit, and thundered across her parlor floor, pushing and shoving their way toward the terrified woman.

Lifting her skirts, Cora ran toward the sheriff's office, screaming. The herd followed the shrieking woman in a ragtag parade through town. Folks stopped to gape at the scene. What they saw were Cora's stick-thin legs as she galloped right down Main Street with a herd of wild pigs chasing her. Her carefully coiffed hair flared around her face in frizzy hanks, her face beet red and sweating. The folks on Main Street also got a good gander at her faded petticoat, the lace hem torn and shoddy.

Jed Thornton opened the door of his office and stepped outside to see what the commotion was all about. Cora burst past him into the sanctity of one of his jail cells and slammed the door, the javelinas right on her heels, scuffling toward the open threshold.

Thornton pulled his pistol out of its holster and shot twice in the air. At the sharp sound of the gun, the animals panicked, scattering like seeds from one end of Main Street to the other.

Horses rolled their eyes and bolted. Children screamed for their mothers. Men jumped out of the way and cowered behind the water trough as the herd flew past. Jed followed up behind them, hollering and swatting at the air.

The large boar stopped in his tracks and spun toward Jed. He pawed the ground and squealed before lunging for him. The sheriff aimed his pistol and shot him between the eyes. It took two more shots to bring him down, right in front of Buttons and Bows, as Miss Emily looked on in shock. She jumped back inside the shop, slamming the door.

A few men joined Jed, and between them, they herded the stampeding pigs past the church and down into an arroyo. A few more shots from their pistols, and the javelinas disappeared down the gully, squealing and bouncing against each other in a riot of sound.

Behind the safety of her closed door, Marian Humphrey laughed until she wet her pants.

The Sanders's garden lay in ruin. Almost every vegetable and flower had been sampled or crushed beneath cloven hooves. Lined up on the fence, a murder of crows settled in and ruffled their feathers, no longer afraid of the half-eaten scarecrow that rested on the ground, part of its gruesome face staring up at the Texas sun.

Down the street in a jail cell, Cora Sanders waited until nightfall to slink home.

MISS EMILY AUGUSTA

EMILY AUGUSTA WATCHED THE CIRCUS Cora Sanders had created on Main Street with amusement. Cora was one of the biggest annoyances in Breyer. Nobody was safe from the woman's sharp-tongued banter. Emily knew she had been singled out time and again by Cora over the years. It was quite rewarding to watch the wretched woman suffer.

She turned from the window of her dress shop and sat at the table where she had pinned a pattern to a lovely piece of silk before all the ruckus. This would be a special dress Emily was making for herself. Something to wear from time to time. To church, perhaps. The lines of the dress were simple, but the stunning peacock blue silk would lend an air of sophistication. It was the perfect combination. The beautiful dress would likely catch Cora's eye and prime the pump for more meddling.

Cora had probed and pried relentlessly since Emily arrived in Breyer. The woman never ceased pestering her in all those years, and Emily resented it.

Emily's philosophy was the less people knew about her, the better. She had no time for gossip or judgments. No time to befriend the town's women and take part in their silly talk. Miss

Emily Augusta planned to make something of herself. Become a woman of culture. Display good breeding.

Her dress shop and house reflected the graceful style Emily invoked. She loved to run her hands along an elegant piece of fabric, or the silky wood of a fine cabinet. She bought books on etiquette and studied the finer art of manners, behavior, and conversation. Emily sent all the way to New York for a set of the finest china dishes and matching teapot. Every day she filled the stately cup with Earl Grey tea, caressing the warmth in her hands as she sipped.

It was pivotal that Emily not engage in anything but exemplary behavior. Every day was a new chance to reinvent herself. Struggling all her life from the burden of a humble beginning, she liked to think she rose above it and had carved out a good life for herself.

Before long, she believed in her own persona. The woman she invented grew more authentic as the years passed, and she reveled in it. Engaging with others might crack through the veneer of the woman she now presented to the world, perhaps exposing things she wished to keep to herself.

So, keep to herself, she did. Emily Augusta was a woman of mystery. A woman of austere behavior, a woman whose cool exterior belied the heat that simmered inside her soul.

Checking herself in the mirror across from the table, she saw a handsome woman with light brown hair and deep blue eyes. A woman who kept her lovely figure supple and enhanced it with corsets and dresses with belts that hugged her slender waist. She wore her hair in a severe chignon instead of letting it flow loose across her shoulders.

Nobody in Breyer knew Emily at all. She was simply an enigma who trailed through town like a ghost, never sharing one moment of her life with the people who engaged with her. Coldly polite and distant, she glided about town on well-shod feet, nodding at everybody but speaking to no one. Nobody knew where she came from and what might lurk in her past.

Emily pricked her finger with a pin and gasped. Blood rose to the surface and spilled across her skin like a liquid ruby. The familiar coppery smell assaulted her senses, and she stirred in agitation.

Rising from the table, she put her finger in her mouth and walked back over to the window. The wild pigs were gone. Main Street was calm. The afternoon sun shone on the citizens of Breyer as they made their way along the dusty street. Although she recognized many of their faces, they all seemed like strangers to her.

And that was exactly how Emily wanted it.

WILLIE SNOW

WILLIE SNOW LEFT THE RANCH one morning with a pocketful of payday and a list from his mother. It seemed he couldn't venture into town without errands to run. But he was happy enough to saddle up Captain and ride the miles into Breyer on a wakeful Saturday. Willie wore a fresh shirt and took the time to rub the dirt off from his boots. He slicked his bright red hair back with oil and wore a blue kerchief around his neck, thinking it made him look dapper.

He left at dawn, so he might capture every minute of his trip, in order to have something to daydream about tomorrow, when he'd be back with the herd. For a young man like Willie, excitement waited around every corner. Even though he was tall and broad-shouldered, he was still a boy.

Willie's first stop was at Buttons and Bows, the dress shop in town run by the severe-faced Miss Emily Augusta. His mother wanted him to pick up five yards of fabric for a chair in the parlor. Miss Augusta had ordered it all the way from New York City.

He entered the tiny shop and peered around. Women's stuff. Miss Augusta had placed dresses, scarves, and corsets around the room in a feminine way. Part of him wanted to finger the silky items, and the other part made him grow red in the ears, just thinkin' about it.

Miss Augusta stepped out from behind a curtained doorway in the back and recognized him.

"Willie, I imagine your mother has sent you in here to fetch the fabric she ordered."

"Yes, ma'am, she did." Willie pulled his hat off, remembering his manners. His mother would frown at him if he didn't treat a lady with respect.

"I have it in the back." She turned, her skirt billowing behind her in a pleasant sort of way, leaving a faint trail of unusual perfume behind.

The last time he'd been in Buttons and Bows, a pretty young woman had caught his eye. She had been looking at hats, lifting first one, then another, off the display in the window and trying them on in front of a mirror on the wall. Her russet hair glimmered in the sunlight pouring through the pane, hair that fell upon a graceful neck in wisps. The girl must have sensed him staring at her because she turned and looked his way.

She put the hat back and squinted at the young man. "Do I know you?"

"No, ma'am, I don't believe so." Just saying those few words was hard for Willie. He always froze up around girls, especially the pretty ones. He fumbled with his hands as though they had nowhere to go. Willie finally folded them in front of him as he stared at the floor.

"Oh, well then, I'm Molly Brewster. You know, from across the street at The Crow Fly?" She held out a dainty hand, but he couldn't seem to unclasp his, so she let it fall to her side.

MISS AUGUSTA INTERRUPTED HIS REVERIE about Molly, just as she had interrupted them the last time he was in the store.

"Here's your mother's fabric." She held out a length of dark green velvet. "I hope she likes it."

Willie nodded, his mind elsewhere. He watched as Miss Augusta wrapped it in brown paper and tied a string around the parcel. He paid her the money his mother had sent with him, then left the shop and secured the package in his saddlebag.

From there he went to the apothecary for some hair oil and a tin of tobacco for his father.

Willie spent the rest of the day watching people parade up and down Main Street. They all looked as though they had somewhere special to go, he thought. Some ambled along while others bustled.

A train whistle caught his attention, and he wandered over to the depot. His horse snorted and crow-hopped as the huge black engine pulling several cars came into view. The brakes screamed as it slowed, then stopped in front of the station. A couple disembarked with a little boy. The boy had dark hair and silvery eyes. He held tight to his mother's hand, walking so close to her that a gust of wind blew her skirt into his face. They peered around as though looking for somebody, then walked across the street to the Breyer Hotel.

By that time, the sun was setting. Willie rode over to The Crow Fly and tied up his horse. Truth be told, this is what he had been waiting for all day. He knew Molly Brewster worked there. He figured she was a singer or dancer, and he didn't want to miss a moment of her show.

When Willie walked in, he saw other cowboys had already drifted into the saloon. In the corner, a dark-haired man played a piano. The tinny sound filled the room with loud music. Ladies walked around the saloon in fancy dresses. Willie blushed a bit, as many of them showed their bosoms more than his mother would have said was proper. He couldn't help but stare.

An older woman in a blue dress with a feathered hat approached him.

"Anything I can help you with, young man?" She had blonde hair, and her cheeks were flushed with rouge. Her green eyes looked Willie up and down. He squirmed under the scrutiny.

Willie pulled his hat off and held it with both hands in front of him like a shield. "Well, ma'am, I was looking for Miss Molly Brewster. I understand she works here?"

The women brightened and pointed toward the corner. "Over yonder, if you can catch her. There's a lot of men interested in Molly."

Willie followed her gaze toward the back, and sure enough, there stood Molly. She wore a bright red dress with white lace around the hem and sleeves. Her breasts rose out of the bodice like pale moons, and her hair floated about her shoulders, shimmering in the lantern light. He'd never seen anyone so beautiful in his life. Like the tide, he was pulled across the bar toward her.

Two men were talking to her, and she threw her head back as she laughed. Molly had hitched up one side of her skirt in a way that displayed half a slender leg. Willie thought she was the most beautiful sight in the world.

Swallowing his shyness, he spoke up loud and clear as he approached her. "Miss Molly, do you remember me from Buttons and Bows last month?"

Each word sounded like a stone falling into a well. He swore he squeaked. The men stopped and stared at him. One nudged the other with his elbow and smirked.

Molly smiled and straightened her shoulders. "No, sir, I don't believe I do, but I am glad to make your acquaintance." She held out her hand, and this time he took it. Her fingers clasped in his sent shivers down his spine. He dipped his head and smiled.

"I'm William Snow from the Five Bar Ranch? Everybody calls me Willie. Pleased to see you again." This time, the words came out with a bit more boldness, and he drew her hand closer, bringing her in toward him. It seemed like nobody else was in the room. Even the music faded away as he lost himself in her orbit.

"Willie." She stood on tiptoe and breathed softly in his ear. "What can I do for you?"

"Well, Miss Molly, I came to see you."

Molly pointed to the older woman in the feather hat. "Go talk to Peg about it. If she says it's okay, come back here."

"Oh, yes, ma'am," he replied, dropping her hand and turning toward the bar. "I'll be back right away."

It seemed to Willie that it was a little odd that he needed to talk to Peg first, but maybe she was a chaperone or something. He approached the woman, who was standing by a potted plant in the corner next to an enormous dark-haired man.

"Miss Peg? Molly said I needed to see you about visiting with her."

Peg nodded, a smile dancing across her lips. "She did, did she? Well, it's three bucks for an hour, ten for the night."

Willie's eyebrows raised in surprise. "Just to watch her? I didn't know that was how it worked."

This time it was Peg's turn to be surprised. "Well, what did you think, young man? Do you think she'd work for free? Pay up or go on your way."

Willie dug his pay out of his pocket and counted out three dollars. Peg stuffed them in a small, beaded bag she wore over her shoulder and nodded to Molly, who glided across the saloon toward them.

Molly took Willie by the arm. "Come on along," she said. "I'll show you a good time."

"Where are we going?"

"Why, upstairs, Willie. You don't expect we'd stay here, do you?"

"I guess not."

She led him up the stairs to a room, opened the door, and walked in. Willie followed.

The space was small, with a dresser, a rocking chair, and a bed. On the bed was a cheerful quilt the color of sunflowers and bluebonnets. Neatly placed on the dresser was a brush and a couple of small pots. A soft rag doll with yellow yarn hair sat in the rocking chair, along with a ruby colored pillow. The window was open. A warm breeze billowed through lace curtains, fluttering the pages of a calendar on the wall. Below on the street, Willie heard the creak of wagons on the road and voices. Willie flushed. It was awkward being in what was obviously the girl's bedroom.

It wasn't until she shut the door, turned toward him and pulled at her dress that Willie realized the truth. Molly was a whore. He just about dropped over, he was so embarrassed. How could he have been so stupid? She stood in front of the door, or he would have bolted right then and there.

"What would you like to do, Willie?" Molly asked. She reached behind her neck and unfastened her scarlet dress. Willie watched, mesmerized.

The red dress floated to the ground. Molly stepped out of it wearing a tight black corset. She pulled down the straps, releasing her breasts. They swayed as she walked toward him.

"I... I think I made a mistake," he said. "I thought you were a singer, not a well... you know. I'm sorry to trouble you, ma'am. I best be on my way."

Molly looked surprised. She laughed, then, a soft little giggle that he swore made his hair stand on end, among other things. Suddenly, Willie didn't want to leave. He was aching to stay.

"Are you a virgin, Willie Snow?" Molly reached for his hand and placed it on her warm breast. "I can help you get over that, sir."

Willie moaned. His hat dropped to the floor. Molly touched him below his belt buckle and he thought he'd explode. He didn't care about anything else. Not the night, or the horse tied up outside with his mother's fabric on it, or the fact that Molly didn't dance. She led him to the bed, and he fell upon her, bruising her lips with eager kisses.

MOLLY LOOKED DOWN AT WILLIE'S sleeping face. They'd been together upstairs much too long. He hadn't paid for the whole night, but she couldn't bear to let him go just yet. Willie was so different from the others who dragged her upstairs for a quick poke. Some didn't even bother to get undressed. Willie was sweet and gentle and held her in his arms as though she were fragile.

But now it was time for him to leave. She nudged him awake, and he fell upon her again with more kisses and groans.

"Willie, you only paid for a poke. It's time you went home. Next time, if there is a next time, pay for the whole night and we can be together longer."

After they dressed, Molly led Willie back downstairs, and he walked through the swinging doors into the night. His horse stood patiently, tied to the post. It seemed like he had been away for weeks. Slowly, the sounds of the night came back. He heard the lively music from The Crow Fly, voices in the saloon, the clip-clop of hooves on the road.

Dazed, he mounted Captain and turned north toward home. Luckily for him, his horse knew the way because Willie had no idea where he was. All he could think about was Molly, her lovely smile, slender legs, and russet hair. Molly with lips like little pillows where he placed his again and again before they traveled down her slender throat then nibbled on her moon shaped breasts until he thought he might burst.

He decided right then and there he'd come back again next Saturday night. And the Saturday night after that. He'd pay for the night and not leave until the birds sang in the rafters at dawn. He'd keep her to himself and not let any other man touch her.

It had been a helluva night. A night when a young man's ritual into adulthood ended in success.

One thing was perfectly clear. Willie Snow was no longer a virgin.

And he was in love with Molly Brewster.

BOY TO MAN

BACK AT HOME, WILLIE'S MOTHER was not happy to see him return from Breyer so late the next morning. But his father defended him.

"Clarisse, let him be. He's a man now. Will works hard all week. If he wants to blow off steam on a Friday or Saturday night, it's good for him."

"Good for him?" Clarisse Snow raised her voice. A tiny woman, sometimes Willie and his father wondered how she could muster so much noise out of her slender throat. Her red hair and green eyes spoke of Ireland. There was a small lilt in her words that carried all the way back to County Mayo.

But even a fiery woman like Clarisse knew when she was defeated. The more Willie grew, the harder it was to part the waters of masculinity around there, and after a while, she rolled her eyes and muttered several warnings, but Willie Snow knew he'd won the battle.

Willie returned again and again to The Crow Fly. He made sure he arrived as soon as the saloon opened, so he could spend all his hard-earned money on Molly.

Upstairs in her room, Willie was pretty sure he'd found

heaven. He and Molly were the same age. Both of them were just eighteen, but where Will had been raised in a structured home, poor Molly had seen the darker side of humanity.

They often snuggled under the sheets and talked and giggled after they had sex. Willie made shadows of ducks and rabbits on the wall with his hands, and Molly sang silly songs, making up the words as the situation suited. Will always left by the back stairs in the dead of night so he could make the ride back to the ranch before dawn.

Sometimes he'd get home and have to turn right around because his mother requested he come with them to church on Sunday morning. Hot and tired, he'd turn Captain's head and go back the way he came, following their carriage into Breyer.

On Sundays, Molly sat in the rocking chair by the window that looked out on Main Street and watched the faithful as they journeyed to the little white church at the end of the street. She kept a lookout for Willie. They made a pact that he'd ride past her window and lightly flick his hat, which was his way of saying howdy. She'd laugh and hug the pillow to her breasts as he rode by.

One night, Willie took her upstairs with a grim face. His hand gripped her elbow a little too hard. When they got to her room, he slammed the door behind him and threw the latch.

"Why, Willie, what's wrong?" Tears sprang into Molly's eyes as she rubbed her sore elbow. Had she offended him somehow?

"Molly, I don't understand why you keep entertaining other men. I can't stand it anymore! Stop!" He sat on the bed, pulled his boots off, and let them drop to the floor with a thud.

"Willie, I have to do it! I have to earn a living! You know what I am, what I do." Molly was defensive. Did he think she wanted to be a whore? Who the hell did he think he was, pushing his way in here and giving her ultimatums?

Willie fell back on the bed in exasperation. The bedsprings

groaned beneath his weight. He clutched at his red hair and moaned.

"This can't continue," he said. Then he sat up and reached for her satin skirt. Pulling her over to him, he buried his head in the soft folds of fabric.

"Molly, you know I love you. I can't stand the thought that you sleep with other men. It's wrong! Just wrong!"

Molly walked over to the door and opened it. "I think you better go now," she said, her voice ragged. "Willie, I love you too. But we come from two different worlds. I have to make a living, and you belong at the ranch."

"Then we'll get married!" Willie walked over to the door and leaned against it with his arms folded across his chest. "We'll get married right away."

"Are you crazy? I've seen your parents every Sunday on their way to church. They're God-fearing people. They'd never abide a girl like me!"

"They would, once they got to know you."

Willie warmed to the whole idea. He'd marry Molly in secret, and then his parents couldn't do anything about it. Besides, if they objected, he'd leave them and the ranch. Take Molly somewhere better. Colorado, maybe. Hell, he was young, but he could break a horse better than anyone else at the ranch. There had to be jobs for a man willing to put in an honest day's work.

Willie tilted the girl's chin up and brushed her lips with his. "Molly, do you love me?"

She didn't hesitate. "I do. I'm afraid, though."

"Afraid of what?"

She swept aside the curtains and peered out the window. Down below, men were entering The Crow Fly. She recognized several of them. They might even ask for her tonight. She flushed and turned away.

"I guess I don't trust people too awfully well," she said.

There were years of heartache behind each word. Trust was

something other people did. She shivered. For the first time in a while, she felt completely alone.

"You can trust me. I promise. We'll get married and you'll quit this job and everything will work out." Willie sat on the edge of the bed, deep in thought.

"Listen, I'll be back on Friday night. We'll talk about it and make our plans then. In the meantime, don't sleep with anyone else but me." He stood and emptied his pockets of his entire month's pay. "Will this be enough for you to stop?"

She nodded mutely and picked up the bills and set them on the dresser. With a soft sigh, she pulled off her dress. Taking Willie's hand, she led him to the bed.

When Willie returned the following week, he had plenty to tell Molly.

"We're gonna get married, Molly! I swear it! I've been thinkin' about it all week, and decided we'll leave Texas and strike out on our own. It's better that way. A new start, sweetheart. Think about it!" He removed his clothes and settled in with her on the narrow bed.

"But, Willie, what about your parents and the ranch? Surely they need you, and eventually you should inherit that ranch."

Willie shrugged. "I love you. That's all that matters. I don't think my parents would ever accept our marriage, the more I think about it. This is just the way it will have to be." His eyes narrowed. "Believe me, I've thought long and hard about all of this. I know my folks. And I know the ranch. And I know you. It's best this way." His lips nibbled on her neck and shoulders.

"I can't let you do that, Willie." Molly turned on her side, away from him. She traced his name on the wall with her finger. "You'd be giving up your whole life on account of me. It would break my heart." She pulled the blanket up to her chin.

"Now, honey, I didn't tell you all this to make you sad. Why, we're going to start a whole new chapter somewhere else where people won't talk and we can live a normal life. With kids and all!"

Willie jumped out of bed and walked over to his pants draped over the rocking chair and reached into the pocket. Molly watched as he strode over to her. His red hair stood on end like a rooster and his naked body glowed in the candlelight. She smiled. He had a man's body, but a boyish face. The combination was charming. Her heart lifted. She loved him. That was all that mattered. She turned away again and drifted deeper under the covers, waiting for him to join her.

"Turn around and look at this, sweet Molly."

She peered over her shoulder. "What's that you've got?"

"It's my late grandma's sapphire ring. Her wedding ring. It came all the way from Ireland. My grandparents and mother sailed here from County Mayo. My grandparents died on the journey. This ring was all my grandma ever had of value, but she held on to it all her life. Good times and hard times, she never sold it. Even when those times were the toughest and they needed money, she refused to part with it. My mother told me she kept it for the woman I marry. It was Grandma's wish.

"Now, it will be yours." He took Molly's hand and placed the ring on her finger. It gleamed in the lamplight. "It's your wedding ring."

Molly touched it. The ring fit perfectly. The stone was still warm from Willie's pocket. It was a beautiful legacy from across the sea. To feel it on her finger was both humbling and exciting.

"Willie, I've never seen anything so pretty in my whole life! Are you sure you want me to have it?"

He grinned and kissed her forehead. "It's my promise to you, honey. There ain't nothing as special as you," he said. "I have to leave early tonight. Startin' tomorrow, we're moving cattle down from the upper meadow and selling some off to market. I won't be back here for two whole weeks. I won't leave my dad in a lurch. I'll work until we sort the cattle out, and then head back to Breyer. That's when I plan to take you away with me. I'll bring a horse for you and we'll ride out of here early in the morning and get married along the way to Colorado. I have some money saved up. Do you?"

Molly nodded. "Yep. A little. Enough to buy us food." She smiled at him. "Do you really mean all of this? Because I've been lied to before. I think my heart will crack wide open if you're foolin' with me, Willie Snow."

"I ain't foolin'. That ring's proof of my love. I wouldn't give it to you if I were fooling with you. But now I have to run. We herd the cattle first thing in the morning."

He dressed and pulled on his boots, taking an extra moment to kiss Molly deeply on the lips.

Willie turned the door knob and winked. "Now, you remember. Two weeks from this Sunday I'm coming for you. That's two weeks and one day from now. Be packed and ready, then slip out the door just as soon as you see me ride up the street at dawn. I'll be here before the churchgoers and my parents arrive, okay?"

Molly nodded. It all seemed too good to be true. She gazed down at the beautiful ring on her finger and, for the first time since she lost her parents, felt hopeful.

"I love you, Willie. I'll be ready."

She watched him walk out the door and his familiar footsteps faded into the night.

MOLLY'S PLIGHT

TWO WEEKS WITHOUT SEEING WILLIE was hard on Molly. He'd asked her not to see any other men while he was gone and she was running out of money fast. As it was, most of the money she saved was used to pay her share at The Crow Fly without sleeping with the patrons. She figured Willie would understand, since she remained virtuous for him.

Molly spent her days wandering around town and at night she lolled in her bed, listening to the sounds of the saloon below while she read one of the many books she'd bought over the years. It was a delicious feeling to relax and know that somebody loved her.

Old Peg pursed her lips when Molly told her she was running off to marry Willie Snow. It was a too familiar tale. Promises were so easily made by young men, and the girls believed them. Peg had seen this happen more than once. Men sometimes got love and sex all mixed up in their brains and said things they really didn't mean in the heat of passion. Molly was an innocent girl in many ways.

"Molly, I know you're happy and excited, but I wouldn't go telling anyone else yet. You know how they can be."

"But I want them to know!" Molly sat on the bottom step of the rickety stairs at the back of The Crow Fly and grinned. Her russet hair caught the last of the afternoon sun. She looked beautiful and happy. Since she wasn't entertaining other men, she wore a simple yellow cotton dress that graced her ankles and made her look young and full of life.

Peg pursed her lips and swatted at a fly with a rolled-up newspaper. "What if this doesn't happen, Molly? Then what? Do you think Kate, or Miss Emily, will be all that happy for you if it does? It'll be tough to hear that you will run off and lead a happy life when theirs may be lacking. Think about them before you announce all those plans. They might not be as kindly as they once were to you. It's best you keep it to yourself for now."

"They'll be happy for me, Peg. Why wouldn't they? They know I've been seeing Willie. It won't be a surprise or anything."

"Just take my advice, and keep it to yourself for a while longer. It won't hurt to wait before you tell them." Peg reached down and picked up a coin somebody had dropped, brushed it off and put it in her pocket. She felt bad, taking the steam out of the girl, but it would be far worse if Molly announced her plans, only to be humiliated by yet another young buck who had no intention of following through on his promises.

Peg's advice hurt Molly. This was the happiest time in her life, and Peg was doing her best to ruin it. She stood and abruptly climbed the stairs.

"Mind you, Molly," Peg said. "Don't be making a fool of yourself. I've seen it before, honey. Men make promises they won't keep. Mark my words, you'll be sitting here all alone come Monday!"

Molly stopped at the top of the stairs and looked down at the older woman.

"Willie's not like that! You're just jealous."

Peg shook her head sadly. "Have it your way, then."

THE SALOON ALWAYS FELT DIFFERENT in the morning. The stale smell of sweat and whiskey coated the walls and silence hung heavy in the air. Molly walked down the staircase to the bar below and let herself out the back door. Today she was going to see Miss Augusta at Buttons and Bows and purchase a new hat. She couldn't afford a wedding dress, but a hat might be just what she needed to look pretty when she married Willie.

The shop always looked so merry, Molly thought. Miss Emily had colorful hats in the window, displayed on a frothy yard of lace. Right in the front was a white hat with an ostrich feather. It looked sophisticated and elegant. If the price was good, it would be perfect.

She entered the shop and looked around. The bolts of fabric lining the walls were almost magical. Lush colors and pretty patterns were everywhere. A girl could spend the whole day here and not see it all. On the counter was a mirror, surrounded by beautiful hair clips. Below, in a glass case, were brooches and a delicate necklace with tiny blue stones in it. Molly looked down at the ring on her finger and thought the necklace was a perfect match.

Miss Emily parted the curtains in the doorway and stepped through. As usual, she had a slightly superior look on her face. If she smiled, she might be pretty and her figure was still fit. Molly imagined she had been lovely in her younger days.

"What can I do for you, Molly?" Emily straightened the gaily colored kerchiefs on the counter. Today she wore a green dress that shimmered in the lamplight. Her hair was worn in ringlets on the top of her head. Molly figured it was the latest look from New York.

"I was lookin' at the white hat you have in the window, Miss Emily. And the necklace here in the case."

"Why, that's a lovely choice. Two of my best pieces."

"Oh. Well, could you tell me what you want for 'em?"

Emily named her price.

Molly's shoulders slumped. She couldn't buy both. And shouldn't buy either. The hat was out of the question.

"Do you want to try them on?" Emily opened the case and picked up the necklace.

"Let me see the necklace. I can't afford the hat."

Emily placed the jewelry on the counter. Molly picked it up and held it to her neck. She walked over to the mirror. The necklace was perfect. It was delicate and worldly, something a sophisticated lady might wear. Something a proper wife might wear.

"Is this for a special occasion?" Emily asked.

Molly remembered what Peg said about announcing her wedding to everybody. Maybe she was right. She sure didn't get the response she thought from Peg. Maybe Miss Emily would be that way, too, and Molly thought she'd burst into tears if one more person threw cold water on her dreams.

"No, not really. I just thought I wanted something pretty." She reached into her purse and brought out several dollars. Now she would only have three bucks left. She hoped Willie would understand. It was her wedding gift to herself. Just thinking about marrying Willie made her heart lift a bit, and she turned and grinned at Emily.

"I'll take it!"

"Good choice. I'll wrap it in tissue for you."

"No, I'd like to wear it right here and now."

"Of course." Emily clasped the necklace around Molly's neck and stepped back. "It becomes you. You have a lovely neck and a beautiful face. I hope you enjoy it for years to come."

It was the nicest thing she'd ever heard Miss Emily say, and she felt a glow inside. Old Peg didn't know what the hell she was talking about.

"I'm gonna marry Willie Snow!" Molly said, then blushed.

Emily's brows arched in surprise. She knew Clarisse Snow, and had serious doubts that Willie was going to walk a whore from The Crow Fly down any aisle. So many young men developed heartthrobs for the ladies they slept with, but when it came to marriage, they'd find a decent woman to wed. She opened her mouth to say something, but changed her mind. After all, let the girl have her happiness, even though it might be short-lived. Emily would not be the one to ruin her day. She'd had plenty of her own days destroyed by heartless remarks over the years.

"Why, that's lovely. I wish you and Willie the best. He's a very nice young man."

Molly smiled and twirled in front of the mirror. "Thank you! It's gonna be the happiest day of my life."

Emily watched as Molly walked back across the road to The Crow Fly. A gust of wind lifted the girl's skirt, and she brushed it back down, dodging a tumbleweed that sailed across the street. A storm was coming. The wind had been teasing Breyer all morning, but now it was serious.

MOLLY

MOLLY SAT IN HER ROCKING chair and drew back the curtains. From the second floor, she looked down on to Main Street and loved watching the constant parade of wagons, horses, cowhands, and Breyer's citizens as they bustled about their day. She smiled as she watched Lara Thornton herding her two daughters on their way to school. The woman always had a friendly word for everyone, including the ladies from The Crow Fly. Not far behind them, and always watching, was Jed. Oh, to have a man like Jed Thornton for a husband! Handsome and sure of himself, he reminded her of a sleeping lion. Quiet, yet strong and ferocious if provoked by gamblers on a Saturday night. Even the roughnecks showed respect when he'd walk into the saloon.

Lara Thornton was exactly how Molly dreamed her life would turn out. She wanted to grow up to become a teacher. She wanted a strong, capable husband, and most of all, she wanted children. Life took such a turn for the Brewsters. A turn her father and mother would have never wanted to happen. And yet, here she was, a whore at The Crow Fly, entertaining men until the wee hours of the morning. Her mother and father would be so sad and ashamed that Molly suffered because of decisions they made.

It wasn't their fault. They were trying to make their lives better. Never would they have thought it would turn out the way it did.

JANE AND ROBERT BREWSTER SAVED for years to buy the plot of land in an unforgiving part of Texas. They didn't know how badly they'd been cheated until they left their small farm in Indiana and made their way out to the hardscrabble acreage so far from home that it all seemed like a bad dream.

Molly was their only child. She was just fourteen when they arrived in Texas. It was a different world from the farmhouse where they lived in Indiana. The lush green meadows and well-traveled roads in the Midwest had been replaced with a dirt trail that wound across a landscape that looked so much like what was over the next hill, a person could get lost for the rest of their lives. And Molly reckoned this was exactly what happened to them.

Back in Indiana, Molly went to school every day. She loved everything about school, from carrying her lunch in a little metal bucket, to the chalkboard where the teacher wrote the alphabet and taught arithmetic. There were children to talk to and play with, and books on a shelf that she could borrow and bring home to read. Her teacher, Mrs. Young, was a pretty woman with jet black hair and blue eyes. Molly thought she was the most beautiful person in the world and spent half her days wishing her chestnut-colored eyes would turn blue. She dreamed of becoming a teacher and worked hard at her lessons.

But Robert Brewster had other plans. A short man with tall ideas, he hankered to live on a larger piece of land and raise horses or cattle, or even sheep. It was no surprise to Jane that his plans took hold and overflowed. He brought home information about land for sale in Texas and Oklahoma. Land where a man might find his mettle and raise his family. Fresh air and blue skies. Despite Jane's objections, Robert's ideas ran away with him.

One day, he came home with a deed in his hand and a triumphant look on his face. "Well, Jane, I did it! I bought one hundred acres in Texas and we're moving before winter!"

Jane spun around from setting the table. She wasn't much bigger than Molly, her dark hair twisted into a thick braid that hung down her back. Her tiny hand rested on her hip as she glared at her husband.

Molly still remembered the cries and arguments that night. She heard their voices rise and fall through the walls. She finally fell asleep, her mother's cries and her father's shouting surrounding her.

The next morning, the air was thick with resentment. Robert had won. Jane was still in bed with a headache when Molly left for school. She felt as though the world was spinning the wrong way.

The Brewsters moved to Texas in September. They lived in tents for months, despite the sometime harsh weather in the winter. After a week or two in the tents, Jane gave up keeping anything clean, and soon they were filthy. And hungry. Robert hadn't thought things out properly, and the only thing that kept them alive were his trips to a nearby town, trading their possessions for flour, meat, and other necessities. He even traded Molly's books for a slab of beef, along with Jane's gold wedding ring.

Robert Brewster was stubborn, and worked hard on his equally stubborn scrap of land. His focus was building the small cabin they eventually lived in. After that, he turned toward the land to see what might grow. The hardscrabble earth was not at all what he expected. It would be almost impossible to raise animals on the acreage he bought. He realized he was naive, and it cost his family dearly. Clearly the only way to survive would be to plant a garden and hope it might grow food in the Texas dirt. Thankfully, seeds were cheap and easy to come by. Packet after packet of seeds were shoved into the ground. Jane and Molly dragged home water in heavy buckets from the small creek that passed through the land. Jane tenderly watered the few sprouts foolish enough to break through the ground, but the earth fought back and kept most of the seeds to itself.

The tender plants that survived were a delicious treat for the wandering rabbits and deer who helped themselves day and night. Robert, Jane, and Molly took turns chasing them out of the feeble garden, and precious else got done around the homestead.

They had no mirror to see their own shocking reflections. Gaunt, dirty, and wide-eyed with confusion, it was likely they didn't even know they were slowly starving to death.

Robert became sick after going into town one day for supplies. He came home with a fever, droplets of sweat on his face, a rash appearing right behind it. He collapsed in bed. When Jane came in from chasing animals out of the garden, she drew back in shock.

"Robert! What's wrong?" Jane set her worn gloves on the hearth and placed her hand on his forehead. He had a raging fever.

Molly's father was too weak to speak. Hunger, unrelenting heat, and sickness rendered him helpless as he lay on the cot.

Like a bolt of lightning that hits with astounding brilliance, and then disappears just as quickly, Robert Brewster died by the next morning. He was so thin that Jane and Molly easily carried him outside for burial. There was no time for tears. The vast array of everything they had endured traveled up their bodies and into their heads, cutting off any semblance of normalcy, and left them numb.

Now it was up to the two females on the hellish land to survive. Jane and Molly immediately understood they needed to leave and move on. The closest town, Breyer, was ten miles away and had very little to offer, but perhaps they could sell what they had left to purchase a ticket back home to Indiana. Perhaps the horse and wagon might be enough to pay for the two of them on the train. They could also load any tools on the property into the back of the wagon for barter, along with what few possessions they had left, and go to town with the idea they would never come back. They began packing.

But by the next morning, Jane couldn't rise from her bed, and Molly felt woozy herself. The two danced between feverish hallucination and comatose sleep. Once Molly heard animals scratching at the door, and the howl of coyotes out where Robert's grave was, but she could only lay there and hope they couldn't find their way into the cabin.

When Jane died, Molly could not lift her from the bed. So futile were her efforts that she fell back to sleep by her mother and didn't wake for hours. When she did, she gathered the few remaining things of any value, then walked on unsteady feet out the door, leaving her mother behind in the hut.

She'd seen her father ride to town several times, so she knew to saddle the horse and ride west, over a scrub-filled knoll. She didn't have the strength to hitch the horse to the wagon. Perhaps somebody in Breyer could help her gather her things left behind once she got better. When she got to the other side of the hill, she saw an endless landscape of brush and dirt. Far in the distance was a line snaking through the scrub, and the closer she got, the more it looked like a path. With no other options, she followed the trail.

Breyer loomed out of the dust like a mirage. Molly was delirious by then. She held on to the saddle horn and mumbled as the horse walked toward town. She heard music and followed the sound to a saloon. The Crow Fly. Molly stopped the horse in front of the swinging doors, and tried to dismount, but fell off onto the dirt of Main Street.

Kate Dawson was walking back from Buttons and Bows when she saw the girl collapse. Lifting her skirts, she ran over to help.

She hollered for the piano player. "Rick! Rick! Get out here!"

Rick burst through the swinging doors.

"What's the problem?" he asked, then saw Molly and jumped off the sidewalk and into the street to help.

They carried her into the cool saloon and placed her on a chair. Peg came downstairs to see what the ruckus was all about.

"Who is she?" she asked.

Kate shrugged her shoulders. "I don't know. She pulled up here on a horse and then fell right off. She's pretty sick. Thinking of her own bout with the pox, Kate shrank back from the girl. The pretty little thing was suffering from something serious.

Peg leaned over and touched Molly's forehead. It was burning up.

"Rick, run get a bucket of cold water and some cloths. Kate, go see if Doc Winters will come over here. Tell him she's a stranger, and not a whore. He might stop in then."

Molly opened her eyes. She had trouble focusing, but turned toward Peg's voice.

"Help me," she said, reaching out her hand.

Peg took it. "You're safe here, honey. Just relax. We're sending for the doctor and he should come soon."

DOC WINTERS RECOILED WHEN HE saw Molly.

"I think it's smallpox. This girl needs to be isolated. She could make half the town sick, for God's sake. Who is she? Where does she live?"

"She didn't say," Peg said. "She's ailing too much to talk. But she's awfully sick and dirty. I don't think she comes from around here. Don't see any of her folks either."

"Well, I'd say keep her upstairs away from everybody until we can figure this out." The doctor shrugged. "I have no room in my office for somebody with the pox. Too many folks comin' in for other ailments could catch it. If you don't take her, I ain't sure what to do with her."

Kate took a step closer. "I'll tend to her. I already had the pox. Rick, help me bring her upstairs."

Rick hesitated. "I've never had the pox. I don't want to catch it either."

Kate frowned. "How the hell am I to get her upstairs?"

"I'll help," said Peg.

The two women inched their way up the flight of stairs and put Molly in an empty room at the end of the hall that was used for extra chairs and cases of whiskey. Kate brought several blankets from a closet, and they laid the girl on the floor.

"Doc says to try to get water down her. Then maybe some soup. She's pretty far gone." Peg had tears in her eyes. Such a sweet little thing. Sometimes life was cruel.

Kate sat by Molly the whole night. It was a Tuesday, so very few customers made their way into The Crow Fly and Peg turned them away. Kate kept cool cloths on Molly's head and dragged a rocking chair into the room, where she sat and rocked and watched over her.

When Molly awoke, the sun was shining through the dirty window above her head. The first thing she saw was Kate in the rocker, the light illuminating her in a halo of dust motes and sunshine.

"Are you an angel?" she asked. "Am I dead?"

Kate woke at the sound of her voice and walked across the room to check on the girl.

She laughed. "No, honey, I am anything but an angel, and you aren't dead. You've been mighty sick, but I think your fever broke. You have the pox. Don't scratch at the spots like I did, even if they itch." She pointed to her own marked face. "Try to leave them alone and get some rest. I'll go downstairs and fetch you some water and soup. What's your name, anyway?"

"Molly Brewster."

"Well, Molly, I'm Kate Dawson. Do you have any kin around here?"

Molly picked at the blanket, tears in her eyes. "My mother and father died of the fever. I don't have anybody else."

Of course. There would be no other reason why such a lovely young girl would wander through Breyer on her own.

"You're safe here with me and Peg at The Crow Fly. It's a saloon. It's quiet upstairs here, though, so you just get some rest and we'll talk more later today."

Molly continued to improve over the next several days. She talked to Peg and Kate and told them her story. They were sympathetic and kind. Molly clung to them as though they were big sisters. She couldn't bear the thought that she was completely alone in the big world, and without the comfort from them, she wasn't sure what she would do. Once she felt better, she followed the two women everywhere. They were kind and tolerant. The newly orphaned Molly decided they were her family now.

Later, Peg would say to Kate she wished Molly's horse had stopped in front of the church instead of the saloon. Or even at Jed Thornton's office. Her life might have turned out differently. Instead, Molly stayed at The Crow Fly and eventually made her life, and her living, with Peg and Kate.

LIFE SURE TOOK A LOT of twists and turns, Molly muttered to herself. Some days were dark and others filled with sunshine, like the whole world was ready to bloom. Today was one of those days. The sky was so blue it took your breath away if you let it, and the slight breeze smelled like promise. Molly looked down at her ring. Only a few days, and Willie would come and claim his bride.

Molly hugged herself in anticipation. She couldn't wait to see him. She had a big secret to share with him. Running her hands along her belly she smiled. Molly was pretty sure she was expecting a baby. She hadn't talked to Peg or Kate about it yet and was too shy to go see Doc Winters. Besides, he frowned on treating the women of The Crow Fly. She hoped with all her heart she was right. Only time would tell, and she and Willie had plenty of that.

LIGHTNING

IT WAS TOO NICE A day to sit inside and wait for The Crow
Fly to open, so Molly tossed a shawl around her shoulders
and set out for the mercantile. She hadn't felt well lately. A little
queasy, a little tired. Sunshine would surely help.

She bought a tin of powders for her upset stomach at the dry
goods store and leisurely walked up Main Street. The town was
bustling with activity. A wagon jostled up the road past Miss
Emily's house. A family she didn't recognize lurched along in it.
The man tightened the reins and clucked under his tongue. One
horse tossed its head and wrestled with the bit in its mouth. The
woman smiled at Molly, then grasped the side of the buckboard
and held on as a wheel hit a rut along the way.

Jed Thornton tipped his hat as he walked by.

"Good morning, Molly. How are you today?"

"Just fine, Mister Thornton." Molly tightened the shawl
around her shoulders. She always felt so small next to the sheriff.
He was intimidating, even though he was kind to her.

Jed noticed the dimples on Molly's pretty face. Why, she
didn't look much older than his own daughters. It was a shame
she worked at The Crow Fly. He thought of his girls, and how his

heart would break if they ended up in a whiskey-soaked saloon in the middle of nowhere.

An ominous noise startled Molly. She craned her neck around in surprise.

"What was that?"

"Oh, I imagine it was thunder and lightning, Molly."

She peered up at a crystal-clear sky. "But it's nice out. Is a storm coming?"

"Nah, it's likely heat lightning and sounds from a storm far away. It probably won't touch down anywhere near town. It won't bring any rain with it, though Lord knows we could use some. The sky's been pouting and turbulent for days now. I wouldn't worry none. It'll go away. The sun will stay out. Just you wait and see."

Jed wanted to give the girl a hug and reassure her. But he knew it would look odd to the people in Breyer. They would not understand that he felt fatherly toward a whore. So, instead, he gave her a smile, bid goodbye, and continued on his way.

Molly hurried back to The Crow Fly. The sheriff was probably right. But she sure didn't want to get caught in a rainstorm and get soaked and muddy.

By the time she got back to the saloon, the noises had quieted, and the sun beat down upon Breyer like it always did.

HERD INSTINCT

WILLIE SNOW'S HORSE, CAPTAIN, STAMPED his hoof impatiently while Willie settled the saddle over the roan's withers. He reached underneath Captain's belly to grasp the cinch and yank it up to slide it into a ring under the flap.

Pulling it tight, he noticed the cinch looked a little worn. Willie peered around the barn for a cinch in better shape but couldn't find anything close by. Maybe his father had some in a shed he kept for surplus saddles, bits, and spare horseshoes. It was behind the largest corral.

Cursing, he tied the horse to a post and walked out of the barn.

William Snow stopped him on his way out.

"I've been looking for you! Let's get going now, Willie," he said. "We're already running late. No dawdling." He frowned and jutted his thumb over his shoulder. "All the rest of the men are ready and mounted up. You're late. Get a move on!"

"My cinch looks frayed," Willie replied. "I was gonna see if I can find a new one in the shed."

"Is it bad?"

"No, sir. A little frayed is all."

"Then mount up and let's get out of here. You can ride back by nightfall and look around for another then. We can't waste any more time."

Willie saw a dozen cowboys waiting on their mounts near the corral. Flustered, he turned back to the barn and finished saddling Captain. Putting his foot in the stirrup, he swung up and settled into the well-worn leather of his favorite saddle.

Captain moved forward and nickered at the horses. A mare whinnied back. Raising his hand, Willie greeted the other men. He and his father led them out into the open fields and they broke into a light jog.

LATE IN THE AFTERNOON, WILLIE wiped his brow with his blue kerchief. It was hotter than blazes under the Texas sun. He and the other cowhands had been rounding up cattle all day. Most of the herd, well over one hundred heifers and steers, were rounded up at the end of the valley and ready to turn toward home. There had been a few stragglers, but Willie figured they had most of them now. Once they sorted them out in the fields near home, they could decide which ones to take to market. Then there'd be a long cattle drive. One that Willie did not plan to take part in this year. Instead, he'd be with Molly somewhere in Colorado. Just thinking about it made him grin. He glanced around for any dawdlers.

One old cow was hiding behind a thorny shrub with a newborn calf. It was the devil's work pushing her out of the brambles. Sulking, the cow shuffled her calf toward the front of the herd, rolling her eyes at Willie. The calf was only a few hours old. Part of the placenta still hung out of the cow in a ropy twist. The calf walked on spindly legs, bumping into the other cattle as its mother hurried him along.

Snow loped up to his son and narrowed his eyes as he studied the cow.

"Seems like that cow might have to be cut out of the herd, but I doubt she'll stay behind. She'll insist on coming with us, I think. We can't nurse her along, son. She'll slow everybody down and I want to get this herd closer to the homestead tonight. We're a good ride away. Guess we'll have to get 'em to move a little faster than usual. Keep 'em in order, though."

Willie nodded and slapped his hand against his thigh. "Here now! Hi-yap!" The other cowboys did the same, whooping and edging the cattle forward. Several steers eased into a trot. One wrangler angled his horse ahead of the herd and turned them in order to slow the pace down. It was never good to incite the herd to do more than walk. A few wranglers broke into song, which seemed to soothe the animals as they moved along.

Willie pulled on the reins and fumbled for his canteen. He took a swig and looked out at the great expanse of the Five Bar Ranch. He'd miss this beautiful place. It's all he'd ever known. It's a pity his parents might object to little Molly. Despite the joy Willie had known here all his life, he would give it up for the woman he loved. Only a couple more days, and he'd fetch her. He took another drink and swiped at his mouth with the back of his hand.

A bolt of lightning sliced across the horizon, a blinding white light that lit up the sky. It arced and split across the plains.

The cattle shuffled and flicked their tails. The old cow rolled her eyes and stamped her hoof in the dust. Willie straightened in the saddle and moved forward with the herd. The smell of ozone permeated the valley. Captain snorted and tossed his head.

Another bolt of lightning and a roll of thunder cracked through the heavy air like a whip. The nervous cattle moved forward behind the cow as she led the way through a dry arroyo and back up along a ridge with an expanse of grass. The herd followed, twisting and pushing into the gully and scrambling up the other side, then fanning out along the ridge.

The next flash of light started the stampede. Anxious and aroused, the cow lowered her head, and leaving her calf behind, bolted. Within seconds, the rest of the herd thundered forward.

"Willie! Willie! Get ahead of that damned cow and try to mill 'em." Snow reined in and cut his horse in the other direction. "Damn stupid cow just left her calf behind. It's gonna get trampled. I should have cut her from the herd when I could. You get going, and we'll flank you along both sides!"

Willie tapped Captain with his spurs. The horse broke into a gallop. He raced toward the panicked cow, hoping to turn her to the right, then press the cattle into a large circle, slowing them down.

Up ahead was a gully with steep banks. Willie didn't want the frantic animals to spill over a cliff. He pushed Captain ahead of the racing herd. Dust billowed everywhere. Cattle bawled and bumped into each other. A steer knocked into the chest of a horse, and horse and rider almost went down in the swirling mass.

Slapping his reins along Captain's neck, Willie pulled far ahead of the herd, then turned and edged closer to the lead cattle.

Suddenly, the cinch broke. It was like riding a gust of prairie wind as the saddle listed to one side and Willie's feet came out of the stirrups. He instinctively grabbed for the horn. His weight pulled the saddle under Captain's belly, and Willie spilled to the ground.

William saw his son fall as the herd swept by in a sea of dust. Captain whinnied in terror and bolted away from the surging cattle.

"No!" Snow screamed and pulled his pistol out of the holster. He raced forward and shot into the air, but the cattle heard nothing over the thunderous noise of the stampede. The frenzied animals continued their breakneck gallop toward the gully. Then several riders flanked the cattle and pushed them into a wide circle, forcing them to slow.

As suddenly as it started, it stopped. The milling cattle slowed to a trot, then a walk, and others halted altogether. Some stopped to sample the grass, tails swishing under a lazy sun. The old cow walked in circles, bawling for her lost calf.

Willie's body lay as still as the afternoon, crushed and broken.

His father fell off his horse and onto his knees, buried his head in his hands and howled.

IT SURPRISED PEG TO SEE Jed Thornton walk into The Crow Fly. The evening had just begun and promised to be a slow one. Most wranglers were out on the range and wouldn't be coming into town on a Tuesday night.

"Peg?" Thornton said, pulling his hat off his head. "Do you mind if we have a little talk? Maybe out back behind the building?"

She sighed. "Jed, if this is about Andy Connor, I've told you everything I know. If you continue to question me, I'll have to start making things up."

The sheriff shook his head. "It ain't about that. Please."

Peg noticed Jed's hand shaking as he gestured toward the back door. Nodding, she followed him outside. He turned toward her, his face half hidden in the shadows. The sun was setting behind a hill. Far in the distance, an owl sounded out, a lonesome cry that stirred the soul.

"Isn't Molly sweet on the young Snow boy, Willie?" Jed asked. "Seems to me I heard they were a twosome."

"Yep." She rolled her eyes. "That young man fell hard for Molly and the two think they're in love. You know how that goes, Jed. First love, and all that. Why do you ask?"

"There's no easy way to say it. Willie Snow got caught in a stampede yesterday. He fell off his horse and was trampled. He didn't survive."

"Oh my god." Peg put her hands to her ears as though she

hoped to stop more bad news from getting in. "Oh, Jed, that's awful." Her stomach churned, and she thought she might retch.

He nodded. "It's a terrible thing, for sure. The funeral will be here in Breyer at the church tomorrow. The whole town will turn out. As for Molly..." he faltered. "She needs to know," he said in a low voice.

Peg closed her eyes and nodded. "I'll tell her. But it won't be easy. Poor girl was thinkin' they would marry soon. Willie gave her a ring and everything."

She patted Thornton's shoulder. "Thank you for telling me. I'll go see her right away before she finds out from somebody who ambles in here. She's upstairs in her room."

Jed stared up at the darkening sky then hung his head. "These are times when I want to ask God just what the hell he thinks he's doing. It isn't fair. It doesn't make sense. Willie Snow was a nice boy." He clapped his hat back on his head. "Go easy with her, Peg. I don't envy you. I'm around if anybody needs me." He held her hand between his for a moment, then walked between the buildings back to his office.

Peg came back inside and peered up at the hallway on the second floor. A light shone under Molly's door. She wiped her sweating hands on her skirt, took a breath, then started slowly up the stairs.

WILLIE'S FUNERAL WAS WELL ATTENDED the next day. Clarisse Snow leaned on her husband as he guided her down the aisle to the front pew. Her fair Irish skin was pale as a pearl as she cried softly with each step. Pastor Green provided the congregation with as much comfort as he could muster. Silence was thick inside the church. It was somber and sad as the citizens of Breyer dealt with the tragedy.

After he spoke, the pastor guided the bereaved to the small cemetery behind the church for Willie's internment.

Outside, a light breeze stirred up the dirt recently dug up in the graveyard. The dust swirled and danced across the bleak ground, as though it wasn't ready to be shoveled back on young Willie's coffin. The mourners gathered in a circle around the open grave. William Snow tossed the first shovelful of dirt onto the pine coffin, then put his arms around Clarisse. Under a petulant sky, crows fluttered into the cemetery and settled on several crosses, preening their feathers and peering at the grievers.

Next to the church, standing behind a cottonwood tree, a young woman watched the graveside ceremony and cried.

Later that day, Molly stood alone next to Willie's grave. She told him he was going to be a father. She told him she would never forget him, and would love him until her last breath. Then she placed a single rose from Miss Emily's garden next to the hastily made wooden cross and walked away.

MOLLY'S BABY

JED THORNTON STARED AT MOLLY Brewster as she walked into the sheriff's office. He hadn't seen her in a while. The young woman worked at The Crow Fly as a prostitute, but clearly wouldn't be working now. Her belly was large and rounded, pushing against an old cotton dress that had seen better days.

The sheriff cleared his throat and rose from his seat. He came around the desk and pulled back a chair for the girl.

"Thank you, Mister Thornton," Molly said, lowering herself into the chair and crossing her ankles.

Molly's deep auburn hair billowed around her face from the breeze through the open door. She always had a smile on her face. But not today. Today she looked tired and worried.

Now Jed understood why he hadn't seen her around town lately. Willie Snow and Molly were in love. Then poor Willie died. Jed didn't know Molly was pregnant. He wondered if Willie knew before he was killed.

Hiding his shock, he sat down and leaned his elbows on the desk. His eyes searched her lovely face. She gazed back at him with a simple quietness.

"I asked you here because I am still working on Big Andy's murder case. I have a few more questions, if you don't mind."

"Of course, but I don't know how much more I can tell you. I heard nothing and saw nothing."

"I know. But I have a few new questions."

Molly straightened in the chair and rested her hands protectively around her belly.

"I guess you can tell I've been shamed, Mister Thornton. Willie Snow and I were set to get married, but he died. Peg and Kate are letting me stay on at The Crow Fly. I do chores for them, such as laundry and cleaning and cooking, to pay for my room and board." She cast her eyes down toward her belly and whispered. "I have nowhere else to go." A shaft of sunlight from the window bathed her face in a soft glow.

Jed nodded. "That must be hard. I'm glad the women are letting you stay. Do you... do you plan to go back to work afterward?"

Molly blushed and looked away. "I don't know. Maybe."

It's a pity, Jed thought. How she ended up in Breyer at The Crow Fly, he didn't know. He heard she was an orphan. Now, she'd be giving birth to another orphan. Waves of protectiveness flooded his soul as he thought of Lara and his daughters should anything happen to him. Somewhere, he thought, is the ghost of this poor girl's father. How he must ache for Molly and his grandchild.

He gentled his voice as much as he could and tried to look less imposing. The girl looked scared out of her wits.

"What I wanted to ask is if you ever noticed Andy regularly leave the saloon some nights, for several hours at a time?"

She nodded. "Oh yes, lots of times."

"Do you know where he went? Was he dressed up? Had he been drinking?"

"I don't know if he'd been drinking, but I'd say he dressed nicer than usual on the nights he'd leave. I don't know where he went.

Most times, it was on a Friday or a Saturday evening. I remember because then the barkeep quit putting water in the whiskey." The corners of her mouth turned up in a sweet smile. "Even the music was happier when Andy left for a while. But he was always there to close up the saloon and count the money."

Jed pulled on his mustache. This was what Old Peg told him too. Clearly, it was a habit of Connor's to leave the saloon on the more popular nights for a while, then come back. Did he have a lover somewhere? Did he visit the other saloons? He'd ask around at the other bars in town and see if maybe Andy was a frequent visitor.

"Okay, I think that's all for now." Jed took his elbows off the desk and rose from his chair. "Oh, one more thing. Did you ever notice a peculiar smell on him? Not unpleasant, just different?"

Molly chewed on her lower lip, thinking. "No, I don't remember. But, could it be hair oil? I noticed he slicked his hair back with something, but I never got close enough to smell him." She giggled, and Jed was struck again by how young and sweet the girl was.

He simply couldn't imagine her shooting Big Andy. There was a purity about Molly that was almost holy, even though she worked in a brothel. He decided to have a talk with Lara about her. Maybe they could help. Lara always had good ideas.

"That'll be all for now," he said.

She struggled out of the chair and he came around his desk and walked her to the door.

"Molly, if there's anything you need, please let me know. My wife Lara could help you in some way," he said.

"Thank you, Mister Thornton. I appreciate it."

Jed wanted to hold her like the child she was and tell her everything would be okay. Whatever tragedy had struck Molly Brewster, she sure didn't deserve this.

He watched as she walked across the road, sidestepping across a patch of mud that lingered next to a watering trough. Then he returned to his desk to ponder the case.

Molly took a deep breath and tried to calm her trembling hands. Jed scared her. He was so tall, and his eyes could look straight past yours to the back of your head, and she swore he'd know if you were lying or not.

Molly had lied. She knew something about Big Andy. Something so shocking it could blow the lid right off the case. She'd stumbled upon it accidently three years ago and decided it best for all involved that she never mention it to anyone. And she hadn't. Not even to Willie. She knew Big Andy had a lover. And she knew who the lover was. Nothing good would come of it if she told the sheriff. Life was already hard enough without Willie. Why turn Breyer upside down?

Willie. Her heart ached just thinking about him. By now, they would have long been married and on their way to Colorado to start their family. She twisted the ring she wore on her finger. The ring Willie gave her as a token of his love. It was to be her wedding ring. Instead, it was a symbol of what could have been, tarnished by a terrible fate.

The baby moved in her belly. The nudge was enough for her to stop and wait until the tremor ended. Soon. Their child was coming soon. A baby created out of love, a true love, she was certain. But now it seemed so common. A story for the ages. The young man sowing his oats. The girl left behind to deal with the consequences. Time and again she wondered if Willie meant everything he said. After all, she was a lady of the evening, as Kate liked to call them.

Her face burned with shame. What a predicament.

The sun beat down on her, and she was more than happy to step back into the saloon and walk into the kitchen, where she helped peel potatoes for supper and rubbed her aching back.

The ache in her back worsened, and Molly figured she was going into labor, but she didn't know for sure. It wasn't until her water broke on the kitchen floor she knew for certain. Her heart thumped in her chest as though horses were clomping down the road.

Frightened, she sopped up the mess with an old towel and went up the back stairs to her room. Pain was getting worse now, huge cramps that left her gasping for breath. Desperate, she looked down at the sapphire ring. They may not have married, but she was having Willie's baby and that child would be brought into the world with the ring on her hand.

She walked to the balcony and searched the saloon floor for the women. Peg was counting the bottles of liquor for the night with the bartender. She looked up and saw Molly's frightened face above her.

"I'm coming," she said, and walked away from Bob. The bartender turned and peered at the balcony. He saw Molly's expression, and watched Peg mount the stairs. Frowning, he went back to counting the bottles.

Peg took Molly by the hand and led her to the bed. The girl was moaning by then and panting. Her fear was palpable.

"Now, honey, just relax as much as you can. The more you tighten up, the more that baby is gonna push back. It's easier if you don't tighten your muscles."

"Why does it hurt so much?"

"That's a question for God, I guess. It seems like women have to go through all this pain and agony to bring life into the world. Remember that it will be over soon and then it will be just a memory." She turned from the bed and stopped in the doorway. "I'm going down to get a basin of water and some towels. Try to relax and I'll be right back."

Molly looked toward the window. The sky was blue with a few clouds scuttling across its great expanse. Then pain overtook her. The next time she looked at the window, stars speckled the night, and still the pain kept coming. Twice she heard Willie's name and realized she'd called out to him. Peg and Kate came in and out of the room, but she hardly noticed. Her body was like a boat heaving on the sea of her mattress, wave after wave, until all she wanted to do was get up from the bed, walk out the door, and forget about trying.

When Molly looked through the pane again, dawn was breaking. Peg slumped in the chair next to the bed, chin nodding toward her chest.

"Peg," she said, her voice a ragged whisper. "Help me."

Peg jolted awake, took one look at Molly's perspiring face, and headed for the door. "I'm going for Doc Winters."

She pounded on Kate's door down the hall.

"Kate, get out here and stay with Molly. She hasn't had the baby yet and I think she needs help." A muffled voice answered from inside the room. Then Peg turned and fled down the stairs and into the street to the doctor's office.

Winters was preparing for his day when Peg knocked. Scowling, he walked over and opened the door.

"What is it, Peg?"

"It's Molly. She's been in labor for a long time and the baby doesn't look like it's coming anytime soon. I think something's wrong."

He pushed his glasses up on his forehead and stared out the window toward The Crow Fly.

"You know I don't get involved with the things that go on over there with you women. The townspeople, especially the ladies, wouldn't appreciate my serving you girls as well."

Peg flushed with anger. "This is an emergency. We'd never come around unless it was life or death. Are you saying you'll stand back and watch a little girl die?"

Doc shuffled uneasily and scratched at his head. Then he nodded. He took an oath as a doctor. It wasn't meant to be selective.

Winters put tools in his bag along with a bottle of laudanum, and straightened his coat.

"I'll walk around the building and come in your back door," he said. "So, look for me in a minute or so."

Peg nodded and hurried back to The Crow Fly. Winters let himself out the door gingerly, looking around to see if anybody noticed Peg had been there. It was early, all was quiet on Main Street. The shops hadn't opened yet. Only a few folks were out on Breyer's dusty street.

He entered The Crow Fly by the back door and showed himself up the stairs. Molly's moans echoed down the hall. When he entered, his heart sank. The girl was ashen and weak. No baby yet. Kate stood in front of the window, silently crying. Peg held Molly's hand, but aside from the moans, the girl lay still under a blue quilt. Sunlight poured through the room, warming it to the point of discomfort.

Doc moved forward and placed his bag on the bed. "Let me take a look here," he said, "and open up the window. It's hotter than hell. It's warm outside, too, but at least we can get some air."

Peg opened the window. Sounds from the street below flooded in. The curtains rustled softly in the early morning breeze.

"Molly, it's Doc Winters. Can you hear me?" He leaned over the bed and rested his hand on her shoulder.

The girl nodded, perspiration trickling down her cheeks and onto her neck.

"I'm going to examine you. Don't worry. I'm here to help."

Winters pulled back the quilt and gently pushed her night-gown up to her thighs and parted her legs. He moved his hand along her flank, then between her legs. She was fully dilated. He prodded her belly and inserted his fingers. Molly squirmed in pain.

It was worse than he thought. The baby was in a breech position. Its feet were at the mouth of the womb. It had to be turned around, not an easy feat and agonizing. He wasn't sure Molly could stand much more.

Winters took a bottle of laudanum out of his bag and held it to her lips. "Swallow this, honey. It will help you relax." She sputtered as it trickled down her throat and turned her head away. He took her chin in his hand and poured a bit more into her mouth. She instinctively swallowed.

The doctor turned to Peg. "I have to turn this baby around. I may need your help."

Peg winced and approached the bed.

"Place your hand here, on Molly's belly. I'm going to try pressing on her abdomen and push the baby into the right birthing position. Tell me if you feel anything."

Peg leaned in and felt Molly's abdomen contract, then relax. The spasms seemed to do nothing to help turn the baby. Doc Winters gently pressed on her swollen belly, hoping to coax the baby to turn inside the womb. Molly cried out in pain, then grew quiet. Peg shook her head.

"I don't feel anything moving now, Doc."

"We have to hurry," Winters said. He swiped at the sweat on his forehead, then continued to press, slowly and rhythmically. "Pray this works."

The room was silent. The baby stopped moving in the womb altogether. Doc wrinkled his brow and gave one more push on Molly's abdomen. He smiled. "It's in the right position now! But I don't know if Molly can birth it. She's too exhausted."

"Molly, help me here," he said. "I know it's painful, but you need to push and push with all your might. Let's get the little fella out of you and into this big old world. Come on, I know you can do it." He peered up at her face from the foot of the bed. The girl did not respond.

Molly dreamed she was helping her father on their small farm in Indiana. They were pushing and shoving bales of hay into the loft of the barn. The hay was itchy and warm and heavy to handle, but she tried and tried. The loft seemed so far away. Her father's voice was far away too. But once in a while she heard him say, "Molly, push. You can do it. Come on now, girl," and so she tried.

And with her last final push, the bale made it into the loft, and she straightened up, but a flash of pain doubled her over. Then the sky went white and lightning flashed and Willie stood at the edge of the bed. His clothes were torn and his blue kerchief hung in tatters around his neck. He was missing a boot. One arm hung by his side.

"Honey, help our baby," he said. "It's not your time. It ain't his either. Please, make me proud." When she looked again, he was gone, but it was enough to make her want to finish the job he gave her. That of bringing his son into the world.

Young Willie Brewster arrived screaming in protest, deftly caught by the doctor with a towel and held aloft for the women to see. The baby had tufts of red hair, just like his father, his tiny face blotched from crying.

"A fine boy you have there," Doc said. "Fine boy. Why, he's a big one too. He's gonna do well, and so will you. Here, relax a minute and I'll cut the cord and help you with the placenta."

Molly's eyes fluttered open. Doc patted her on the shoulder. "It's over now, honey. You're gonna be fine."

He separated Molly from Willie with a quick snip of his scissors and handed the infant to Kate. She wiped him dry with a cloth, then held him up for the new mother to see.

Molly raised her head and smiled. There was no shame in this baby. He was the replica of Willie Snow. They made him from love, and no whorehouse in a dusty town in Texas could ever say this new life wasn't precious. She felt one last spasm, then fell asleep, despite the voices and bustling in the room.

The piano started downstairs in the saloon. Peg and Kate locked eyes. It was time to clean up and go downstairs. Doc had left an hour ago, and the baby was sleeping in Molly's arms. Their two chests rose together in harmony. Peg thought about her own son with a wave of sorrow so deep she thought the floor might collapse beneath her. She turned to Kate.

"The hell with the customers. We're both staying up here tonight to help with the baby. Cocheta can have the night off too."

"Can we do that?" Kate asked. "They'll be expecting to see us."

"Why else did we decide to run this place, Kate? To be at the beck and call of a handful of men on a Saturday night? I don't think so. I think this is our call to make. I'll send word down to Shorty and Rick. They can handle questions. We'll tell them we all took sick."

Kate nodded. "You're right. Sometimes I forget what we're doing here. This place is ours. Not theirs." She peered down at Molly and little Willie. "What's going to happen to them, do you think?" She tucked the quilt up under the girl's chin and touched the soft downy head on the baby. "There is no place for them here. We have Cocheta now. We can't have that little boy grow up in a saloon. It just ain't right."

Peg walked over to the window and closed the curtains. A few patrons were straggling in already, their horses stirring up dust on Main Street. It wouldn't be long before the saloon was in full swing.

Weary, she turned toward the door. "I don't know, Kate. But I know one thing. This little girl ain't gonna do this alone. No matter what happens, we're all together."

Then she tucked her hair behind her ear, took a quick look in the mirror, and bustled down the stairs.

The baby slept through his first night in The Crow Fly, stirring only long enough to latch on to Molly to feed, then sank back into the folds of his blanket. Kate swore when he opened his eyes and saw her standing there, he winked.

Molly woke the next morning to feel the baby move by her side. She guided Willie to her breast and gazed at her son through the light pouring into the room. Little blue veins pulsed under the baby's skin. His tiny fingernails looked like seashells. The sunshine lit up his red hair like a candle. Pressing her lips to his head, she inhaled the sweet smell of him.

He was a joy. But never had she been so filled with trepidation. When her parents died, leaving her as an orphan, it was tough enough. Somehow, she survived. But now there was a little person she was responsible for, and she had no resources aside from what she did at The Crow Fly.

She held back tears. It would do no good to cry and possibly make things worse. Sometimes when a person made themselves vulnerable to emotion, they'd learn there is no safe place to fall. So, she lifted her chin and tried to enjoy the fact that she and her son were in a warm bed, and she had several weeks to figure things out before she needed to go back to work.

That evening, Molly heard the piano strike a chord and play a lively tune. Usually, she would be on the saloon floor, walking among the customers and making sure they were having a good time. And, of course, they wanted something more than a few drinks and a game of cards.

Shame washed over her. She remembered she birthed Willie in the same bed used for all those men, and tears started afresh. This time, she could not hold them back.

THREE WEEKS WENT BY IN the hazy time after childbirth. Kate or Peg often stopped in to watch Willie so she could leave the cramped room and go outside for a quick walk in the fresh air.

When there was a sharp tap at the door, Molly figured it was one of the women.

"Come in," she said, bringing Willie onto her chest and sitting up on her elbows.

Molly was shocked to see Miss Emily walk in. As always, she looked fresh and pressed, wearing a striped skirt and a frothy white blouse. Her hair was worn loose on her shoulders today, instead of the severe bun she usually wore. She looked years younger. Emily was lovely. There was a tiny smile across the woman's lips as she stepped to the foot of the bed.

"Hello, dear. I heard about the baby, and I wanted to bring you a little something."

"Why, thank you, Miss Emily. That's awfully kind."

Molly dimpled, her brown eyes crinkling in the corners. Emily handed her a package, tied up in the prettiest blue bow she had ever seen.

"Oh, I don't want to open it and ruin this pretty bow," she said. "It looks like somebody wrapped it in heaven!"

Emily laughed. "Breyer's about as far from heaven as you can get, my dear. Do go ahead and open it. You can save the ribbon for your hair."

Molly carefully untied the ribbon, opened the parcel, and gasped in delight. Inside was a soft blanket, yellow as a baby duckling and just as downy.

"Oh, it's beautiful! I love it! Did you make this?"

"Yes. I sent for the fabric before Willie was born." She cleared her throat. "Of course, none of us knew if it would be a boy or a girl, so I thought yellow might be bright and festive."

"It's beautiful! And Willie will love it, too!" The girl stroked the blanket against her face and grinned. "I've never had anything so nice in my life. Thank you."

Emily smiled, then turned and walked briskly toward the door. The thought of Molly and the baby choked her up. It was silly, really. But these feelings came through, no matter how hard she tried to tamp them down.

Setting her mouth in a firm line, she opened the door. "Have a good day. Get some rest and enjoy your little boy."

Molly snuggled deeper under the covers, the baby at her breast. She was now over the trauma of labor, and resting in the warm bed was almost like having a proper home. What was she going to do? Maybe work at the hotel? Or somewhere else, anywhere else, but here at The Crow Fly. Or, maybe she could work in the saloon, just for a short while, and save all her money so she and Willie could leave town and go to a bigger city where there might be work for a girl like her, without selling her body.

She hung her head. Willie deserved better. But it all seemed so impossible. A tear slid down her cheek, pooling into her neck. She wiped it away and looked down at her son.

"One of these days, my little baby. Someday it will get better."

Then she spread the new yellow blanket over her son's back and held him tight.

BREAKER JOE

BREAKER JOE HANSON REINED IN the gelding and gazed across the valley. *No matter how you look at it,* he thought, *this part of Texas is ugly.* Tufts of sage and tumbleweed cropped up like whiskers across the endless miles of tawny earth. Deeper in the valley, sweet grass grew, a green oasis amid the boring landscape.

The Five Bar Ranch splayed along the corridor of land, fed by a wispy trickle of water that tumbled down from a small mesa in the distance. It was enough to water the cattle and horses, he figured. It flowed along the gullies and turned a dingy brown, carrying the Texas earth with it downstream in an unappetizing way.

Joe shrugged. Why anybody would want to live out here was beyond him. He was glad just to be passing through. A Wyoming man, his heart ached for the grand snow-capped mountains and the lustrous blue of a cooler sky. But, the Snows had sent for him, and the pay was good. Good enough for him to saddle Teton, his favorite horse, and travel the miles to Texas.

The Snows lost their only son, Willie, a while back in a tragic accident. Part of the ranch business was buying and selling horses along with the cattle Snow raised, and Willie apparently had a good hand with the horses. Mr. Snow didn't want to work with them, age catching up to him along with the grief. The hired hands broke a few horses, but they turned into poor mounts, shying and bucking at the slightest provocation. The men just didn't have the right hand with an animal, so he sent out feelers for a professional horse trainer.

Word was, Breaker Joe was the best around. He could read inside a horse's soul, people said, and know just how tender, or how tough, to treat it. Truth be known, Joe never treated a horse harshly. It would always come back to you in the end. Some horses needed a slow hand, while others had to be taught who's the boss, but he was never cruel.

Joe broke each horse differently. As a result, by the time he was finished, the horse was his friend, and willing to take on whatever job that needed to be done. He'd pass the animal on with plenty of advice for the new owner, and by and large, customers were satisfied.

This would be a four-month job. The Snows had ten horses roaming the paddocks, eating their fill of feed and not earning their keep. They could be sold, but it would be at a loss unless they were broken to saddle and worth a buyer's while. William Snow also hoped to get Joe's help sifting through the horses for sale at the stockyards in Fort Worth, picking out animals with the best potential.

Joe liked geldings. They didn't fuss like a stallion, although a stallion was a fine mount. Their fire and temperament led to the potential for a good racehorse or breeder. But they were worthless on the trail, or herding cattle, in his opinion. Their minds were set on mares and little else once they were used for breeding.

The mares were worse, he thought. Their moods waxed and waned with the seasons and when they came into heat, they were flighty as hell.

As a result, he only chose a good gelding for his own purposes and often advised ranchers to geld most of their male horses unless one stood out as a stud.

The ranchers often bought a horse because of its initial attraction. A young stallion put on quite a show at the sales, tail set high, chest expanded as it trotted around the corral. Joe estimated at least seventy percent of the horses he encountered to train were males, and of those, most needed gelding.

The Snow ranch was no exception, he soon learned. Joe tied Teton to a post and wandered up to the ranch house. William Snow answered the door, shook his hand, and they went straight away to the corral, where Snow had all the horses on display.

The ten horses eyed him suspiciously. It was spooky. They sensed a power in Hanson that others simply didn't possess. It was as though Joe himself were a stallion, come to cut the rest of the horses out of the herd and calm things down.

Four of the horses were male. They were ready for the saddle, but still quite young. Joe figured all of them needed to be gelded. Not a one of them had nice enough lines to cover a mare, and the way their bones rode under their hide, few could outrun a good gelding on steady land. It pained William Snow to hear it, but he recognized their lack of worth.

"Okay then, Joe, we'll geld these horses tomorrow and while they heal, let's go after the six mares." William rubbed his cheek and poked at the dirt with the toe of his boot. "I have to tell you, I was looking for a good stud in the bunch here. Maybe next month we can ride into Fort Worth and you could help me pick out a good one. I need to start breedin' here on the ranch rather than having to shell out money to somebody else for these animals."

Joe nodded. "We'll find you a good stallion. But, I warn you, the one I pick out will probably cost a lot of money and then he shouldn't be used for other things. You cut cattle with him or use him as a trail horse, and he could break a leg and ruin your investment. He should just cover the mares."

William nodded, his mouth set in a grim line. A stallion who didn't work except for breeding was a luxury. But, likely worth the money in the long run. He waved across the railing at the six mares. "Take your pick and start working on them in the morning. In the meantime, we'll get you set up in the bunkhouse and Cook will conjure up some food for ya." He tossed a pebble into the corral and clapped Joe on the shoulder. "I respect your opinion. But let me say this. I would like these horses trained and ready to sell within a few months, then help me acquire more for breeding and selling. That's a lot of work, but your reputation precedes you, and I'm sure you can do it."

After supper, Joe wandered back to the corral. He already had his eye on a rangy gray mare who stretched her neck across the rail and let him pat her on the forehead. She was intelligent. He figured that out right away. Solid for a mare, with a big chest and haunches. She had sturdy legs that could carry a man anywhere. She'd be the first he'd tackle in the morning.

Breaker Joe wasn't a tall man, but he made up for it by his calm demeanor and confident ways. Folks always thought he was bigger than he was because he was a born leader. His black hair and deep-green eyes made many a woman swoon. Truth be told, he tamed women the same way he did a horse. Some needed a softer hand, while others worked better under a tighter rein. He could tell right off which ones were quality and which ones to leave in the pasture.

Life was lonely as a traveling horse trainer. There was no room in it for a wife and children. He often journeyed from home for weeks at a time, sometimes months. So, he spent his time and money in the saloons on a Saturday night, and more often than not, with a whore. He'd already heard about The Crow Fly and the women there, and in his mind's eye, Saturday night couldn't come fast enough.

The week flew by, and by the end of it he had the gray mare working under the saddle like a dancer. He started two other mares. One he tamed with a whisper, the other with a low, commanding voice. The horses already nickered when he walked nearby. He was establishing himself as a leader. This would be an easy job, he figured. Then he'd find William Snow a good stud and wander back to Wyoming.

Saturday night in Breyer was all Joe hoped it would be. Merry music flooded into the street. The saloons were lit up. Golden light poured out from the swinging doors. The arid land looked best in the dark, and now Breyer shone like a pretty woman. He felt the usual tug of the lonely heart as he tied Teton up to a hitching post and wandered into The Crow Fly.

He noticed Cocheta right away. She stood out from the other women in the room. Long black hair cascaded down her shoulders, and light from a lantern on the wall played along her face like sunset. She was Apache but clothed in a white woman's purple dress that moved like a living thing and shimmered when she moved. She wore an eagle feather in her hair with a fancy filigree hairpin holding it in. Cocheta was all angles and softness at the same time, the way an artist might paint a deep canyon at dawn. Joe didn't bother to look at anybody else.

It didn't take him long to find Peg and shell out the money to spend the entire night with the girl before anybody else could stake their claim.

Cocheta came to him quietly, her wide brown eyes taking him in with just a bit of distrust around her mouth and a tightness in her shoulders.

This one needs a gentle hand, he decided. Without even talking to her, he sensed abuse that went deep. He bet she carried a knife. Best to stroke her with kind words and gentle fingers than to force himself upon her.

He picked up her hand and tucked it under his arm. Leading her up the stairs, he was careful to remain by her side, not ahead like a leader, and certainly not behind like he imagined other men would walk, in awe of her beauty. He smelled the light scent of citrus on her neck and placed his hand on her tiny waist. She stiffened a bit, then took a breath and led him into her room.

The room was just as he imagined. It was neat and clean, with a fresh sheet on the bed and a small jug on a table filled with Texas bluebonnets. Draped over a chair was an Indian blanket, woven in rusts and cream, a design that spoke of comfort and healing. Sighing, he sat in the chair and pulled at his boots. She was already in bed, her dress in a puddle on the floor.

By morning, Breaker Joe figured he had her tamed about as well as could be. She smiled at him once or twice, which made his heart sing. The few words she spoke sounded light and angelic, as though heaven lived in her heart. When he stroked her leg, she shivered, then softened. His own head spun with a delight he savored.

Later, he dressed and leaned down to kiss her. "I'll be back next Saturday night, if it's okay with you."

Cocheta pulled the blanket around her neck and nodded, then looked away before he could see the longing in her eyes.

Joe smiled on his way out of town. The sun was dancing across the horizon, and the smell of the night and the woman hadn't left yet. The cool breeze still carried her scent as he turned Teton toward the ranch and let himself drift into sleepy thoughts. Cocheta was one of many women he'd handled over the years. It would be a nice, gentle ride with her. When he'd leave her behind in four months, his thoughts would go elsewhere to the next conquest. All in all, it had been one hell of a satisfying week.

WORK ON THE RANCH WAS gratifying. He told William to sell a mare—a skittish bay—and take the loss. It took him a week to figure it out, but the horse was half blind in one eye and would never work out on the trail, spooking at every movement or gust of wind. Somebody might use her for a brood mare, although in

Joe's mind she lacked the right lines. He didn't think Snow needed the aggravation.

Two more mares worked well under his hand. One was small, less than fourteen hands high. Her calm nature would be ideal as a lady's companion and to pull a light buggy.

The four geldings were healing up nicely. Joe knew it would take a month or two for their hormones to drain a bit, and then they'd take to the bit and saddle in a reliable way. One gelding liked fast changes in gait and would make a fine cutting horse for a cowboy who needed to cull through a herd of cattle.

Every Saturday night, Joe returned to The Crow Fly. He made sure he arrived ahead of the other men, so he could take Cocheta's hand and lead her upstairs for the entire night. One evening, he arrived too late. A lanky wrangler claimed her and pulled her up the stairs. Joe flushed with anger. That man was going to try to master her, he thought. He could tell by the way he clasped her hand in his, and how her delicate shoulders tightened. Joe wanted to follow them to her room, punch the man's lights out and take Cocheta out under the stars, where he'd make love to her with the scent of sage all around them. He walked out of The Crow Fly and rode into the night, where he camped out until dawn and let his temper cool.

The next week he arrived so early he had to wait outside like a schoolboy until the saloon opened, then pushed his way through the swinging doors and walked straight over to Peg to pay for the night. Cocheta glided down the stairs in a green dress that reminded him of a Wyoming meadow. He felt a yearning in his heart. It was all he could do to not reach for her waist and pull her to him. She smiled, and it was like a Texas cloudburst, raining happiness down on him like he'd never felt before.

"I brought you this," he said, pulling a small locket out of his back pocket. It was heart- shaped, connected to a delicate chain. When he placed it around her neck, it sparkled in the candlelight. The joy on her face made him feel guilty. *What the hell was going to happen between them?* he asked himself. He'd be gone in a couple of months, walking away from this woman who had captured his imagination and flooded him with thought.

Joe stayed away from The Crow Fly for two weeks while he festered with emotion, grappling to understand. Yes, she had fallen under his spell and made a fine companion. But, after he made love to her, he couldn't shake her from his memory. *She's just a whore*, he reminded himself. But the thought of her, the scent of her, lingered all week as he worked Snow's horses.

By the third week, he returned to the saloon. There she was, standing along the bar as always, one dark leg peeking out from frothy lace under a red dress that made her look dangerous and sultry. They came together in a rush of breath and smiles. That night he smothered her with deep kisses and freed the bodice of her dress the way he'd loosen the reins on a horse that needed to run.

The next morning, Joe knew he hadn't trained her at all. Instead, she had him under a light rein, while he bucked beneath her and yearned for a certain freedom that would take him a lifetime to understand.

The horses were working well at the ranch. William Snow had already sold two of them. The sheriff's wife, Lara, needed a gentle horse to pull a small carriage for herself and daughters. One gelding made a fine riding horse for Lyle Confort, a businessman in Breyer who wanted something reliable under his squat legs. He needed a patient horse who didn't mind the harsh twist of the bit as Confort used the reins to keep his balance and flopped about in the saddle like a bag of flour.

The horse sale was coming up in Fort Worth the following week. Joe purposefully stayed away from Cocheta that Saturday night. Instead, in a flash of rebellion, he chose Kate Dawson for a quick poke, noticing with satisfaction the pained look on Cocheta's face as he held Kate close to his side and gave her a squeeze. Kate was a different sort of woman, he figured. Smart and feisty, she left little to his imagination. He longed to go back in time that night and be with Cocheta instead. Afterward, when he walked down to the main floor, he noticed Cocheta was gone. She was probably upstairs with someone. He walked out into the warm Texas night and rode Teton hard through the brush.

FORT WORTH WAS SWARMING WITH ranchers, horses, and cattle. The sounds and smells were overwhelming. William Snow and Joe walked past the bulls and heifers and ambled toward the lower corrals, where the horse sales were. Joe's heart sped up. The chance to look at so many horses all at once was exciting. A long-legged roan mare stood out right away. He thought he might buy her for himself. She'd suit him perfectly, but he had two other horses back in Wyoming, and Teton. It was easy to convince Snow to buy her instead. She was a beauty.

Finding a stallion would be harder work, and the two men spent two days shopping around until Joe found just the right one. The horse was perfection. Tall, at least sixteen hands high, the horse's ebony coat gleamed in the sunlight. He had a small white blaze on his forehead and one back fetlock with a white sock. Calm, contained, the stallion blew softly through his nostrils as he surveyed the stockyards with confidence. Joe ran his hands down the horse's legs. They were sound and muscled. His chest was wide, neck thick, yet elegant. He stood quietly while Joe examined him, but he knew the horse had the power to break free and jump the corral fence. His long black tail brushed along the ground and his forelock fell toward his muzzle in handsome wisps. There was no question this should be William Snow's stud.

Joe walked over to the seller and shook hands. "Has this stallion been proven?" he asked.

"Yup, three mares dropped foals this spring, all out of Bandit here. Good lines, strong legs, one looks just like his sire. He covered each mare only once or twice too. Potent stud."

"So, why are you selling him?"

"To be honest, I'm selling my entire ranch. Moving my family back to Ohio. I'm hoping to get enough money from the ranch and livestock to buy a nice farm."

The price for Bandit was high, but Joe was sure he was the right horse, and William agreed to buy him. Joe talked the owner into throwing in one of Bandit's yearling fillies as part of the bargain. They left the next morning for the ranch with the roan mare, yearling, and the black stallion in tow. When they reached the valley where the ranch was and approached the barns, the stallion tossed his head and whinnied. A mare answered across the meadow. William and Joe smiled at each other. The horse yanked on the rope, eager to get to the mare. The investment was already paying off.

The next morning, Joe saddled up Teton and walked over to the ranch house. William was out on the porch and stepped down to talk to him.

"I believe your horses are all in good shape now, including the new roan mare." Joe nodded toward the barns. "And that stud of yours is going to be sought after, I promise."

Snow grinned and clapped him on the shoulder. "You did well, Joe. You trained the horses to perfection, and I know I'll be growing a fine herd with Bandit. We'll miss you around here. Are you going straight back to Wyoming?"

"Yep. You paid well enough for me to winter over at my place. I always ride down to Colorado come spring to the Hayes Ranch. More often than not, they'll be needing me to work some of their horses and I usually spend a couple of months there. Then I'll see where my fortunes take me."

The two men spoke for a while, then shook hands and parted company. It made Joe happy to think he'd done a fine job and that William Snow was pleased. He mounted Teton and loped through the valley, smelling the last of the sweet grass before climbing out of the valley and into the scrub.

There was just one more thing to do, and his heart thudded in his chest. He turned Teton toward Breyer and urged him into a steady trot.

It was a warm Tuesday morning. The Crow Fly sat silent on Main Street. Joe rode around to the back stairs and tied Teton to a railing. He knocked on the door. Peg answered.

She gestured toward the thick blanket roll tied behind Teton's saddle. "You headin' out?"

"Yeah. I finished up at the ranch this morning." He looked down at his feet, suddenly shy. "I'd like to talk to Cocheta if I could."

Peg nodded and ducked inside. It seemed like an eternity before the door opened again and Cocheta stepped into the morning sunshine. Dressed in a sky-blue calico dress buttoned up to her neck, she looked young and vulnerable as she stood before him. She wore her black hair in a braid over one shoulder. A few tendrils fluttered softly about her face. Joe's heart skipped. He longed to reach out and brush the wisps away from her lips and bring her in close to his chest.

His mouth went dry. "I'm headin' back home this morning," he said. "Thought I'd stop on my way out of town and say goodbye to you."

Cocheta didn't look into his face. Instead, she turned her delicate neck and focused on a flock of birds flying overhead. She held herself still, like a fawn. The two stood in silence for a while, until a loose-limbed dog trotted up to Joe and sniffed his hand, breaking the spell.

"Well, I guess that's all I wanted to say. It's been awfully nice knowing you." He winced at his awkward words. A slow flush moved up his neck and into his face.

Cocheta quietly reached behind her neck, unfastened the heart-shaped locket and held it out to him.

"No, no!" he said, tears springing into his eyes. "It's yours! From me. I bought it just for you. You keep it." It pained him to think that she didn't know how he felt, but then again, how could she? He'd kept his feelings to himself, and she expressed nothing to him but her sweet smile.

The girl clutched it in her hand and stared at the ground. Her thin shoulders hunched forward as though protecting herself from a blow. When she looked up and into his face, Joe felt something clear down to his boots. Then she turned and walked inside, closing the door on his heart forever.

The sounds of Breyer getting ready for the day pulled him from his thoughts. He must have been standing there for a long time as the sun was higher in the sky and sweat trickled down his back. Teton stamped his hoof in the dust and shook a fly off his neck.

Even Joe's breath felt lonely as it passed his lips. He didn't remember mounting up or turning Teton toward the west. So strong was the struggle with his emotions, the horse tightened beneath him, nervous and jumpy. He turned Teton around at least three times on his way out of town to look back at The Crow Fly in confusion and indecision. Then he tapped the gelding with his spurs and galloped over the ridge. Breyer slipped out of his sight, and, he prayed, soon forgotten.

Inside The Crow Fly, Cocheta clasped the locket back around her neck, then watched out the window as Joe disappeared over the hill.

COCHETA

COCHETA RAN A BRUSH THROUGH her black hair until it shimmered like spun silk. It hung past her shoulders and rippled when she walked, like a river in the Texas hill country. It was Sunday. A day of rest at The Crow Fly. Old Peg often dressed up and walked to church on Sunday mornings, but Cocheta had no ambition for such things as the white man's God. To her, there were too many rules, punctuated with hypocrisy. The fact that Peg sat in the back of the church away from the congregation annoyed Cocheta. If their God was so good, why did the town judge the women of The Crow Fly then? So many rules, so divided.

She spent her free time in her room, sitting in a chair by the window or lying on the bed. *Strange*, she thought, *it seems like I spend most of my life on this lumpy old mattress.* The irony didn't escape her.

But Sunday evenings were different. Each week, after lying about all morning and afternoon, she'd amble downstairs and over to the Breyer Hotel, where she ordered a lovely dinner and brought it back to her room. Her mouth watered as she wondered what they were serving each Sunday. It could be anything.

She loved the surprise. She never asked ahead of time. It spoiled the moments of anticipation and excitement. For Cocheta, there wasn't a lot of excitement in this vague town nestled in a sea of sand.

The other women who worked at The Crow Fly felt burdened by their careers as prostitutes, but for Cocheta, it was easy. She enjoyed the simple life here. Sometimes a man became too full of himself, or maybe was born mean, and that was intolerable for the Apache beauty. But most of the time the men were gentle and respectful. Cocheta smiled at the thought. She had entertained many of the men in town. Men who lived respectable lives with wives and children. Men who walked to church every Sunday with their families. And yet, they'd never acknowledge the whores if they saw them on the street, even though they knew them well.

She'd seen the look of need and want on their faces. She'd satisfied their desires. But when they sat at the hotel restaurant with their wives, their eyes never wandered. It was as though Cocheta were invisible.

That was fine with Cocheta. Invisible. She wished she were. She wished she could fly over the rooftops and never return. Maybe sneak up on Breaker Joe before he'd hightail it out of Texas. Her throat tightened at the thought. Once. Only once in her young life had she given her heart away, and that was to Joe. She was a dark-skinned fool. An Indian who didn't know her place. What was she thinking, to imagine that a white man would love her in a serious way?

Cocheta peered out the window. Jed Thornton and his wife, Lara, and their daughters walked up the middle of the street on their way to the church. Lara held on to Thornton's arm as the girls skipped ahead.

"He's a handsome cuss," she said out loud. "But I'm glad I'm not in his line of fire."

Jed Thornton had not interviewed her yet about Big Andy's

murder. She hadn't arrived in Breyer until Andy was long dead in the old cemetery. Jed interrogated all the women more than once. She figured at some point he'd talk to her, just in case she heard something and could impart more information. The thought made her nervous.

Thornton had never come to The Crow Fly except on business. He kept to himself and clung to his wife. Lara was a beauty. And nice too. She always had a smile for everybody in town, including the whores.

Her eyes followed Thornton down the street. Yes, it's too bad he didn't come to her. She would enjoy it. But maybe then she'd have to hurt him if he got too close to her and her secrets.

Life in Breyer was not too bad. It would be a shame if the sheriff knew about her. She'd seen his eyes travel down her body. Sometimes she wondered if he was looking for her soul in there.

Instinct told her to be very careful if she wanted to stay in Breyer. And she was. Because no matter what happened at The Crow Fly, it was nothing compared to what she had already endured. Sometimes she wanted to tell the other women to shut up and stop complaining. Because Cocheta knew things could be far worse.

Memories flooded in, and with them came the familiar pounding heart and sweaty palms. No matter how hard she tried, she could not keep those thoughts at bay. It was only with Breaker Joe that she released her demons and allowed herself to feel anything but numbness. Now Joe was gone, and he took the last of her dreams with him. Try as she might, she descended into darkness, a tug like the current on the Rio Grande, so strong and cold that she thought she might lose herself forever in the past....

A SHIFT IN THE WIND

L IFE WAS GOOD GROWING UP in the small Apache village where Cocheta lived with her parents and younger brother. A person knew what to expect every day. Every season. Every year. Cocheta had several friends and a beautiful pony named Twig. She'd ride out into the desert every day with the other children. One boy, Tarak, seemed to like her. He was the son of a tribal elder and handsome. Cocheta hoped he'd choose her as his wife one day. Tarak always rode alongside her with sidelong glances that caused her to blush. He was seventeen years old. Almost a man. Cocheta was only fourteen. But she hoped he might find favor with her.

It was a beautiful day in spring. The desert showed off like a beautiful woman, cacti blooming in colors of pinks and reds. Even the smallest beast enjoyed the sunny weather. The desert was awash with animals, roaming about on trails that led to their dens, their tracks scattered throughout the valley. Cocheta and her friends rejoiced in the day, feeling like wild things themselves.

The desert floor darkened as the sun slipped behind the mountains to the west. It was time to return home. But the air was so pure, and their young selves so gay, they rode far past the usual rocks and gullies that were familiar and found themselves in unfamiliar territory.

Tarak held up his hand, and the group of friends halted. Already, he was the leader. Cocheta smiled. Some day he would be a great warrior.

"We need to turn around now. As it is, darkness will come before we're home." He turned his horse toward the village. He laughed and nudged the pinto with his heels. "Race you home!" He took off, riding low over the horse's neck.

The others laughed and shouted. The race was on. Cocheta dug her heels into Twig's side and tightened her legs. The animal responded with a small hop, then straightened and thundered after Tarak. She let out a whoop and felt the cool wind on her face, the warm pony between her legs. *I will never forget this day,* she thought as she leaned into the wind. It was locked in her memory forever.

But in the space of a few moments, the memory morphed into a nightmare that captured her again and again in its web.

When Tarak fell off his horse, it looked as though his mare had stumbled. Cocheta slowed and reined in Twig. The other horses galloped by amid childish laughter. Cocheta was still grinning as she dismounted and approached her friend, but her mouth went dry when she saw he was not moving. Then his chest blossomed with blood.

Cocheta approached him. "Tarak? Tarak?"

Suddenly, the valley erupted with shouts and whoops. The five other children ahead of her tumbled off their mounts one by one. Two horses fell to the ground, straining to get back up.

Out of the dust rode four men, shooting rifles and pistols and howling. The noise was terrifying. It was as though demons were fighting their way past the setting sun.

Before Cocheta could turn and run, an arm as thick as a tree limb reached down and snatched her off the ground and flung her over the horse in front of him.

It's strange what one remembers in the midst of terror. For Cocheta, it was the smell of the horse's sweat and the warm heat of the man who held her against him. She felt his breath. She tasted the salt on his skin when she raised her head, and he locked his elbow around her neck.

They galloped up into the nearby hills, where he and the other three men pulled their horses behind large boulders, breathing heavily and peering around the rocks across the valley floor.

The captors were rogue bandits, up from Mexico. They had formed a cruel gang of like-minded men who warred with just about anybody, and did not care who they hurt. The bandits murdered the other children that day. They spared Cocheta.

She trembled as strange hands lifted her from the horse and carried her over to a large boulder. The abductor set her down firmly beside it, then tied her hands behind her back with rawhide. She tried to stand, but he slapped her so hard her ears rang.

"Stay. Or I will kill you." He ripped the deerskin dress down to her waist, as if he wanted to show her his threat was real. He knocked Cocheta on to her side and walked up to the others.

"Anybody following?" he asked.

"No," another said, peering around the rock. He looked back at Cocheta as she lay on the ground. "But they will soon."

All four captors nodded in agreement.

"We rest for a few more minutes, then we leave. Straight over this hill and down behind it. That way, nobody will see us when they send out a party to find them."

Cocheta was terrified. Where would they take her? She was not familiar with the red rocks cradling the foothills of the mountains. How would she find her way home? She thought of Tarak, and her friends, and a faintness enfolded her. Closing her eyes, she concentrated on her breathing, stifling sobs that rose in her chest.

This time, when the kidnapper lifted her on to his horse, he had her ride astride in front of him. His arm slid around her waist and tightened like a vise. Her head rested against his chest. She heard his heartbeat through his shirt and flinched at the intimacy.

They rode in darkness through the boulders. Cocheta noticed deer trails that led around the small mountain like a road map and tried to commit it to memory, but it was useless. Once they broke free of the hills and rode into the open again, the land was unfamiliar. The boulders gave way to desert again. Now they rode hard, talking and laughing among themselves.

After several hours, they stopped in a small canyon. Deep in the shadows, the men dismounted and tied the horses to trees that grew in a ring around a patch of grass. The bandit lifted Cocheta from the horse and placed her in the middle of the grass.

Two men chuckled.

One of them spoke. "You go first, my friend. You carried her all the way here. It's only fitting."

Her captor nodded and smiled, though it never reached his eyes. In one swift motion with his knife, he cut through Cocheta's dress and laid her bare. Startled and frightened, she tried to hide her body from the men, but with her hands behind her back, she could only lay there.

What happened next destroyed her soul. He introduced a young girl who lived a life of innocence to sensations so searing, so painful, that she screamed again and again.

When the outlaw finished with her, he rose, and the next man approached. And the next. There was a great deal of cruel laughter and pinches and torture as she stared up at a starless sky and wished she had been shot like Tarak.

At some point she lost consciousness and when she woke, the men were returning for more. It wasn't until the sun came up before they stopped and tended the horses, preparing to ride out again.

One man chuckled. "She's a pretty one. She's worth her weight in gold, I think."

The others nodded as they mounted their horses. Cocheta

was placed with her captor again, naked and bruised. Every step the horse took shot pain through her limbs.

It took several days to reach their destination. Each day was agony. Each day was abuse and torture. The men were careful not to mar her face or pull on her long black hair. They wanted to keep her as beautiful as possible.

Nothing in Cocheta's imagination could prepare her for what happened next. In a dusty town in Mexico, her captors sold her into slavery with a cruel man who ran a bordello. His name was Jose Ruiz. He rendered the women helpless through drugs and other measures. None of them were there out of choice. The bordello was a popular destination for men of all sorts. Over time, Cocheta met them all.

Twice she tried to run away. Both times she failed. After that, Jose kept her tied to her bed several hours every day when she wasn't entertaining men and often sedated her in order to keep her from escaping.

How long Cocheta endured the abuse, she didn't know. Days melted into one another, then weeks, and finally, years. When she wasn't in a drug-induced haze, her mind struggled constantly to figure out how to rid herself of this life.

One warm November night, several men tied up in front of the bordello. Cocheta peered out the window and recognized one in particular, a vaquero named Pablo, who had frequented her bed more than once. She watched as he tied his pinto to the railing and ambled into the bar. Cocheta cringed. Pablo liked to pinch and slap her, then afterward would fall asleep in her bed, unable to rouse after hours of drinks and sex.

That night was no exception. He entered her room with a flourish and nodded at the Apache woman.

"How are you, my beauty?" he asked as he pulled a ragged hat off his head and reached for his guns and holster. He laid them on the table next to the bed and sat on the edge of the mattress, removing his dusty boots and climbing out of his pants. He kept his shirt on, made of rough fabric that scratched at Cocheta as he mounted her.

Tonight, he did not hurt her. Instead, he rolled off her and fell asleep, his soft snoring echoing through the room.

Slowly, Cocheta rose from the bed. Pablo did not stir. Looking out the window, she scanned the street on this Saturday night. It was busier than usual. The noise downstairs became louder as the men grew rowdier.

Cocheta saw three vaqueros stumble out into the night, holding each other up. One drew his pistol and shot into the air. The other two laughed. Cocheta noticed the piano did not even slow in its merry play, and the voices below never ceased.

It was at this moment that Cocheta knew what she would do. Not allowing herself to think about it, she loosened the pistol out of Pablo's holster, thrust the barrel against his temple and pulled the trigger. His body bounced under the weight of the bullet. He never woke up. Below in the saloon, the laughter and music continued as loud as it had before.

Trembling, she picked up his holster and tied it around her waist, thrust the pistol inside, then tossed on her clothes. She forced herself to drive her hands into Pablo's pockets. She found a fistful of money, then tore a gold ring off his hand.

There was no going back now. With the bravery that only the truly terrified can conjure, Cocheta lifted the window, threw a leg over the sill, eased herself out, and dropped.

Landing was painful. For a moment, she thought she couldn't walk, but somehow, she stood, then limped over to a watering trough on the side of the building and hid in the shadows. Seconds counted. Pablo's pinto waited, tied in front of the bordello with several other horses. Crawling on the ground, she found her way under the bellies of two geldings who snorted and stamped their feet in surprise.

Rising next to the pinto, she untied him and placed a trembling foot into a stirrup and lifted herself up and into the saddle.

Still, the music played on and nobody came outside. "God is on my side tonight," she whispered as she turned the horse into the street, then dug her heels into its side and sped away. She didn't take the main trail out of town but galloped headlong through the briars and cactus that made up the darkened landscape. She remembered her captors had crossed a large river running from north to south, so she found a star to follow and guided the horse through the night. At dawn, she crossed the river, water sluicing around her legs, cold and clean, washing away the past.

Cocheta shivered. She had killed a man. It was a sin. Then grim resolve took over and she knew she did what she had to do in order to live. Tears of relief and shame mingled and wet her face as she urged the horse into a gallop and didn't slow until his sides heaved and he trembled with exhaustion.

It took several days before Cocheta found the town of Breyer. She had not eaten, her body and soul ebbing away. The young Apache stopped the horse in front of The Crow Fly. Men paused and stared at this apparition, muddy and stick-thin, as she limped up to the bar.

"Food," she whispered. The startled bartender brought out a loaf of bread and a block of cheese and placed it in front of her.

"Is this America?" she asked in broken English.

"Yes, ma'am," he said. "What else can I get ya?"

"Work."

After her recovery, Cocheta worked on the floor of The Crow Fly every night. She kept to herself and quietly observed what was going on around her. When she spoke, her voice was high and lilting, like a flute. Never once did she speak of her past. It was best left behind. Cocheta doubted she would ever get over the fact that she killed a man in order to live. It all seemed so distant now, the abuse and torture. The endless days. The drug-induced haze. Sometimes she even wondered if it ever happened. But one thing she knew with surety.

If she had to, she would kill again.

LYLE CONFORT

JED THORNTON LEANED AGAINST A post and watched Cocheta glide by. When he nodded, she glanced away, her dark eyes downcast. Jed knew where she was heading. Lyle Confort lived in the big house on top of a hill at the west end of town.

Jed scowled. Confort had broken no laws since he moved to Breyer but angered more people than a summer downpour at a picnic. A burly man with little manners, he blundered and pushed his way around town like an angry bull, buying up businesses and pestering the shopkeepers with rent hikes and daily harassment.

Confort now owned the building that housed The Crow Fly. He used his iron will to manipulate the women with rent hikes and constant intolerance, often calling upon Jed to tamp down the merrymaking on a Saturday night. Not because the noise bothered him, but because he hoped to take over the saloon and get rid of the women who owned it. If he could get Jed to chase the customers off on a Saturday night, the women would make less money. If the man had been in Breyer at the time of Big Andy's murder, he would have been a prime suspect, Thornton thought. There would have been quite a competition between the two men over The Crow Fly.

Cocheta was part of Confort's ornery logic. He paid for her to come to him in his home every Friday and Saturday night, keeping her all to himself. Men were disappointed to find the dark-haired beauty missing. The lovely Apache was a big draw, and now Confort had her all to himself.

Jed clenched his fists. He wished there was something he could do as sheriff to make Confort's life uncomfortable. Maybe uncomfortable enough so he'd leave town, but it was just a pipe dream. Lyle Confort was here to stay, weaving his web over the entire town. Thornton pushed off from the post and ambled down the street, hoping to get a cup of coffee at the hotel before they closed up after lunch.

LYLE CONFORT PEERED OUT THE window of his bedroom to the town below. Amid the people wandering around on Main Street, Cocheta stood out like a beacon on a stormy sea. His throat tightened. The young woman was exciting and made his nights special. He came the closest to loving her than anyone in his life. But love for him was simply feeling less cruel than usual.

He snorted and coughed into his handkerchief as she approached the front porch. Straightening his shirt and slicking down what hair he had left with a trembling hand, he lumbered down the stairs, opened the door and smiled, his wolfish grin never quite reaching his cold eyes.

"Cocheta, my dear, come in."

The Indian woman stepped across the threshold and gave him a quick, cool nod. She wore her silky hair loose and had chosen a simple green dress that clung to her body like hungry hands.

"Sit, please." Lyle gestured toward a flowered chair in the parlor. He liked it when she sat in the chair, ankles crossed and hands clasped like a lady would, posing for him, her brown eyes boring into him without expression. Perhaps he would have the maid serve tea in his finest china, just to watch her slender dark hands hold the delicate creamy porcelain, a startling contrast that never ceased to arouse him.

"How was your day, Cocheta?"

She cocked her head. "Why do you ask, Lyle? It is always the same. I am always the same. Shall we go upstairs?"

Confort flushed. Cocheta was not intimidated by him, nor his fancy house. Didn't she know how powerful he was? Why, he could take her slender neck between his hands and choke her, and she'd be dead in an instant. Or he could wrap pearls around that neck and kiss her with reverence. He was capable of both.

Instead, he pulled on her hand roughly until she rose gracefully from the chair and escorted her up the stairs, loosening his tie with one hand and placing his other on her slender waist.

Afterward, when he'd sated himself, Confort traced circles on her breast with his finger, and leaned back against the headboard.

"I'm finished with you for now, but you can't go back to the saloon. I'll call you if I need you again. Why don't you go downstairs and find a book to read? You do know how to read, don't you?" Cocheta nodded. Peg taught her the basics, and she caught on quickly.

Confort stayed in bed a while longer after the girl left. He smiled. Cocheta was the best idea he'd had in a long time. Not only was he cheating The Crow Fly out of a desirable whore, but he enjoyed it in more ways than one. He frowned. A man of his portly size and ornery disposition would never entice a woman who looked like Cocheta to be his lover unless he paid for her. He flushed with anger, tossed the sheets aside, and rose from the mattress.

Staring at his body in the mirror, he frowned. He was young once. Young and spry. The kind of man women looked at with admiration, not disgust. But age and lifestyle caught up with him in an unforgiving way.

Confort shrugged. The best he could do is what he did best. Build an empire. Build wealth. And woe be to those who might stand in his way, including those stupid whores at The Crow Fly. A small spider crawled across the floor. He stamped it out with his bare foot and grinned.

"Watch out, Breyer, Texas," he muttered. "There's more where that came from."

Confort walked downstairs to his study and unlocked a tall oak liquor cabinet. He poured a finger of brandy into a crystal glass that sparkled when he held it up to the lamplight. From the doorway, he saw Cocheta curled up on the fine chair, her nose in a book. He chuckled.

"I doubt she can read," Lyle muttered to himself.

Then he sat at his desk and pulled out a thick leather ledger. The numbers swam before his eyes in the afternoon light. He didn't stop to fuss with adding and subtracting. He was profiting off this one-horse town in ways that nobody might imagine. Now at least half the town had accepted Confort's money, for a variety of reasons. Need. Greed. Breyer's residents were either beaten down by depression, or harbored hopes of a new start somewhere else.

Soon, he knew, The Crow Fly would buckle under the weight of his pressure. Between the high rent he put on the building, and other factors, such as keeping Cocheta to himself, before long those stupid women would come to him to unload their precious business, and he'd be ready to offer them a pauper's sum for it. And they would take it.

Confort laughed out loud at the thought. He grunted as he rose from his chair.

In the parlor, Cocheta raised her lovely head and looked at him.

"Go back to the bedroom," he said. "I have need for you again."

Nothing made Lyle Confort more amorous than thinking about destroying lives and making money. Taking his brandy with him, he climbed the stairs.

OLD GRINGO

MISS EMILY AUGUSTA OPENED THE door to the Buttons and Bows and breathed in the cool air. After a dusty summer, the freshness was a welcome respite. One more hour, and the shop would close for the night. She grabbed an old straw broom and swept the floor, depositing the endless dirt back outside where it belonged. Wiping her hands on her skirt, she peered up and down Main Street. Night was closing in. Soon the sun would carry itself over a Texas hill and the windows in town would shimmer with candles and lamplight.

"He should be here by now," she said.

It wasn't like him to be late. Not at all. Folks said you could set your watch by Old Gringo. Why, he was the one steady presence in Breyer. Something you could count on. And every afternoon, folks awaited his arrival. Old Gringo never failed to comply.

A lonesome bray shattered the silence. Emily grinned. The old fool must have spent too much time down at the hotel. Even a woman of sophistication such as Miss Emily enjoyed Old Gringo. She marched back into the shop and took out several pieces of horehound candy kept in a jar on the counter.

Old Gringo walked directly up to the shop. He knew better

than to clout through the dressmaker's tidy store and track mud or dirt. Instead, he stood politely, like any well-bred gentleman would do.

Emily stepped off the boardwalk and walked up to Gringo.

"So, there you are! I was wondering." She opened her palm and offered the candy.

He took it from her hand, then shook a rusty mane, stamping a small hoof in the dirt.

Old Gringo was an ancient donkey. Nobody in town knew where he came from, or how long he had been there. He belonged to nobody, a fact he couldn't hide because of his matted hide and filthy tail. Gringo's hooves were too long, turning up on the ends like an elf's boot. His rheumy eyes wandered as though he were trying to drink in the town in one big gulp.

Every afternoon, Gringo made his way through Breyer like the town crier. He brayed and snorted, tail twitching as he sauntered from place to place. Starting at the hotel, he wound his way down Main Street, ambling all the way to the end of the road and past the saloons, then finally turning off near the schoolhouse, and disappearing.

Children tried to follow him out of town, but he eluded them every time. Some folks said he was a ghost, and he could turn into a jackrabbit and hop away. Others said he belonged to an old miner who lost his way in the Texas sage and died. Most folks didn't care. He was just there, like the sun rising every morning overhead.

The whole town fed Gringo, which was apparent, due to his barrel of a belly that waddled from side to side as he went about his business. He didn't mind a pat or two and stood still like an old dog with his head down, especially loving having his large ears scratched and his back rubbed.

Gringo was friendly with everybody and tolerated by all. He didn't stir up the horses or aggravate the dogs. He didn't shove his enormous head into anybody's belly or kick out in anger. Children swarmed him, rubbing his head and hugging his furry neck. Women gave him sweet treats, and men grinned at his approach.

There was only one thing Old Gringo didn't like. When some fool got it in their head to groom him. He would politely draw away, shaking his massive head and snorting. But if they persisted on using a brush on his rough hide, or lift his feet to trim them, his tail would swish back and forth, then he'd open his mouth and bray. The stench from his breath was a mixture of sweet grass and smoke, as though he slept near a campfire at night. Nobody wanted hot breath in their face and an angry donkey, so aside from the occasional roundup, where the townspeople roped Gringo and insisted on cleaning him up, he was by and large left alone.

Gringo had been near Big Andy when they found the saloon owner's body. He stood under an old cottonwood tree next to The Crow Fly's back door. He didn't leave, even when Miss Emily screamed like a banshee and ran from the corpse. Nobody even noticed that Gringo was there. Nobody except Jed Thornton, who wished like hell donkeys could talk.

"He'd probably be the most honest witness I'd encounter," Jed said, when he helped the undertaker pack up Andy and haul him over to the livery where the smithy would build a coffin for him.

After that, the donkey wandered more frequently into town. For a time, he edged his way along the buildings, keeping to himself. But lately, he made himself known, presenting himself to Breyer every afternoon and begging for handouts.

Thornton watched as Gringo made his journey down Main Street. The sheriff stepped onto the rutted road and whistled. Gringo turned his head, then ambled toward him. Jed stopped to pat his soft muzzle on his way to the bank. The old donkey nodded his head and brushed against him with a gentle nudge. They walked together in companionable silence. Then Gringo stopped, turned around, and waddled back toward the saloons.

Jed chuckled as he watched the animal. Gringo was intriguing. Everybody wanted to know where he came from. Nobody took the time to follow him, Jed thought. Although he interested everyone, the citizens of Breyer soon took him for granted, and didn't work too hard to investigate. Gringo was simply a part of Breyer, and a welcome sight each day.

Thornton looked at his pocket watch. If Gringo were on schedule, he'd probably leave town in about an hour. The sheriff chuckled. Why not follow the old thing? He'd ride well behind him and let the donkey have the lead and see where it went.

He laughed at the thought. "What a stupid thing to contemplate."

But as he went about his business at the bank, his mind turned back to Gringo. The more he thought about it, the more he liked the idea. After all, it was a Monday night. The town was quiet as a church, and Lara didn't expect him home for dinner for a couple more hours. He was curious, and he had the time.

For starters, Thornton followed the donkey on foot. The animal had regular stops. First was the hotel for scraps of lettuce and carrots tossed behind the building. Then he'd move on to Buttons and Bows for a horehound delicacy from Miss Emily. After that, he made his way to the general store and brayed outside the door until rewarded with a neck rub and an apple from old Mr. Dobbs, who worked behind the dry goods counter.

He rounded out his afternoon at The Crow Fly. There he would stand by the hitching post next to the horses and wait patiently for somebody to notice.

This evening was no exception. The donkey burrowed his way between two mares at the hitching post and stood quietly in their shadow. Jed stepped back and hurried to the sheriff's office. His horse, Flyer, waited outside. On impulse, Jed loaded his pistols and grabbed his hat off the rack in the office. He locked the door with a brass key and tossed it in his pocket, then mounted Flyer and turned toward the saloon and waited. He watched as

Kate came bustling out through the swinging doors and gave the donkey several cubes of sugar and a pat on his swayed back.

It took a while, but eventually Old Gringo eased his way out from between the horses and turned south toward the schoolhouse. He didn't appear to be in a hurry. Jed nudged Flyer forward at a slow walk and followed.

The donkey's ears fluttered back and forth as though listening, and sure enough, he came to a halt and turned his large head, peering behind him. Jed reined in Flyer and stood stockstill while Gringo assessed the situation. The minutes ticked by. Nobody moved. Then a wagon jostled past on its way back to a nearby ranch. Jed nodded and tipped his hat. The wagon slowed, and he exchanged a few pleasantries with them.

This was Gringo's opportunity, and he broke into a portly trot toward the back of the building. Jed followed.

When Thornton rounded the corner, Gringo was nowhere in sight.

"Damn! Where could that scoundrel be?" Thornton turned Flyer first one way, then the other, looking for donkey prints. The ground was messy from the countless children who played in the schoolyard. But just as he was about to give up, Jed found a small set of prints heading out to a small arroyo behind the school.

"Of course. Gringo steps down and into the arroyo and walks through the gully! Only, which way?"

Jed stopped and listened. The faint sound of hooves ringing on rocks to the north broke the evening silence.

"I gotcha now, you old sod. We're going to find out where you call camp."

He kept a fair distance from the donkey, although once in a while the animal's big ears showed above the rim as he wandered through the shallow arroyo. It was easy to track him.

The sun was going down. Soon it would be dark in the gully. *Perhaps this was a fool's errand,* thought Jed. *Nobody cared about this crazy old animal. Why put yourself in danger out here in the dark?*

"Where the hell are you going, Gringo?" Jed asked, and leaned back in the saddle, stretching his arms above his head. Flyer snorted and tossed his mane.

As if in answer, Jed saw the donkey climb out of the gully and away. Nudging Flyer with his heels, he loped along the arroyo until he found a well-worn path that cut through the bank. He pointed the horse up the steep trail.

They crested the rim. It surprised Jed to find another trail that led to a small cabin in the distance. Old Gringo was working his way toward the dwelling and seemed to ignore everything around him. Jed followed. The donkey swiveled his ears but kept walking.

Gringo halted in front of the cabin door. Behind the hut was a small corral with the gate open, and after taking a turn or two along the porch, he ambled into the corral and lowered his head.

Jed approached the deserted-looking cabin and rested his hand on a pistol. He broke the silence, his voice thin in the wind.

"Hallo in there! Anybody home? This is Sheriff Jed Thornton from Breyer. I followed the donkey here. Just wanted to talk to somebody. Please?"

There was no answer. Jed didn't expect one. The cabin was tired-looking, as though nobody had taken care of it for a long time. A shutter swung by one nail near a broken window, glass lying on the ground in a hapless fashion.

Frowning, Thornton stepped off Flyer and tied him to a porch railing. He'd never seen this cabin before. It was well hidden behind a stand of trees. One would have to look hard to find it.

Gringo snorted and stamped his hooves. Then he buckled his knees and rolled in the dirt on his back, snorting and tossing his head to and fro.

Jed rapped on the front door. Silence. "Ain't nobody here, nor has been for a long time. It's deserted," he said to himself. He rapped again, then tried the knob. It didn't open. He walked over to the broken window and peered inside.

The one-room cabin held a single bed, a table and one chair, a fine-looking cabinet, and a cold fireplace. As he watched, a mouse skittered across the floor and scurried under the bed.

It was almost dark now. Maybe a half hour left before it would be too dark to make his way home down the arroyo safely. Lara would be worried if he lingered much longer. Making a hasty decision, Jed broke the rest of the glass off the windowsill and climbed inside.

Clearly, the cabin had not been used in quite a while. Dust and cobwebs were everywhere. He ducked under a spider's web and peered around for snakes.

"There's gotta be a few critters living in here." He shuddered, then gazed at his surroundings.

The room was spare. A beautiful ebony cabinet stood out like a beacon in the drab room. Although the table and bed were simple, the cabinet was elaborate, with inlaid wood and a brass plate. An elegant key hung listlessly from the door. Jed didn't have to use it. The door swung open on a well-oiled hinge.

Inside were papers and a metal box. Jed reached for the box. It groaned as he opened the lid. The box housed two pearl-handled pistols nestled in velvet.

He whistled. "These are mighty fine. Why would somebody leave these behind?" He pursed his lips and peered around. "It doesn't make sense. Unless, maybe, the owner met with danger and never made it back home."

Two sets of papers lined the other shelf. One had been tied with a purple ribbon. The other papers had a piece of rawhide wrapped around them.

He reached for the rawhide bunch first and pulled away the knot.

Jed stared in surprise at what appeared to be bills and receipts from The Crow Fly. There were orders for whiskey, food, and monthly tallies. There were also bills and receipts for another house in town, as well as the saloon. A copy of the deed to the house was neatly folded between the other papers, but the light was fading, and Jed couldn't read very well in the shadowy room.

"This cabin had to belong to Andy Connor!" Jed said. "But why the hell did he keep the papers out here instead of the saloon's safe? There must be something he didn't want the women or the bartender to see." He stood and paced in the coming darkness.

"Clearly, I need to bring these back to Breyer and read them. It might cast a light on the investigation, and they'll just end up ruined here." He stopped his pacing. "So, what other dwelling did Big Andy own in Breyer? This doesn't make sense. Andy lived on the second floor of The Crow Fly. I didn't know he owned another place in town. And why all the mystery?" Jed scratched his chin as he talked to himself, trying to make sense of it.

Jed stuffed the papers in his shirt, then reached for the other set. The purple ribbon shredded between his fingers. It was tied around several letters. Letters that gave off a familiar perfume, even after all this time. An aroma that Jed had encountered some-where before.

Jed opened one letter, and his mind reeled as he read it.

"Well, of course," he muttered, sitting down hard on a chair. "It was right in front of me all this time," he said. "How could I be so stupid? This changes everything."

Jed crawled back out the window and came around to the corral. Old Gringo brayed and swished his tail. On the fence post was a halter and rope. There were a few wisps of leftover hay in the corral, but the water trough was empty.

He thought about roping the donkey and bringing him back to town but left things the way they were. Instead, he filled a bucket from a nearby stream and poured the water into the trough, then scratched the old donkey's neck. Gringo leaned into him and nudged him with his soft muzzle.

"Old Gringo, you sod, you've lived for over two years without Big Andy. You've been making sure you're well-fed and taken care of in town. I ain't about to stir up any more trouble until I finish this investigation. I'll just leave you the way you are and know you'll be coming back to town tomorrow. If you ever don't show up, I'll come searching for you."

As if he understood, Gringo blew softly through his nostrils and flapped his ears back and forth.

Jed mounted and turned Flyer back down the path. In the distance, a coyote yipped for its pack—a cold, foreboding sound.

But nothing was more chilling than what Jed read later that night by candlelight in his office.

LITTLE WILLIE SNOW

PEG SMILED AS MOLLY BUNDLED little Willie in a soft yellow blanket, then held him up to the window.

"See, Willie. Your daddy lived way over yonder, behind that hill on a big ranch. He's in heaven now, but I can tell you he would have loved you all the way to the moon!"

The girl dimpled as she rocked the baby in her arms. Peg thought nothing was prettier than the sight of those two. It was alarmingly pure. Having Molly and the baby living at The Crow Fly was like watching flowers bloom in the desert. It was so out of place, so different, and it made the women feel good, the way it feels when love catches up to you.

Even the cold, silent Cocheta had a warm smile for Molly and the baby and often brought Molly little treats from the hotel on a Sunday.

Peg frowned. It just wouldn't do to have Molly go on living here forever, sitting up in her room and playing with Willie all day long. At some point, she'd have to go back to work, and then what would she do at night with the baby? Peg shuddered. This was no place for a sweet young thing like Molly and her innocent baby. Something had to be done.

As Molly pointed out the sights from her window, it occurred to Peg that she might need to take matters into her own hands and make this right. Later that evening, she walked downstairs to talk to Rick.

"Rick, do you still own that little buggy and horse? I haven't seen you driving through town in quite a while."

"Yeah, I own it, but there's nowhere to go around here in this godforsaken place." He stopped rifling through his sheet music and turned his attention to Peg. "Are you interested in buying it? I'd sell the carriage for a good price. I dunno what the hell got into me to buy that fancy little thing. It'd suit a lady more. Not sure I'd want to part with the horse, though. I still ride her."

"Nah, I don't want to buy it. Just wondered if I could borrow it for a brief trip outside of town? Wouldn't be more than a few hours. I'd pay you."

Rick sat down at the piano and plucked at a key, cocking his ear. Satisfied with the sound, he looked up.

"Sure, I don't care. Just maybe pay for some extra oats for Blanca. She's down at the livery right outside of town. It's not too far to walk there and fetch her. Do you mind if I ask where you're going?"

"I don't mind, but I need to talk to Molly first. Then I'll tell ya."

The next morning, Peg knocked on Molly's door. She straightened her skirt and patted her hair. This talk may take some doing. She had to be careful what she would say to the girl.

"Come in!" Molly's voice rang out. Peg smiled. The baby must be awake.

Inside, the room was warm. Sunlight splayed through the curtains and left shadows on the floor. The bed was placed by the window. It looked cozy, set up with extra quilts. Willie cuddled by his mother's side, snug in his yellow blanket. The two looked content. Peg couldn't help but smile.

"Hi, Peg! How are you today?" Molly tucked her hair behind her ears and grinned up at the older woman.

"Well, I'm just fine, honey, and I see you and Willie are too."

Molly beamed. She rubbed the baby's back, and he gurgled.

"He's bigger every time I see him," Peg said, then threw back her head and laughed. "And I see him every day!"

Molly lifted him up and into Peg's arms. The older woman held him close to her chest, while a sad look passed across her face. She hid it with a smile and jostled the baby up and down gently. When he burped, they both chuckled.

"So, honey, I was thinking of something," Peg said, rubbing Willie's head with a gentle finger. "Maybe we should take a ride out to the Snow Ranch and talk to Willie's parents. After all, little William here is their grandson, and maybe they'd like to help you out, with your Willie passing and everything."

Molly's smile dimmed. "I've thought of that. I really have. Many times. But what good would it do for me and little Willie? They would never want to admit to having a grandson by a whore from The Crow Fly."

"Well, then why did their son come here anyway?" Peg asked. "Answer me that, Molly! Nobody forced him to visit here every Saturday night. He was just as responsible as you were when it came to getting pregnant, you know. So, don't go selling yourself short. If there's any wrongdoing, Willie Snow was right there with you."

Molly looked at her baby, then up into Peg's face. She got out of bed and lowered herself into the brightly painted wooden rocking chair the women gave her as a gift. Peg brought the baby over and placed him in Molly's lap.

"I guess I never thought of it like that," Molly said. "I thought maybe I was an evil person. You know I'm not." She spoke so softly, Peg had to lean down to listen.

Tears brimmed over and trickled down Molly's face. Peg knelt and cradled the girl's head against her shoulder.

"You're not evil, sweetheart. You're a nice girl. Things just happened. Things you had no control over, and you did what you had to do to survive. And still do. Why, Willie Snow saw the good in you! He wanted to marry and live with you forever. He loved you. No, Willie didn't just love you, he absolutely adored you. He was willing to give up his entire life at the ranch, and his parents, in order to have you as his wife." She brushed a wisp of hair away from the girl's face.

"I think we need to ride out to the Snow Ranch and show them your son. Talk to them. Don't hide from them, honey. Willie deserves better than that. You deserve better too. And the only way to find out is to sit down and talk to them."

"I'm afraid," Molly replied.

"I understand. But I'll be with you, and if you aren't up to talkin', I'll pipe up. Don't be afraid. Be brave." Peg toyed with the tortoise shell brooch on her chest. She took a steady breath. "I'm thinking we should go out there tomorrow. Rick has a carriage I can borrow, and you and the baby could stand some fresh air. It'll do you good. Will you say yes?"

Molly thought for a long time. She closed her eyes and rocked back and forth. Once in a while, a tear slid past her closed eyelids. Her mouth puckered up once or twice as though she might cry, but she kept rocking. Finally, the rocking stopped and Molly opened her eyes.

"Okay." She brushed the tears away and smiled. "Okay."

CONFRONTATION

THE NEXT DAY BLOOMED AS pretty as any day Peg had seen in a long time. Rick's horse Blanca was a steady mare who pulled the buggy slowly on the well-worn trail out of town. It was a good distance out to the ranch, and would take a while at their pace, but Peg wasn't about to make the horse go faster and jostle them until their insides ached and stir up the baby.

Molly sat next to her, holding Willie in her arms. She swaddled the baby in the yellow blanket Miss Emily gave him. His shock of red hair rose above the blanket like a small flame. Molly took every care to clean him up and brush his downy head. The gentle movement of the buggy rocked him to sleep.

They turned onto a trail under a wooden sign that read *Five Bar Ranch*. Both women marveled at the vast amount of land, and the large number of cattle grazing, flicking their tails in the morning sunshine. The trail widened into a well-maintained road that led the women through a grove of cottonwood trees before opening into a large meadow.

In the middle of the clearing was a two-story house. Handsome, it had been freshly whitewashed and displayed a large porch with rocking chairs and potted flowers on it.

Molly fell mute. Her eyes took in everything.

"So, this is where my Willie grew up! This beautiful ranch. Oh, what a wonderful life he must have had here."

"Yep," Peg said. "But remember, honey, he wanted you more. Never forget that. In particular, don't forget it today of all days." She patted the girl's knee for reassurance.

A large man appeared on the porch and waved. Waving back, Peg guided Blanca off the main trail and onto a cleared area with several hitching posts. Nervous, she stepped down from the carriage and tied the horse to the post, taking care to do it just right while she gained her composure. When she looked up, the man was only ten feet away.

"Hello! I'm William Snow. What can I do for you ladies today?"

He walked to the side of the buggy and put out his hand to help Molly down. Willie stirred and let out a thunderous wail. Snow took one look at the flaming hair and stopped short. His outstretched hand retracted into a fist.

"Who are you?" he asked, his icy glare fixed on Molly's face.

Molly tried to shush Willie while working her mouth to talk, but nothing came out except the air she had been holding in ever since she saw the house.

Peg cleared her throat. "I'm Peg Rutherford. This is Molly Brewster, and this, Mister Snow, is your grandson, William Snow the third."

If a snake had slithered out from the barn and bit him, Snow wouldn't have been more agitated. His countenance shifted as first one thing, then another, crossed his mind. It ended with a scowl as he realized these women were from The Crow Fly.

"You ain't welcome here, ladies. Best you turn around and go home. I don't know what you're up to, but you won't get anywhere with me. My son didn't go to whorehouses. My son was a nice boy. He didn't mingle with you women, and he didn't have a son."

"Mister Snow," Peg spoke through gritted teeth. "I knew your son, Willie. He'd come every weekend to see Molly, and they were aiming to get married. He loved Molly with all his heart, and you should love what he made with her."

Snow flushed at her frank talk. "That's enough language like that around here. Now, leave and take your tricks with you before I take you back to Jed Thornton myself and press charges." He reached for the pistol on his hip but stopped short of pulling it out.

Molly trembled and turned to Peg. "Please! I can't do this. I can't talk to them. Take me home!" She buried her face in Willie's blanket and the baby wailed louder. Blanca flattened her ears and shifted her feet in agitation. The buggy lurched forward, then stopped abruptly behind the horse's rump. Blanca flicked her tail and tossed her head.

Snow took a menacing step forward. "Get out of here and take that little bastard with you. You won't come here again and tell lies about our only son, may he rest in peace. You hear?"

Molly straightened and looked into Snow's eyes. Her usual sweet face was stormy. She held Willie tighter to her chest.

"He's not a little bastard. He's Willie Snow, and he deserves better than what you just said." She waved her left hand, where Willie's ring rode on a shaking finger. "We were engaged!"

"What are you doing with my wife's mother's ring?" Snow flushed and the veins on his neck popped. "What the hell did you do? Steal it? Give it to me! It doesn't belong to you! Why, I should wrench it off your damned finger!"

Molly burst into tears. Blanca rattled the reins at the post. Peg moved forward, took Willie from Molly's arms, and rocked him as he screamed.

"We'll leave right now," Peg hissed. "Look what you've done to this poor girl. This is your loss, Mister Snow."

"Stop right there!" A voice rang out from behind the buggy, and everyone turned. A tiny woman with scarlet hair stood with her arms crossed against her chest. Her eyes, the color of the open sea, were fixed on the little boy. Then they shifted to Molly. Trembling, she walked toward Peg and put a tentative finger out to little Will, who immediately stopped crying.

In the sudden silence, the woman turned toward Molly. In a lilting Irish voice, she reached for her hand.

"Come in. We'll talk. I have no idea what any of this means, but I think we need to get to the bottom of it. If you knew my Willie, I want to hear what you have to say. Please."

"Don't, Clarisse," Snow said. "These women are shysters. They need to leave." The man gazed sadly at his wife. "Stop looking under rocks and behind buildings for Willie. He's gone, my love, and he's not coming back."

"Hush now, William, they're coming in, and that's all there is to it." She reached out and helped Molly down from the buggy, then turned toward the house. The women followed.

Clarisse led the way into a parlor filled with plants and paintings. On the sofa, a sleepy white cat peered at them, then jumped down and stalked away, tail in the air. The room was lovely, decorated in soft colors. It was shady and cool, a contrast to the Texas morning. On a table sat a silver tea service. Next to it was a book.

Molly gazed around in awe. It was so peaceful and lovely. How could Willie leave this place? She was aware of her ragged dress—a faded gingham shift with stains on it. Molly wore her hair loose instead of piled into an elaborate hairstyle. She wore no rouge. The effect was that of a young, innocent girl that belied what she did at The Crow Fly.

"Do sit. Would you like tea or coffee?" Clarisse's voice was pleasant, controlled, but her eyes had darkened into storm clouds.

Molly and Peg sat next to each other on the sofa and placed the baby between them. He squirmed in his bunting, then settled into the soft cushion, chubby fingers in his mouth.

Clarisse looked hard and long at what was before her. Peg certainly looked the part of an aging prostitute. There was a sadness about her that overtook every bit of her. Even when she touched the baby, her hand rested protectively about his tiny head in almost a fearful, sorrowful way.

The girl looked fresh and lively. Even though she had recently birthed the little boy, she was wildly attractive, with hair the color of autumn leaves and a sweet dimple that deepened when she smiled.

And the baby. *Oh, the baby!* Clarisse thought as she touched her own scarlet hair, then looked at a portrait of Willie hanging over the fireplace. There was no doubt this was her son's child. No doubt that Molly had come by her mother's ring the honest way. Willie would never have given her the ring if he wasn't sincere. It was too special. That this girl sadly used her son at The Crow Fly did not erase the fact that Willie's son, her grandson, was here, in this very house where she raised her own wonderful boy.

Now, she had to find a way to keep him here where he belonged, on the Five Bar Ranch.

CLARISSE

CLARISSE GAZED AT THE BABY, now sleeping between Molly and Peg on the parlor sofa. There was no doubt in her mind that Willie was her grandson. Besides sporting a thatch of red hair, the baby looked so much like Willie did as a newborn that Clarisse felt like she had taken a step back in time.

She longed to reach for his sweet body and cradle him. Longed to keep him here and let him grow up on the ranch, let him hear the sweet sounds of the cattle lowing in the fields, the lazy way the breeze danced through the meadow, the warmth and smells of a good home.

As Molly leaned over the child and fussed with his yellow blanket, Clarisse saw why Willie fell in love with her. A beautiful girl with an innocent smile, it was no wonder she turned her son's head.

Clarisse peered over at her husband. William's jaw was set hard as Texas clay. He still didn't believe the truth. That their son loved Molly Brewster. But it was the truth. She knew it was. Just as she knew that she already loved her little grandson.

Clasping her hands together, she sat back in her chair. There were so many questions, and in the end, the answers might color the direction the Snows were going to go with the information.

"So, Molly, tell me what happened between you and Willie," Clarisse said, her voice soft and comforting.

Molly dimpled. "Well, ma'am, we didn't meet at The Crow Fly. We met at Buttons and Bows. I was in the shop when Willie walked in one day and we said a few words to each other. I told him I worked over at The Crow Fly."

William Snow shifted uncomfortably in his chair. It bothered him that his wife would learn about a whorehouse from two of the very denizens themselves. He prayed they wouldn't resort to swearing or explicit language. Why, Clarisse might swoon and faint. But Clarisse was leaning forward in her chair, listening intently to the pretty girl on the sofa.

"It was a couple of weeks later, and Willie showed up at the saloon and asked for me." Here she stifled a smile. "My gosh, Willie thought I worked there as a singer or a barmaid." Then her face tightened with shame. "He didn't understand what I was." Now her face was bright red, and she felt an uncomfortable tightening in her throat.

Peg interjected. "That's right. Willie didn't know. And the two of them were just as cute as any other young couple who was courting." She turned toward Clarisse. "Why, he was so sweet to her, Missus Snow. We all knew they were in love and Willie asked her to marry him and gave her that ring."

Molly picked at her skirt, and her voice lowered. "Willie didn't think you would approve of me, so we planned to run away to Colorado or somewhere and get married. He was planning to come back that very weekend, the weekend he died in the stampede." Now the tears came, and Molly couldn't stop them. "He didn't know about our baby. I hope he does in heaven."

She swiped her eyes with the back of her hand. For the first time, a look of defiance came over the girl. She sat ramrod straight on the sofa and looked Clarisse Snow in the eye.

"I loved Willie with all my heart, and I am proud to bear his son."

"Don't you have family anywhere, Molly?" William Snow asked, his voice a little gentler.

"No, sir. My parents died of the fever, and I got sick myself. I ended up in Breyer with no place to go. Mama told me to go to a church if I ever needed help. Only, nobody was there that day. The churchyard was empty. I fainted and fell off the horse. That's where Kate Dawson found me and brought me to The Crow Fly, so I had a roof over my head and something to eat. They took care of me."

Molly dipped her head and whispered. "One thing led to another, and I didn't want to leave The Crow Fly. I know it sounds strange, but it became a home for me. Big Andy wouldn't let me just stay there forever without pitching in, and well...." Her voice trailed off.

Peg shifted on the couch, her eyes locking onto Clarisse's. "Now, don't go judging this little girl. Life can be cruel to women who have nobody to protect them. Did she make a mistake or two? Of course she did. But who hasn't? What would have happened to her without our help? Hmm? Where would she be now with not one person in this entire world to turn to?"

Clarisse sat silently in her chair. She remembered her own situation as a girl. On the ship coming to America from Ireland, both her parents had perished from dysentery. It was the most traumatic experience she had ever known. The final days of the voyage, she spent curled up in a corner of steerage by herself, heartbroken and frightened. She still remembered the swaying of the ship, the creaking of the boards, and the rank smell of others in the close quarters below deck. She remembered the scarcity of food, and the stale crusts of bread filled with weevils. During the daylight hours, she could go up on deck, but the nights lingered in darkness and foreboding.

One night, two men approached her. It was clear they had

bad intentions. One reached out and touched the top of her head, then let his hand travel down her arm toward her waist. Clarisse cowered with her head between her knees, terrified. Fortunately, another man on the other side of the ship walked over to the corner where she was sitting and rescued her. He kept her next to his family for the rest of the journey. Had it not been for that family, she shuddered to think about what might have happened. She was lucky.

Good fortune shined upon Clarisse again. When she disembarked, her aunt and uncle were waiting for her. She stayed with them in their warm home on a quiet street in New York City. Their two younger children loved Clarisse, and she loved them too. Gradually, her sorrow lessened, replaced with contentment. Her aunt found her a job cleaning houses for wealthy families close to their neighborhood. She made friends with two girls she worked with, and they often saw each other on their days off.

Two years later, William Snow visited New York and met the young Irish girl through a family member. They fell in love and were married. William brought her out to the Five Bar, where they settled and built a wonderful life together.

When she gazed at Molly, she saw the same primal fear in the girl's eyes she had once known on the ship so long ago. How small the girl looked! How vulnerable! And there on her lap was little Willie, the spitting image of his father, his fingers wrapped around a lock of Molly's hair.

Clarisse opened her mouth to speak, but William cleared his throat.

"May I say something here?" His voice boomed across the parlor and landed at Molly's feet.

Snow rose from his chair and walked closer. He reached out a large hand and touched the baby's head.

"I don't know how much of your story is true, Molly. But I know two things. The first is, this is Willie's son. There's no doubt in my mind now. He has the same crooked toes sticking out of his blanket that Willie had. Hammertoes, I think they call 'em. So do I. The second thing I know is, if my son loved you, then you were very special to him. Willie was a good judge of character, even at such a young age." He returned to his chair and settled back with a sigh. "You're welcome here anytime you want to bring Willie out to the ranch for a visit if you plan to stay in Breyer. We'd very much like to see Willie from time to time."

"No, William, Molly won't be visiting," replied Clarisse. "This is our grandson. Our beloved Willie's boy. He will be staying with us here at the Five Bar."

Molly and Peg looked startled. Peg jumped to her feet, her mouth open in protest. Molly threw her arms protectively around the baby.

Clarisse held her hand up. "Calm down, everybody." She looked at William, then over at Molly. Taking a deep breath, she explained.

"What I mean to say is that Molly and her son are both welcome here in our home. They simply cannot return to The Crow Fly. It isn't fitting for Willie's son and for the girl he loved. They both need a decent home."

She turned to Molly. "You and the baby can have two rooms upstairs. One for you, one for little Willie. They're clean and dry and you should be comfortable there." Her voice caught with emotion. "One room was Will's. Now, I can't make promises we will all get along, but it's a start. Willie needs a stable home, and you need a home too. I think we should try it for a while."

Molly stammered. "But, what... what if you don't like me? Will you try to take Willie away from me?"

Clarisse shook her head and sat down on the sofa next to the baby. "No. No matter what happens, Willie is your child, but I hope and pray you will find it in your heart, as I am finding it in mine, for you to live here with us at the Five Bar."

She touched Molly's russet hair, and the girl burst into great sobs of relief. Both Clarisse and Peg put their arms around her.

William Snow nodded. "You're right, Clarisse," he admitted. "We'll send somebody behind Peg to The Crow Fly and gather your things, Molly. In the meantime, you need to rest and take care of this little guy. Why, he looks all tuckered out. Maybe his grandpa can hold him for a while?"

Clarisse and Peg walked together to the carriage. William Snow was inside with Molly and the baby. The two women eyed each other, taking their measure. Both their gazes softened.

Peg looked away from the other woman. She patted Blanca and untied the reins from the post. The horse nuzzled Clarisse's hand. Peg cleared her throat. Her words came out in a whisper.

"I had a little boy once, just like Willie," she said.

"You did, Peg?"

"Yes. Gunfire killed my boy during a train robbery. He was only five years old. I... I don't talk about it much. His name was Jody. Jody Rutherford. He's buried out on the Nebraska prairie along with my husband."

Peg's eyes filled with tears. "Take care of the people you love, Clarisse. As we both know, nothing is guaranteed. Molly is a lovely young girl. Don't hold her past against her. I hope someday you can love her the way Willie did."

Clarisse nodded, then enveloped Peg in her arms. "Godspeed, Peg, and you are welcome to visit anytime. Thank you for bringing them to me."

TWO WEEKS LATER, THE SNOWS entered the church in Breyer with Molly and Willie. Clarisse walked proudly down the aisle to their favorite pew, Molly and Willie trailing behind. William Snow followed, hat in hand.

"Welcome, Molly and Willie Snow," Pastor Green said, then nodded to his wife, who opened with a song on the piano. A song about hope, forgiveness, and everlasting love.

SATURDAY NIGHTS

JED THORNTON STROLLED UP MAIN Street on a Saturday night, his belly full from the hearty stew Lara served him for supper. A few cowboys rode past on their way to The Crow Fly, stirring up dust, their voices ringing out as only the celebratory can.

The Crow Fly. It had been a lot quieter since Molly Brewster moved out to the Five Bar Ranch with her baby. *Thank God the Snows took that poor girl and her baby in,* thought Jed. He and Lara had even talked about taking care of her themselves. It was a pitiful situation. But now she and little Will had a good home, and it warmed the heart to think about it.

Lyle Confort kept Cocheta up at his house every Friday and Saturday night, which rankled the patrons of the saloon. That left only Kate. Peg was the manager now and had retired from whoring. Disgruntled, the men dwindled away. Business had slowed to a trickle. Now, the stragglers who lived close to Breyer rode in for a game or two of cards and a few drinks, then took their other business elsewhere.

It was a relief in some ways. Sometimes it got mighty rowdy around Breyer. Men became fools the more they drank. The good citizens of the town did not like handing the night over to the boisterous patrons and complained regularly to Jed. There was precious little he could do about it. Most of the time, they weren't breaking the law, and they were usually harmless, although the racket the men made was enough to send people scurrying to their homes and locking their doors. Lately, though, it was more peaceful on a Saturday night.

All the better for Jed because now he could spend more time wrapping up that old murder. Big Andy was hardly worth the effort, but Thornton was a lawman, and a man of the law had to do his job, although nobody else seemed to care about Andy's demise.

Big Andy's deserted cabin out of town revealed many answers. But it didn't behoove a detective to run willy-nilly, claiming the case solved and arresting people, until he could prove it. Or at least squeeze the truth out of somebody.

He told nobody about the cabin where Old Gringo lived. Best to wait and see what might come forth on its own without nudging it along. In the meantime, he kept his eye on the suspect more closely, though the killer showed no signs of bolting, nor even of guilt.

Despite the outward appearance of Breyer, there were a few bad actors in town, and they preyed on Jed's mind constantly. He never knew what one of them might do next.

As if summoning the Devil, Confort strolled by and tipped the brim of his hat toward Jed. "Evening, Constable." He shifted his eyes away, casting them toward The Crow Fly as he shuffled past.

Thornton nodded at the man and watched him elbow his way into the saloon. The bastard was probably going to raise the rent again. Eventually, the women would give up and Confort would control one more thing in Breyer.

"He'll never control me," Jed vowed as he stepped back into his office and closed the door.

PEG GLIMPSED HERSELF IN THE mirror behind the bar. It was time to order another dress from Emily Augusta, she thought. This one looked as tired as she felt. Truth be told, she rather enjoyed the fact that business was slow. It was calmer, quieter.

Shorty still stood in the corner near the potted palm but was seldom needed to restore law and order in the saloon. More often than not, he and Peg sat at a small table and talked to one another. It was clear to Peg that Shorty loved her, but she herself held back. Never dreaming that she would care for another person after losing her husband and son, any feelings she had for Shorty she tamped down before they bloomed. And besides, what prospects did the man have? He lived in a tent not far out of town and had few friends. Of course, here she was, a madam, wondering about a man's prospects. Why, she should be happy that anybody even found her attractive.

She looked again in the mirror at her reflection. Peg thought about Molly and wished that she herself had found a soft place to land over the years. The girl had a good chance of thriving with little Will out on the ranch and maybe someday find a good man. People had short memories sometimes, and the townspeople took Clarisse Snow's lead and treated Molly with an air of acceptance. It was a good start. Molly at least had an inkling of a future. There would have been none at The Crow Fly.

Kate spent most of her free time over at Buttons and Bows. Once Emily learned Kate had a flair for design and a love for dressmaking, the two formed a bond of sorts. The austere Emily certainly didn't befriend Kate but enjoyed the other woman's ideas and company. Kate spent as much time as she could helping her sew clothing for the ladies of the town.

Cocheta was nowhere to be seen most days. When she wasn't

working in the saloon or with Lyle Confort, she holed up in her room. She filled her space with books and candles and sweet treats she purchased from the hotel across the street. She was never friendly, but then again, she wasn't unfriendly either. Like a graceful ghost, she floated through The Crow Fly, her delectable body and beautiful face leaving a trail of desire throughout the saloon. Now that Lyle Confort paid for her on their busiest nights, the saloon was much quieter.

Confort saw his opportunity and continued to press the women for more money. He raised the rent constantly. It forced the bartender to water down the liquor, which only ended in angry cowpokes who left through the swinging doors amid cusswords.

Like a noose slowly tightening, the women struggled against the inevitable. Lyle Confort was a force to be reckoned with. He had no intention of easing his iron hold on the saloon, or most of the town, for that matter. He could simply evict them, but this was far more satisfying. He'd buy their business for a token, keep the name, and The Crow Fly would flourish.

COCHETA AND LYLE

"**H**E'LL NEVER CONTROL ME," COCHETA mused as she looked out the window toward town. Lyle was off to The Crow Fly but told her to stay at his house. He did not want her returning until Monday, he informed her.

Cocheta shuddered. Confort had her stay here with him longer than usual. She shifted in the chair in his vast parlor and watched the doings on Main Street. The people were too far away to make out clearly, so she guessed at some of them by their gait and the clothes they wore.

Peg had a limp from a stiff hip. Cocheta watched her step down into the street and walk across to the Breyer Hotel. Like Cocheta, Peg often enjoyed buying food from the hotel, and bringing it back to the peace of her room at the saloon.

Jed Thornton was recognizable because he was lanky and walked with a distinct military stride, smooth as a cat. Not for the first time, she wondered what the handsome man would be like in bed. He was one of the few men who she thought was trustworthy and kind. Lara was a lucky woman.

Fingering through the books on the shelf in the parlor, Cocheta touched her bruised cheek and winced. Confort had never hit her before. Last night, his ire was palpable. She wasn't sure why he became so angry, but one thing she knew. If he did it again, he'd be sorry.

She sat down heavily on the damask sofa with a book in her hand. Though the afternoon sun poured into the room like amber, and the book looked promising, Cocheta was as restless as she had ever been in Breyer. Usually on Saturday nights, she entertained several men. She should be happy, she thought, that she only had to deal with Confort, who, half the time, was content to just hold her, then fall asleep. He was a monster, though, and Cocheta knew it. Something about him emitted fumes of cruelty. Time and again, she wondered what he had done and what he could do. He was already destroying the businesses of Breyer for his own greed. Soon, he would own the entire town.

"But if he tries to own me, he is mistaken," she said in Apache, then deliberately tossed the book into the fire and watched it smolder, then turn into wisps of ashes that settled on the burning logs.

KATE DAWSON LOOKED UP FROM behind the bar and winced as Lyle Confort strolled in. Nothing good ever came of his visits. He was a bad wind. A tainted seed. A constant ache in the heart of town.

"Anything I can do for you, Mister Confort?" she asked.

"Is Peg around?" He tipped the brim of his hat with the head of his cane, then looked around in a proprietary manner. Grasping the edge of the counter, he sat down on a barstool and groomed his mustache with an arrogant finger.

"She's over at the hotel, but I suspect will be back soon." Kate rubbed at the counter with a cloth, then turned away, her back to the man. She couldn't bear to look at him. "Do you want to leave a message?"

Confort sighed and tapped his cane. "Well, I guess so. It's a long walk back and I don't have all day." He ran his hand through sparse brown hair and shifted his haunches on the stool.

Narrowing his eyes, he smirked, then chuckled. "Tell her I'm keeping Cocheta until Monday. Seems she can't live without me."

Kate didn't smile. She slammed a glass down on the counter. "I'll tell her. Anything else you need, Mister Confort, before you leave?"

Confort rose from the stool, his face red. "Nothing from you, that's for sure." He tapped the counter with his walking stick, just missing Kate's fingers, and walked away.

Kate swore under her breath. The man was maddening. Just the sight of him was enough to enrage half the folks in town. Kate was no exception. She didn't like being squeezed into submission by the man, with countless rent raises, complaints, and monopolizing Cocheta. With Molly living now out on the Five Bar Ranch with the Snows, she and Peg were the only women left on a Saturday night. And Peg was no longer interested in entertaining the men.

The only good thing that came from the debacle is that Kate was making a lot of money. She paid her share of the expenses for The Crow Fly but still had plenty left over. She even opened a nice account at the bank and loved to watch her nest egg build each week. Kate spent very little. That was okay with her because she had a long-term plan. One that involved her sewing skills, Miss Emily, and Buttons and Bows. Her dream was to buy into the dress shop. Emily may not want to partner with her, and Kate was prepared for the rebuff. The other woman could be incredibly irritating and snobbish. Emily catered to the town's women and had little time for anything else.

If she refused to allow Kate to invest in the dress shop, there were a few things Kate knew that likely would convince Emily to let her in. Kate snorted at the thought. There was a lot she knew. And not just information on Emily Augusta. Why, there was plenty of scandal to go around in Breyer, Texas. Men's tongues loosened up in bed. She was a good listening post.

Kate wandered to the swinging doors and peered over them, checking to see where that snake Confort might be hiding. Plain as day, she saw him lumbering back up the hill to his house, where he kept the Apache girl.

"The joke's on you, Lyle Confort. You might be a snake, but you are sleeping with an eagle. Sleep with one eye open, if you value your neck," she said. Then she walked back to the bar and picked up another glass to wash.

CONFORT OPENED THE FRONT DOOR of his house and took a deep breath. It was always good to be home, wherever that may be. He'd made his home in many places. Usually, he entered a town like Breyer, a down-in-the-mouth town bleeding out with weariness and lack of ambition. Then, he'd buy up everybody's broken dreams and, in turn, profit from them. He'd raise the rents on the shops, take over the saloons, own all the horses in the livery and run people out of town he didn't like. He didn't like any of them, truth be told, but some irritated him more than others. Take, for instance, Jed Thornton. A straight shooter, if there ever was one. Noble. Righteous. The kind of man who could not be bought for any price. A nuisance. If Jed Thornton would nest under his wing, things would move forward smoother. Without him, Confort could not tell him to turn the other eye when things happened.

So, instead, without Thornton's cooperation, he had to weave his web carefully, slower than he'd like, but safer.

Normally, he would have left this stinking little town in the middle of nowhere months ago. He would have moved on to the next downtrodden place. But this was going to take more finesse, and a good while longer.

In the meantime, he enjoyed watching people squirm beneath his thumb. It was intoxicating to be that powerful.

Pouring himself a glass of brandy, he thought of the beautiful Cocheta squirming beneath him and called out.

"Cocheta! Where the hell are you?"

There was no answer.

He tried the parlor, but it was vacant, just the acrid smell of paper burning in the fireplace. A quick trek around the house produced nothing. Not even the cook had seen her. He dashed out the front door.

"If that little Indian bitch went back to The Crow Fly, I'll kill her. How dare she ignore my orders to stay here! Why, she's asking for it! What a bother she is!"

He stormed back in and jammed a hat on his head. This time, he'd ride into town on a horse. No sense wasting all his energy walking, just to punish Cocheta.

As he shuffled toward the stable, he caught sight of Cocheta on a swing fastened to a cottonwood tree. The previous owner had made it for his children. When he sold out to Confort for a good price, the family simply left the old swing where it was.

Cocheta sat with her head down, studying her feet as she lightly pumped up and down. Her black hair flew out behind her like smoke. The wind rustled her skirt, showing her knees. Across the yard, Confort heard her singing a sweet tune.

She looked so young, Confort thought. Young and innocent. The way he imagined their child would look like if he and Cocheta had one together. His heart softened. He yearned to walk across the yard, hold her in his arms, and stroke her beautiful head.

"Cocheta," he said softly.

She stiffened, suddenly mute, and stopped swinging. Peering over her shoulder, her eyes narrowed when she saw him.

"Cocheta, dear, it's getting late. Come upstairs with me."

Sullen, she rose from the swing and nodded, then walked toward the back door with a sigh of resignation.

Confort watched her as she went. If only, just for a moment, the woman would speak to him in that same lilting voice she used to sing. If only she loved him. He would give her the world. Was it that hard to do? To love him?

Sadly, he trudged toward the house and up the stairs, where he knew Cocheta would wait for him, not with open arms, but only with open legs.

GOOD MORNING, BREYER

BREYER, TEXAS, WAS SHOWING OFF. The town was usually content to look like a puckered spinster, dusty and wan. But this morning, it donned a blue sky and a cool breeze. Birds flew overhead in formation, a string of pearls around the neck of the horizon. The sun was warm, but not raging, a demure type of day that made the residents feel squeamish about all the complaints they registered against the town.

Jed Thornton took his time saddling Flyer, breathing in the pure air and feeling the breeze on his face. *Kisses from heaven,* he thought. He tightened the cinch and led Flyer away from the hitching post. Mounting, he nodded at Peg as she stepped into the street with her hands full of pamphlets.

He rode over and halted in front of her. "What's that you have there?"

"Hi, Jed, how ya doin? These papers are advertising exciting things happening at The Crow Fly. I plan to post them around town, if that's okay with you?"

"What kind of things?" Jed leaned down and took one from her outstretched hand. He looked thoughtfully at her. Peg was a handsome woman. If a person didn't know where she worked, she could pass for one of the town's ladies. He peered around. Shorty was usually close by wherever Peg went. He guarded her like a hungry dog, waiting for the few bones of joy tossed to him from her as she went about her day. Sure enough, the giant of a man was leaning against the water trough near a hitching post. He nodded at Jed, then straightened a buckskin jacket around his enormous shoulders and gazed up and down the street.

"Oh, well, we hired entertainment on Saturday nights! We have Rick, of course, but now we've also contacted traveling shows and such. A few of them have agreed to come into Breyer and put on a performance. Two are lady singers, one is a magician, and then there's an entire troupe of folks who sing and dance."

"Well, Peg, that's a great idea. I know folks will show up, for sure."

Peg sobered. "I wish we could shut down the saloon altogether and build a playhouse. A theater. Like they have back East. I bet the whole town would come because we'd keep it proper. We're talking about it, you know? Emily is interested in investing, and she's giving us advice." She tucked a wisp of hair behind her ear. "Well, that's a pipe dream, I suppose, but sure is worth dreaming about."

"Why not? I think maybe the whole town could pitch in and help build such a playhouse." Jed tucked the pamphlet inside his shirt.

Peg cocked her head and grinned. "That's a good idea! I think I'll mention it to Emily at our next meeting." Her eyes crinkled at the corners as she looked up into Jed's face. "I gotta get along now and get these posted here and there. The first show will be in three weeks! I hope you will stop in for a spell to watch some of it."

Thornton nodded. "Of course I will. Sounds exciting."

He tipped his hat as Peg marched away with a purposeful stride. Jed held little hope for The Crow Fly. Lyle Confort made the women's lives miserable, and it appeared he was winning in his plan to shut them down. As far as saloons went, The Crow Fly ran smoothly and tried to be as respectable as possible. Two new saloons had emerged in Breyer, The Lucky Lady and The Ruby Slipper, both much wilder on a Saturday night, although The Crow Fly was the only brothel in town.

However, whenever he thought of The Crow Fly, he thought of Big Andy and his demise. After following Old Gringo to the rundown shack across the arroyo and discovering letters between Andy and somebody he knew well, he thought the case was sewn up. And yet he hesitated to pursue it and make an arrest. First of all, he had no concrete proof, but what he knew was damning. There was little doubt in his mind who the killer was.

Thornton nudged Flyer down Main Street and peered into the windows of the shops and saloons as he passed by. For the first time in his career, Jed was conflicted. He knew everybody in Breyer. Some were scoundrels, but the majority were decent folk and he liked them. He and his wife did business with them. As sheriff, he knew a lot about them and their backgrounds. Arresting one of Breyer's own would be painful. And was it truly necessary? The killer probably had a good reason. Abuse? Swindle? Blackmail? Big Andy was capable of almost anything, he figured.

"Damned if I do, and damned if I don't," muttered Jed as he made his way up past the schoolyard and watched as Lara rang the bell to start the day in the classroom. The clear sound pierced the air, as clean and as hopeful as the morning was. Breyer, it seemed, was on its best behavior, but as any lawman knew, that could change as quickly as a prairie storm.

BUTTONS AND BOWS

KATE DAWSON AND EMILY AUGUSTA had their heads together as they leaned over the counter and studied the pattern of a dress Kate had drawn. It was ambitious, flowing, sophisticated, and noteworthy. Emily got excited just looking at it. "Why, it will be stunning made up in silk or velvet." Emily thought it was one of the prettiest designs Kate had ever made.

"Kate, this is beautiful! I think it's your best yet. I can just see it on one of the fine ladies of Breyer," she said. "Lord knows where the woman could go in that dress around here, but maybe she can convince her husband to take her to Dallas or Houston."

"Why stop there?" replied Kate. "Let him take her to Paris."

Both women laughed at the thought. Here in Breyer, Buttons and Bows was about as elegant as any of the ranch wives would ever see. And yet they yearned for new fashion and were willing to pay for it.

Kate spent most of her spare time at the dress shop. She loved talking fashion with Emily. Kate's designs were flawless, lovely drawings of beautiful gowns. She had a good eye for color, too, and helped Emily pick out new fabrics from catalogs out of New York.

Despite the differences between them, Emily welcomed the company. She had spent many years running the shop on her own. Now, with Kate's input, things ran smoother. Kate often helped her sew, and once in a while helped in the shop, although many of the women in town disliked seeing a denizen from The Crow Fly in Buttons and Bows.

Looking at Kate's face steeped in concentration as she gazed at her design, Emily chewed on her lower lip. She thought lately of partnering with Kate, offering her a piece of Buttons and Bows, where they would invest together in the dress shop, but hesitated. Kate could leave The Crow Fly then and have a respectable job. But, of course, everybody in town knew what Kate did for a living. It might be hard to convince folks to do business with her.

Sometimes Emily thought of leaving Breyer and starting up somewhere else. She had no real ties here. However, it was a comfortable life, and the extra money she made managing The Crow Fly's finances helped buy more inventory. Things had been going along smoothly until recently. Molly leaving the saloon to live on the Five Bar Ranch was wonderful for the girl and her baby, but with Cocheta up at Lyle Confort's home most Saturday nights, and Peg retired from prostitution and managing the saloon instead, any profits were dwindling.

Then there was the issue of Lyle Confort himself. The man kept raising her rent. He wanted her out of the building so he could control the space. He did this all over town. First, he would offer the owner of the building a good price for the property, and many folks in Breyer folded like cards when he waved cash in front of their faces. Once he owned the property, he concentrated on running all the businesses out of town so he could replace them with his own, holding them hostage so he could squeeze every last penny out of them first. He desperately wanted to break the women at The Crow Fly so he could take over, and sadly, he might get his way. Business was dismal, and with Molly gone and Cocheta unavailable most of the time, it was sad indeed.

Emily looked up from the counter and groaned as she saw Confort weaving his way across the street toward the shop.

She nudged Kate with her elbow. "Here comes trouble," she said under her breath.

Kate gazed out the window and shuddered. "I can't stand that man," she replied.

The little bell above the shop door tinkled as Confort shoved his way over the threshold. He stopped and tossed an oily smile at the women and tapped his walking stick on the floor, as if to announce his arrival.

"Afternoon… ladies," he said, emphasizing the word as he stared at Kate.

Kate frowned and turned away, fingering the spools of thread behind the counter.

"Is there something I can do for you, Mister Confort?" Emily stared at him the way she would at a rattlesnake, never taking her eyes off him.

Again, the oily smile. "Well, Emily, I was thinking of purchasing a surprise for Cocheta. She's been a very good girl." He smirked, rubbing his abundant stomach with his hand, as though the very thought of the Apache woman whetted his appetite.

Emily bristled at the remark. "What did you have in mind?"

"Oh, maybe a pretty frock. Something elegant. A dress she can wear for me when we dine. Something special."

Emily led him over to a rack of dresses, and he pawed through them with his meaty fingers.

"These dresses are for schoolmarms! Isn't there something more, well, shall we say, enticing?"

"Kate and I were just looking at this design of a beautiful dress." She pushed the drawing and pattern across the counter. "I have some burgundy velvet in back that might be perfect on Cocheta."

She excused herself and walked behind the curtained doorway, leaving Kate with Confort. He looked at her with narrowed eyes.

"So, how are things at The Crow Fly?"

"You know how they are, Lyle. But we have ideas on how to improve business."

"Oh yes, I saw your attempt to bring entertainment to the town. A lovely idea. I may have to build a playhouse myself here. Call it Confort Theater. Has a nice ring to it, doesn't it?"

Kate's fists clenched in her pockets. She wanted to throw the spools of thread at him and watch his face turn red with anger. She wanted to yank his walking stick out from under him and see him fall like a walrus onto the floor. How dare he steal their ideas!

Emily reappeared, carrying a bolt of burgundy that shimmered in the late afternoon light pouring through the window.

"This will be lovely against Cocheta's skin," she said. "All it would need is a pearl choker and she would look like sunset and dawn, all at the same time."

Confort smiled. Between sunset and dawn was the best time he spent with the Apache woman. To see her in this color certainly would make his blood rise. It was perfect.

He twisted his waxed mustache. "I like it. How soon can you make it?"

"Well, bear in mind that the fabric is expensive, imported from France. And to sew it as a rush job, I fear it might be costly."

"Name your price."

Emily did. Kate hid her smile behind her hand. Emily charged Confort three times what she normally would.

His eyes widened in surprise, but then he set his stubborn chin. "Fine. I'll take it. But make sure you get this dress finished within the next couple of days."

Reaching into his gray waistcoat, he pulled out a roll of dollars. He peeled the amount off and tossed it on the counter.

"Paid in full, Miss Augusta. Now, get to work. I hope you understand I want it right away."

"Of course. I will put my other jobs aside and start on this immediately."

Confort tipped his hat and walked to the door, then stopped and wheeled around.

"By the way, Emily, I'm afraid I need to raise your rent again. Another ten percent." He shrugged his shoulders. "You know how things are. It's so expensive to maintain these properties. I'm sure you understand."

"I've understood from the beginning, Lyle," Emily replied. "Good day."

Confort snorted and stepped back, flourishing his walking stick. "Have a lovely afternoon, Emily. Kate."

Emily walked over to the door and locked it behind him. "The nerve of that man! I'm closing down early today. I'll get started on his bloody dress. But I am doing it only for Cocheta, as I cannot imagine what she's going through with that awful person."

She placed her hand on Kate's arm. "Do you mind if we use your lovely new design for Cocheta?"

Kate fingered the velvet cloth. "No, it's fine. But only because of Cocheta, as you said. Besides, I would like to see the finished product."

"If you help me sew the dress, Kate, I will split the profit with you. And as you might imagine, the profit is generous."

The women laughed. Then Emily rolled the fabric out on the cutting table, and they went to work.

DAYS IN THE SUN

BREYER, TEXAS, LOOKED THE SAME as always, Lyle Confort thought. It drooped in the sun like an old union suit on a clothesline and smelled almost as bad. The lack of wind the past few weeks left a stench of surrender, as the residents wandered through Main Street past several closed businesses. Confort had driven out several shops and now had his eyes on The Crow Fly, where he hoped to impart the killing blow soon and get those pesky women out of the saloon so he could run it himself.

He'd keep whores in it, naturally, but the ones who were there needed to leave. Old Peg managed the saloon, and it was a good thing, he thought, because nobody would want her. And Kate? Well, Kate was like the luncheon special down at the hotel. The same thing every day, until you wanted to smother it with gravy. It was so boring.

Then there was Cocheta. The prize. He now kept her five days a week at his house, paying handsomely for the honor, but it didn't matter worth a hill of beans as far as The Crow Fly gaining any profit. They were losing ground, and fast.

He peered over the rim of the book he was reading in the parlor. Cocheta sat on the sofa in the burgundy dress from

Buttons and Bows. It fit her perfectly. Around her neck was a silver heart necklace that glimmered in the firelight as though it were alive. The Apache woman wore it day and night. Confort frowned. Maybe he'd get her a pearl choker, like Emily Augusta suggested. Then she truly would outshine the moon.

As if she read his mind, Cocheta gazed across the room at him and fingered the silver heart around her neck. She didn't mind the early evenings. Confort joined her in the parlor from time to time, although he usually left her to her own interests until nightfall. Tonight was an exception. He spilled over the sides of the chair like melted butter, his scalp shiny and damp, as he held a book in his hands and pretended to read. Cocheta knew he just wanted to be near her. It curdled her stomach. She touched the burgundy dress and shuddered. The gown was beautiful. A loving gift from the talents of Emily and Kate. Paid for by her captor, Lyle.

That's what Cocheta felt like. A captive. Lyle took over most of her life now. During the day, she wandered through his big house or sat on the swing in the yard. At night, he had his way with her. Sometimes he was cruel in bed. Pinching her or pulling on her silky hair. Other times, he held her as though he were a sinking ship, and she was the only life raft.

Suddenly, Confort sprang to his feet and reached out a meaty hand, grasping her around a slender wrist.

"I want you right now. Let's go," he said, pulling her from the sofa.

She rose like the weary moon and followed him up the stairs.

THE NEXT MORNING STARTED FRESH enough. A light breeze made its way past the bedroom window, bringing with it the smell of another perfect day. But here in Lyle Confort's bed, life remained as stale as ever.

Cocheta wanted to cry, something she seldom allowed herself to do. She learned long ago that if you weren't strong, the wolves of opportunity would devour a person and leave nothing but the bones. If Cocheta had learned anything at all, it was that she would never allow herself to lose her soul and turn into bones.

Lyle Confort was a puzzle. Staying with the man in his fine home most of the week was better than entertaining the strangers who shadowed her bed—men she could not, would not trust. Not that she trusted Confort, but he was reasonably predictable. He was always surly, always selfish, and seldom had a good word to say about anyone. Besides the few times he physically abused her, he was content to let her wander his property at will. Christiana, the long-suffering cook and maid, prepared the finest food available and kept the house immaculate. Christiana confided once in Cocheta that she would have left his employment months ago. But the money was better than anything she could earn elsewhere, she said, so she'd put up with his nasty temperament. However, the cook confessed, she did not like the man. She wiped her fingers on a crisp apron. Then turned back into the immaculate kitchen and lined up a handful of carrots to slice.

"I just don't like him," Christiana said, her knife chopping into the carrots with violent strokes, sinking the blade well into the wooden board, leaving marks in the oak like cat scratches. She clucked her tongue and tossed the carrots into a pan. "I don't like him at all."

Cocheta despised him. She hated how he looked, how he smelled, how he touched her in bed. Hated his grunts and groans and selfish needs. Yet, where would she go? She suspected when the time came, and The Crow Fly went under, Confort would take over and expect her to work for him in his new brothel. She would not do it. She would leave.

So, why not leave now? Why not wander off in the dead of night with one of his horses and disappear? Cocheta still knew the Indian ways. The silent ways. Perhaps she could find her village. She looked down at her ample bust pushing up through a low-cut bodice and knew it would be hard for her to go back to her family, now that she appeared to be half white. They might find her too different now. Perhaps not welcome her at all. The thought made her sad.

Then, there was always the fear that her parents and brother were killed by the roving bandits. If Cocheta went near their territory and they caught her again, she would be lost forever. No matter what Lyle Confort did, it was nothing compared to what happened in Mexico.

She walked outside to the little swing and sat down, spinning in slow circles while she dragged one toe in the dirt. That was the reason, of course. One toe in the dirt. No matter what might happen in life, Cocheta was no longer a whole person. Not a full Apache. Not a full woman in the white man's world either. She had one foot in each life. Because she wrestled with the shadows of her past, and danced with the memories of things she could not change, she was half a spirit.

Her fingers rested on the silver locket around her neck. The metal warmed between her fingers. She missed Joe every day. Missed him terribly, even though she meant so little to him. Even though he went away and left her with nothing but the silver necklace. He still lived between her heartbeats and always would.

Confort's hunting dog, Zeus, approached Cocheta on the swing. He pushed his warm nuzzle into her lap and wagged his tail. She reached out and patted him on the head, then threw her arms around his neck and buried her face in his soft fur.

"Oh, sweet Zeus, you understand, don't you?" she said. The dog stood quietly as she hugged him, as though he knew she was broken in some way. The warmth of his body comforted the young woman. For a moment, she didn't feel so alone.

"Zeus," she said in a whisper in Apache, "one day I will leave this terrible place and this terrible man. Someday I will leave

Breyer. I don't know where I'm going, but I'll find a way. You wait and see."

She stroked the dog's silky ears and left the swing, her hand trailing along Zeus's neck as he walked beside her. The sun was warm on her face, and she shielded her eyes as she stood on Confort's front step and gazed down at Main Street. She loved to watch the children as they rushed to the little white schoolhouse when Lara Thornton rang the bell. Sighing, she remembered what it was like to be so young, so innocent.

Lyle Confort opened the front door, breaking into her reverie. He lumbered up to her and gazed out across the town.

"There you are. It's Monday morning. I have business to do. I think I want you to go back to The Crow Fly this afternoon for a day or two. In the meantime, come back into the house. I have need of you."

He stroked his ample belly and sneered. "Wear that red dress I gave you."

Cocheta nodded, and followed Confort up the winding stairs, his shadow blocking any light on the wooden treads.

THE RETURN OF BREAKER JOE

BREAKER JOE STOOD ON WILLIAM Snow's front porch and shook hands.

"Joe, I can't tell you how glad I am to see you! That stallion you picked out for the ranch is a clear winner! Why, ranchers as far away as Dallas are bringing their mares here. He's been standing at stud ever since you left." William smiled as he swung the door wider for Joe to enter. Inside the cool entryway, the delicious aroma of stew simmering in the kitchen stirred his stomach until he thought it might leap out of him and dance in the waning light.

Joe grinned. "Yes, he's a fine piece of horseflesh. If you hadn't taken him, I'd have bought him myself."

Snow threw his arm around Joe's shoulder and pointed toward the barn. "Come on, let's go down and take a look at him."

Joe gazed around at Five Bar Ranch. It was as beautiful as he remembered, a jewel in the middle of a Texas crown, surrounded by sweet grass and cattle, the lazy buzz of bees, and the fresh promise of a good year.

In the distance, a girl with russet hair caught his attention. She sat on a blanket along the side of the house with a baby. The crook of her smile was instantly recognizable. He stopped in surprise.

William followed his gaze. "That's Molly and her baby, Willie. She was supposed to marry our son, but he died, if you recall. She and little Willie live with us now."

Joe nodded, hoping to hide his shock. He remembered seeing Molly at The Crow Fly. Although he never met her, he knew she worked at the saloon.

"How nice," he replied, then turned his attention to the horse trotting in proud circles in the corral. The stallion. Such a beauty. A great addition to Five Bar Ranch.

The men walked over to admire him. The horse blew through his nostrils and bolted to the other end of the corral, neck arched and tail set high.

"So, Joe, what brings you back to Texas? Have a job around here? Sure wish I had some work for you, but for now, things are goin' smoothly. If I ever need your services again, I'll contact you. You can count on it."

"Thank you. I'd like to work with you again." Hanson's steps slowed as he approached the corral and whistled softly for the stallion. The big horse shook his mane, then walked over and thrust his head over the fence. Joe stroked his velvety nose. "I have some unfinished business here and there, and since I just sewed up a job in New Mexico, I thought I'd take some time and head this way."

"Well, that's great. Say, would you like to stay for supper? Clarisse would love to see you again, and Molly has heard plenty of stories about you and what a great magician with horses you are."

Joe thought about Molly, and how awkward it might be.

"I'd love to stay, but I actually have an appointment in Breyer before the sun goes down, so I best be on my way. I won't be in town too long, just a couple of days. Maybe I'll stop in on my way back to Wyoming."

He clasped Snow on the shoulder and the two walked back to the house. Teton nickered as he approached. Saying goodbye, he swung into the saddle and pointed the horse down the path.

Molly waved at him and smiled. He waved back. He was pretty sure she recognized him.

"Good for that little gal," he said to Teton. "She deserved a better life for sure."

He thought about The Crow Fly and nudged Teton into a lope. The gelding covered the ground swiftly. Joe watched the Texas landscape unfurl as it drew him closer to town.

It was late afternoon before he trotted down Main Street. The town looked the same. Awkward and dusty, with several store-fronts boarded up, Main Street looked like a worn-out soldier with a few teeth missing. He laughed when he saw the same kids playing with the same half a hoop they dragged behind them, leaving tracks in the dirt that looked like crescent moons.

He walked into the hotel and got a room, then ordered something to eat. Joe was famished. And tired. And wondered for the hundredth time why the hell he was here. Settling in his chair with a cup of coffee, he waited until early evening, then paid the check and wandered across the street to The Crow Fly.

It was quieter than usual. Rick sat at the piano, playing a mournful tune. Bob, the bartender, hunched over the counter on a stool with a book and didn't bother to look up.

Kate Dawson had her back to him. She turned around at the sound of his footsteps. A flicker of recognition crossed her face. She patted her hair and straightened her bodice.

"Breaker Joe! Well, welcome back." She walked over and put a warm hand on his arm.

Joe smiled and studied Kate's face. It was a good face. An honest face. She was a decent woman, he thought. He flushed as he remembered taking her to bed one night. It was sweet. But not as sweet as the girl he left behind, the girl who cried to see him go and clasped the silver heart around her neck so tenderly.

"Hiya, Kate," he said. "Good to see you too. Say, where's Cocheta?" He was in no mood to mince words now that he was here. He wanted to find Cocheta before the sun ran out. Before he could get nervous. A shadow of doubt crossed his mind. "She's still working here, isn't she?"

Kate twisted a lock of hair around her finger and looked past the swinging doors. "Well, yes, in a way, she is."

"What do you mean?"

"Come sit over here in the corner with me and I'll tell you the whole story."

Afterward, Joe leaned back in the chair and rubbed his day-old beard. Lyle Confort. He remembered the name. Snow sold him a horse he'd trained. He vaguely remembered the man. The walking stick with the silver handle stood out in his mind. Confort was a virtual stranger. And yet he possessed the thing he wanted most in the world. Anger and jealousy nibbled at his soul. *So, he was keeping Cocheta to himself*, he thought. *But not for long.*

"Where does he live?" Hanson asked, his eyes narrowing as he gazed out the window.

Kate peered into her glass of whiskey and swirled it around. "Up on the hill in that big white house. But Joe, you wouldn't be welcome there. Nobody is."

"This is no social call, Kate. I came here to find Cocheta, and that's exactly what I'm going to do." He rose unsteadily from his chair. The long ride, the blistering heat, and the news about Cocheta made him weak in the knees.

"I'd wait until Lyle sends her back to The Crow Fly. Probably by tomorrow or the next day," Kate said. "It would be much easier to talk to her here in the saloon."

He tipped his hat goodbye. "Maybe you're right, but I ain't listening."

He strode through the doors and untied Teton. The horse groaned as he mounted, tired from the long day. Joe nudged him, and the gelding broke into a trot, heading straight up the hill to the house that crouched in the waning light.

BY THE LIGHT
OF COCHETA

JOE FOUND HER IN THE orchard behind the big house, spinning in lazy circles on an old wooden swing hanging from a weary tree. She wore a burgundy dress and no shoes. An Irish Setter sat in the meager grass nearby. The slant of the sun in the early evening made her look as though she were lit from within.

He pulled on the reins and gazed at her. She was even more beautiful than he remembered. His heart sped up as he nudged Teton closer. The horse snorted, and Cocheta looked up. Then stilled.

"Joe."

"Hello, Cocheta. I'm mighty pleased to see you again." He swung his leg over the saddle and jumped down, tying Teton to a tree branch in the shade.

Joe took a step closer, and Cocheta rose from the swing and scowled.

"You won't be welcome here," she said, glancing behind her at the back door of the imposing house.

"So I've heard. I just want to talk to you. Please."

"Why would you want to talk to me?" she asked, smoothing

the velvet dress along her slender body and fingering the silver locket around her neck.

He smiled. "I see you kept the locket."

She dropped her hand and turned to go. "You best go back where you came from before you're asked to leave," she said.

He took a step closer. "I need to talk to you."

"Seems you used up all the talk, and said all you wanted the day you left town."

"Cocheta, please don't make this hard on both of us. I'm sorry I left you behind. Sorry I rode away. I don't know for sure why I ended it the way I did, but I've had time and time again to think about us... think about everything, and I'm here now."

She cursed in Apache and turned toward the house. Joe reached out and grasped her elbow. She spun around, on guard, her face filled with a wild fear. He dropped his hand.

"I ain't gonna hurt you. You know that. Give me a chance to tell you how I feel, to explain to you what the time apart from you has been like, and to ask if we can somehow work on this?"

She hesitated. There was a silence in the orchard as though the trees were listening to them. Tension was thick as fog.

Joe saw her shoulders relax. Just like the countless horses he'd trained, she took a tiny step toward him. Then another. He let out a breath of relief, then picked up her hand and brought it to his lips.

"Just give me a chance, please. Let me speak from the heart."

"Do I know you?" Lyle Confort's voice cut through the air like a whip. "Cocheta, is this man bothering you?"

She shook her head. Joe stepped back and faced Confort.

"You don't know me. I'm Joe Hanson, a horse trainer that comes around these parts from time to time. I worked for William Snow at the Five Bar."

Confort frowned. "You're on my property, Hanson. Cocheta's busy right now. She was about to join me for the evening. You have no business up here. It's best you leave."

Joe's hand rested loosely on his holster. Confort stood calmly appraising him, the way he might look at a building for sale.

Joe heard a metallic click and turned. Another man brandished a rifle aimed straight at his heart.

"Stand down, Carlos. Mister Hanson here was just leaving. You were, weren't you? He won't cause any trouble." Confort stepped forward and grasped Cocheta's wrist. He pulled her toward him. She hesitated and wobbled, almost falling. Joe reached out for her arm, but Confort pushed his hand away, as though he were swatting at a pesky fly.

"Come along now, my dear. Dinner is almost ready. You don't want your food to get cold."

Confort nudged her toward the house. Cocheta looked back at Joe. Her ebony hair gleamed in the coming sunset, as she walked through the door with Lyle.

Joe mounted and turned Teton toward town. He'd figured Cocheta might still be upset with him, but he hadn't expected that he couldn't even talk with her. If he could sit down and tell her how he felt, she might understand. But Confort's man had pulled a rifle on him, and it was clear he wasn't safe up there on the hill. Anger flashed through him in waves. How dare Confort threaten him! But he knew from long experience that you didn't argue with the wrong end of a bullet. You save your anger for another day. Besides, Cocheta didn't seem to want him anyway, so why risk a hardscrabble moment with Lyle Confort? Dejected, he turned back toward The Crow Fly.

Hanson tended to Teton, then wandered back to the saloon. Rick was playing the piano, a jaunty tune that drifted out into the street and drew him inside. Peg walked over and patted his arm in greeting.

"Breaker Joe! Welcome back! Kate told me you were here. I hope you got to see Cocheta and talk with her."

Joe gave her a hug, then walked over to a table in the corner, where he sat down with a thud and ran his hands through his hair. He looked up at Peg with bleak eyes.

"I saw her all right, but she wasn't interested in talking much. Then I ran into Lyle Confort. He was not happy to see me, and neither was the rifle pointed at my chest."

"I'm not surprised," Peg said. "That man is a nightmare. I'm sure Kate filled you in on his hopeful takeover of The Crow Fly and how he's mistreated half of this town. Part of his strategy is keeping poor Cocheta up there several days a week so that we lose business down here with the men."

Peg blushed. She knew Joe had tender feelings toward the Apache girl. It must bother him to hear that she was a private plaything for Lyle Confort. She put her hand on his shoulder.

"What are you having, Joe? The first drink is on the house."

He ordered a whiskey, then sat back and observed the patrons of The Crow Fly while Peg walked up to the bar.

Kate sauntered around the saloon, looking elegant in a powder blue dress that accentuated her bosom and slender waist. There was an almost glacial look about the woman that could tug at a man and make him want to keep her warm. But she was no comparison to Cocheta. While Kate was sophisticated-looking and cool, Cocheta looked wild and untamed. Dressed in that splendid velvet dress he saw her in today, her beauty was lit within like a firefly in a jar. And, just like that firefly, Confort held her captive.

Molly was living out at the Five Bar with her baby and would never come back. Chances were slender for the saloon. Confort was circling The Crow Fly like a vulture and would soon deliver the final blow. The women hung on by a thread, waiting for either an eviction or an insulting offer for their hard-earned business.

Joe clenched a fist. He'd had months to think about Cocheta, and he knew what he wanted. She haunted him while he broke horses, haunted him on his journeys from ranch to ranch. And, haunted him in the arms of other women. In his saddlebag were gifts he'd bought for her. An ivory comb to glide through her ebony hair, and a plaid woolen shawl to drape around her slender shoulders. And, a ring made of the finest silver, set with three round turquoise stones. He bought it at a trading post from an old Apache woman, who sat in the sun outside the store making jewelry and baskets.

The ring, Joe hoped, would serve as a wedding ring. He intended to marry her and be together forever. He brushed his drink aside, queasy at the thought of Confort and the bitter reaction from Cocheta. His eyes were grainy and his spirit low. It was time to wander over to the hotel and get a good night's sleep.

The day had not gone as planned. But one thing Joe knew for sure. He wasn't about to give up. Not tonight. Not tomorrow. Not ever.

JED THORNTON

JED THORNTON WATCHED AS BREAKER Joe rode up the hill to Confort's house, then ride back alone. He remembered Joe had a love affair with Cocheta a while ago. But he also remembered that Hanson rode out of town and left her behind.

"Good luck, Joe," Thornton said under his breath as he rolled down the office shade for the night. "Confort isn't about to let her go easily. Be careful. The man is a snake."

There were two bad actors in Breyer during Jed's time here as sheriff. The first one was dead. His replacement was a worse person, if ever there was one. Big Andy was a blowhard. A man who talked just to hear words flow from his mouth and who had few scruples. A thick-skulled jackass that people ignored for the most part, except those he swindled. Andy wasn't as dangerous as Lyle Confort, and yet somebody saw fit to murder him. He supposed it wouldn't be much of a shock to anybody if Confort met the same fate one day.

Of course, it was Jed's job to keep Lyle safe, just as he had to keep all the citizens of Breyer safe. He hoped Joe wasn't the sort of man to get aggressive and ride up there again to see Cocheta with a fire under his tail. Lyle, or one of his men, would kill him. Then

Jed would have to tease it all out, and God knows, Confort could probably plead self-defense.

Jed stood in the doorway as lights came on up and down Main Street. The Crow Fly was in full swing now, as were the other two saloons in town. This was the time of night Thornton dreaded. The time when Breyer lifted the coarse petticoats she wore during the daylight hours and revealed a darkness underneath. A darkness that occurred in most towns. But in Breyer, it was particularly noticeable because it was such a small town and held such big secrets.

This brought Big Andy back to mind, and the inevitable conclusion of his murder. Every day he didn't do something about the killer was a dereliction of duty. Jed Thornton was never one to back away from the confines of the law. It was what it was, and he needed to arrest the killer soon.

A loud noise from The Ruby Slipper jolted him out of his musings. It sounded like a gun went off, followed by shouting. Cursing, he slammed his hat on his head and strode out the door.

"Damn! I thought I'd be home for supper!" he said. "Now I have to break up some sort of disagreement in the saloon and deal with drunk, angry cowboys."

On his way down the street, he decided to visit a few people in the morning to talk about Big Andy again. "I'll catch 'em while they're fresh. Before they hide behind one lie or another."

SEWING IT UP

KATE DAWSON AND EMILY AUGUSTA were together at Buttons and Bows when Jed walked in. They were hemming a dress on a mannequin, a pretty frock as blue as Lara Thornton's eyes and boasting embroidered flowers all over the fabric.

"Morning, ladies," he said. "That's a mighty nice-looking dress you have there."

Emily smiled. "Good morning, Jed. I think this dress would look beautiful on your Lara." She rustled the skirt with her hands, and the flowers seemed to dance.

Jed pictured Lara in it, and on impulse, reached out and touched the sleeve.

"You read my mind. How much, Emily?"

She quoted him a price. "I know it's rather expensive, but it's custom designed and made of the finest cloth. I would charge more for somebody else, but I can picture Lara wearing it in church on Sunday morning. It's perfect."

Jed thought about it. It was a hefty price, but her birthday was coming up. Lara never complained about living in Breyer, even though the town was bereft of many joys. She raised their daughters with a loving hand and taught the children in town with a smile and a big heart.

"I'll take it, ladies. But I ain't sure what size she wears."

"Not a problem. Lara bought a dress here two years ago, and I keep all the information in my ledger. We can take it in or let it out. I'm happy it's finding a good home! It will be ready in a week, if that suits you."

He nodded. "That suits me just fine."

"Was there anything else, Jed?"

"Well, I'm glad to have the both of you here this morning. I'm still working on Andy's murder, and I was hoping to talk to both of you again."

The women looked at each other uneasily. Emily gestured across the room to an upholstered chair in the corner.

"Have a seat. We're happy to help in any way we can. Right, Kate?"

Kate picked at her fingernail with a pin. "Maybe I should wait outside for my turn?" she asked, not looking up at the sheriff.

"Nope. I can talk to both of you at once."

Jed settled into the chair and clasped his hands on each knee, leaning forward. His gaze settled on Kate.

"I know we've talked before, but I keep hoping you might remember something else the night Big Andy died. Somebody murdered him in cold blood, then left him to die behind the saloon like an animal."

Kate flinched at Thornton's harsh words. His eyes narrowed as he studied her face.

"Seems to me somebody's keeping secrets," he said. "If either of you ladies know something, now's the time to tell me, before things get more... shall we say... complicated?"

Emily walked behind the counter and fussed with a bolt of fabric. She turned it one way, then the other, finally set it down and met Jed's gaze.

"Well, I told you everything I know. I'd closed up the Buttons and Bows at five o'clock and went straight home. I made dinner, had some tea, then fell asleep quite early that night. The next morning while walking to church, I took the shortcut behind The Crow Fly and that's when I saw Big Andy." She shivered and her hands trembled. "It was awful. I'll carry that image with me for the rest of my life."

"I know it was terrible, Emily, and I'm sorry you went through it. But please try to remember if you saw anything out of order besides Big Andy's body."

She frowned in concentration, then brightened. "Old Gringo, the donkey, was there. He was standing under the cottonwood tree. I remember now!"

"I know. I saw him, too," Jed said. "Anything else you can remember?"

"No. Frankly, it's something I want to forget, not dredge up every day. I try to put it out of my mind."

Thornton nodded, then turned to Kate.

"Anything more you want to say?"

"No. I've thought about it and thought about it. The only thing I recall is after we were closed for the night, I went back downstairs. I'd lost a hair comb and thought I may have dropped it on the floor. The bartender and Shorty were there, but Rick wasn't. Usually, he's one of the last to leave. After the saloon shut down for the night, Andy paid him extra to clear up the floor and stack the chairs back around the tables. Things like that. But he was gone and hadn't straightened up the saloon."

Jed leaned forward twisting his mustache. "Is that something out of the ordinary for Rick? To leave The Crow Fly and go home without doing his job?"

"Come to think of it, Rick was always the last to leave. I'm pretty sure." Kate chewed on her lip. "I... I hope I didn't get Rick into trouble for saying that."

Emily patted her arm. "Of course not. Jed understands that

sometimes people leave early. Maybe Rick had a headache or other business to tend. Right, Jed? It's nothing. Truly."

Jed sat back in the chair. *Oh, but it is something, ladies,* he thought. Maybe something important. More important to him than what the women said, was how they reacted to the questioning. Yep, it was a morning that bore fruit, and Jed was one step closer to solving the case. He was sure of it.

When he left Buttons and Bows, Thornton felt a twinge of uneasiness. In a strange way, he felt a little like God. He held somebody's future in his hands. He could make their life miserable or set them free from worry.

Jed doggedly traced his steps over to The Crow Fly. He didn't like this power he had. He didn't like the knowledge he possessed.

For the first time, Thornton questioned if being a sheriff was the right job for him. Life in Breyer was becoming complicated.

A few clouds scudded closer to town. Rain clouds. He wondered if they would make it to Breyer or just rain out where they were.

"We could use a good cleansing," he said to himself, then hollered over the swinging doors of the saloon in the midmorning heat. "Anybody in there? It's Sheriff Thornton."

THE PIANO MAN

RICK JAMES LOOKED UP FROM the piano as someone called outside the door. Normally he didn't arrive at The Crow Fly until late afternoon, but new music had arrived all the way from New York, and he was giddy with excitement to play the songs. A bit of practice, and he'd be able to introduce some of them tonight.

Rick was a quiet man, not one to loosen his tongue, but when he talked, he was always respectful and kind. He wore his dark brown hair slicked back with oil and waxed a graying mustache until it curled up at the ends with a flourish. Bright blue eyes, the color of a Breyer sky, peered out behind black eyebrows, giving him a romantically dangerous look. Folks might say he was a dandy, and he certainly looked the part. After all, he was a performer, and he wanted to impress the customers.

He pushed back from the piano bench, walked over and loosened the latch on the swinging doors, then stepped back as Thornton walked through.

"Hey, Sheriff," he said with a smile. "If you're looking for Kate or Peg, I don't know where they are."

"Aw, Kate's over with Emily," Jed said, "and I don't need Peg.

Actually, I was hoping you were here this morning, Rick, because I'd like to talk with you for a spell."

James gestured toward a table in the corner. "Have a seat. Let me just straighten the papers on the piano and I'll be right with you."

He turned and grinned at Thornton. "New music! Makes my heart sing."

"I suspect it would. You play a good piano, Rick. The best in town. I'll have to wander over some night to hear the new pieces."

Rick sat across from Jed, his long legs sprawled around the table legs. He tilted the chair back in a practiced way and tapped the tabletop lightly with his fingers in a steady rhythm.

"So, what do you need to talk to me about?"

"Aw, it's the same old tired stuff about Big Andy. I was hopin' you might shed a bit more light on the night he died."

"I told you everything I know."

"Well, I am always looking for more clues. I was wondering if you could remember what you did after the saloon closed that night."

Rick looked away, then back at Thornton. He cleared his throat and tipped the chair forward, grounding himself. The silence was so thick, Jed could hear a dog bark clear over at Marian Humphrey's house.

"I already told you. I did the usual things that night. We closed up the saloon, and I stacked the chairs and swept the floor before I went home to bed."

"What time was that, do you think?"

"Oh, it must have been three o'clock in the morning before I left."

"Did you go straight home?"

"Yup. I'm usually pretty tired and it's a bit of a walk down to my room at the boardinghouse."

"And you didn't see or hear anything unusual that night?"

"To be honest, Sheriff, I hardly remember what I did that

night. It only became memorable when they found Andy's body. Then all hell broke loose. But before that, it was the usual Saturday night at The Crow Fly."

Thornton nodded, then rose from the table. Rick stood with him, and the two men walked to the door.

"Well, if you think of anything, let me know. Sometimes people remember little things that they don't think matter, but they do."

Jed tipped his hat and walked outside into the blazing morning sun. He tingled inside, senses alert as a raptor. Either Rick or Kate was lying. Interesting. Which one could he break first?

SWEAT TRICKLED DOWN RICK'S NECK. The saloon was already warm, but warmer still was his encounter with Jed Thornton. His happy morning with the new music was shattered by the sheriff's appearance. Damn him. It was just like Thornton to keep chewing on this murder, the way a dog does with a bone. He eased himself back in the chair and took a deep breath.

When the doors swung open again, he spun around, thinking it was Thornton again. It was Kate, wandering in with a sweet smile on her face. In her arms was a bolt of deep purple fabric.

She saw James and stopped. "Why, Rick, you're here awfully early."

"I got some new music from New York and wanted to practice a bit."

"Oh, great! Would you play for me?" Kate asked.

"Already played several, and my fingers ache a little. Guess it's the rheumatism or something. I better save my hands for tonight."

Kate nodded. "Sure, I'll wait until tonight to hear it then."

She started up the stairs, then turned around and came back. She put a hand on Rick's shoulder.

"It's probably nothing," she said. "But Jed Thornton was just over at the Buttons and Bows and asking us more questions about the night Big Andy died. I hope I didn't get you into any trouble, but I told him you weren't here after the saloon closed that night. I came downstairs later, and you had already left. No big deal, I'm sure, but wanted to let you know what I told Jed."

Rick nodded and shrugged. "I hardly remember that night. Funny that you do. Are you sure you didn't see me? Because I recollect I was here as usual and then I walked home."

Kate frowned. "Huh. I could have sworn you weren't here. I guess you should know. After all, it was a pretty frantic morning after Emily found Big Andy, and I think we all got shook up and forgot things." She patted his arm. "Don't worry. I'm sure you're right. I was wrong."

She walked up the stairs. Rick watched her go. His hands trembled as he reached for his cup of coffee. What she told Jed was not what he told the sheriff, and yet Thornton didn't let on. The sheriff had kept a straight face.

Rick walked over to the piano and picked up the music sheets, shoving them into a small valise. He strolled out the back door of the saloon and over to the boardinghouse.

THAT NIGHT, JED FELT LIKE something was amiss. It was a Saturday night, and everything was in full swing. Horses were lined up at the hitching posts, the saloons filled to the rafters with revelers, their boisterous voices sailing out from the swinging doors and echoing into the street.

Jed hummed a tune as he locked up his office and prepared for a final walk through town before going home for supper.

That's when it hit him. No music was playing over at The Crow Fly. He hurried down Main Street and pushed his way through the doors and peered around. Several men stopped what they were doing to stare as he walked over to the piano. The top was down, and the sheet music was missing.

"Evening, Jed. What can I do for you?" Peg said, pushing away from the bar.

"Where's Rick? Is he sick?"

"We don't know. Kate said he was here earlier today, rehearsing new songs. But he hasn't shown up tonight. I was thinking of sending Shorty over to the boardinghouse to check on him."

"Don't bother. I'm heading that way. I'll just stop in."

Thornton strode out the doors and trotted to the end of Main Street to the boardinghouse. He had a knot in his stomach. He already knew what he'd find.

He burst through the door, startling Sarah Goodman, the owner. She set down the teapot she had in her hand and walked over.

"Evening, Sheriff. Is everything all right?"

"I ain't sure. Have you seen Rick today? He didn't show up for work tonight at The Crow Fly. Thought I'd check on him."

Sarah frowned. "He left town today. Said he had another job lined up in New Mexico that sounded mighty good to him. He paid me in full and took his leave."

"New Mexico. Huh." Jed's heart raced. "Do you know how long ago he left?"

"He didn't show up for dinner, so it was before then. Why do you ask?"

"No reason. Just checking. I'm sure he told somebody at The Crow Fly he was leaving. Have a good night."

Jed walked home, fists clenched. Damn that Rick! The piano player had at least a seven-hour head start, and Jed didn't know which way he'd ride once he left town. There was no way to track him, either, with all the hoofprints throughout the town.

"Like hell you went to New Mexico, you bastard! I can't even begin to think where you ran off to, but one thing's for sure. When things settle down around here, I might just come after you, even if I have to go to every saloon between here and the sea."

As if in answer, a coyote called out from a small knoll on the outskirts of town. It sent a shiver down Jed's spine. The predators of truth were closing in. And Rick James was far from innocent.

COCHETA AND BREAKER JOE

LYLE CONFORT SCOWLED WHEN HE opened his front door and saw Kate Dawson standing there.

"What is it, Kate?" he asked, one hand on the knob and his foot wedged between the door and the jamb.

"Good morning, Lyle," Kate said. "I would like to talk with Cocheta, if I may."

"This can't wait until I send her back down to The Crow Fly?"

"No," Kate replied. "This won't take long."

"What's your order of business?"

Kate stiffened. "Well, I don't think it's any of your business, but it's about female health problems, if you must know."

Confort flushed. He swung the door wide and stepped back.

"Come in then and sit in the parlor over there. I'll tell Cocheta she has company."

Kate walked in and turned into the parlor. She settled herself on the edge of a wingback chair by the fire and looked around. It was lovely. Deep-colored walls and rich fabrics adorned the room. The elegance and good taste were not at all what one might expect from Confort. He seemed the type to like black drapes and candelabras with dripping tallow, not the warmth and beauty displayed in the room. It was midmorning, and light splayed across the parlor as though painted with honey.

Confort and Cocheta entered the parlor. Kate stood and smoothed her skirt.

"You wanted to see me?" the Apache asked in her lilting voice. She stood quietly next to Confort, much like a fawn in the woods, not daring to move in any direction.

"Yes, there's a problem I need to discuss with you." Kate looked pointedly at Lyle. "Please, this won't take long, and I would appreciate some privacy."

He nodded and turned toward the stairs. She heard him walk about halfway up, then hesitate.

"Cocheta, it's good to see you," she said, while jutting her chin up toward the stairs and shaking her head.

Cocheta nodded in response. "It's nice to see you too. Is there a problem down at The Crow Fly?"

"Well, yes, somewhat. I needed to talk to you about Peg. You know, she's been having deep pain in her lower belly, and I'm worried about her."

Kate continued to shake her head and pointed toward the stairs. She went on. "We're worried it might be her womb."

"Is that so? That's not good," Cocheta replied.

Kate took a step closer. She reached for Cocheta's hand and pressed a note inside her palm, again pointing to the stairs. Cocheta put it in her pocket and nodded.

"So, we were wondering if you knew of any Apache remedies that might ease her pain?"

"No, I don't think I do. Maybe a tea or poultice made of birch bark? Has she gone to the doctor?"

"No," Kate said, then took a step back as she heard Confort lumbering down the stairs. He appeared at the door and scowled.

"Are you ladies about through?" he asked through gritted teeth. "I have work to do."

"I'll let myself out, Lyle. Thank you." Kate walked gracefully toward the door. She turned and nodded to them both. "Good day, Cocheta. I'm glad I had the chance to talk to you. I'll check into the tea you mentioned."

Confort watched as she walked down the hill and back along Main Street. He snorted. "That woman puts on airs, just like Emily. You would think they were high born or something." He turned toward Cocheta and put his hand on her hip, perilously close to her pocket. "They're not like you. You at least accept that you're a whore and will be nothing more than that."

He pinched her tender buttock through her skirt, then turned away. "If you need me, I'll be in my study."

Cocheta stood near the fire until she heard him settle ponderously in his leather chair across the hall. She picked out a book and perched on the edge of the sofa, then reached into her pocket and smoothed out the note and tucked it on the page, posed with the book in her hands, and read.

Meet me tonight in the orchard after everyone's asleep. I will be waiting. Love, Joe

Cocheta's heart thudded. This was dangerous. Should Confort catch wind of Joe, he would undoubtedly kill him. And maybe her as well. What could Joe possibly have to say to her? He left her once. How could she trust him now? Was it even worth the risk of meeting with him? She wadded the note into a ball, tossed it into the fire and watched it burn to ash.

That night, Lyle told Cocheta to wear the burgundy dress again. He seated her at the dining room table, poured a glass of wine and offered it to her. She tilted her head and declined.

"You don't know what's good for you, Cocheta. A little wine will loosen you a bit, so you're not as stiff and strong-willed."

He lifted the glass to his nose and sniffed. "A fine wine, my dear, and here's to an equally fine evening with you as my consort."

Lyle drank several more glasses of wine before he pulled Cocheta up the stairs. He was eager to bed her, but as she stepped out of her dress and unlaced her corset, he fell into a deep sleep, his rotund belly rising and falling in a rhythmic pattern. Cocheta sat by the window and stared out at the orchard for a long time. It was dark as pitch, etched with foreboding. She wondered if Joe was waiting out there. Turning toward Confort, she shuddered. He would never let her go. She knew that. She stayed at his house more than at The Crow Fly these days. It brought her no happiness—only repugnance—and the knowledge that one day he would tire of her and then dispose of her like the empty wine bottle on his dining room table.

On impulse, she grabbed the velvet gown, then pulled on an old gingham dress and glided out of the room, moccasins in her hand.

THERE WAS JUST A SLIVER of a moon that night, not even enough to hold a cup of water. The orchard was bathed in darkness. A strong wind blew through the grass, enough to hide the sound of footsteps. The leaves twirled and twisted on the branches, as though wanting to escape.

Joe stood behind a gnarled tree. He'd tied two horses far below the orchard to an old fence post. Joe had been there since the sun set, watching the stars appear, hoping she'd come. He couldn't blame her if she didn't. After all, he left her at The Crow Fly and rode off months ago. The man shook his head at his own stupidity. Reaching into his pocket, he felt for the box with the silver and turquoise ring in it. Joe carried it with him day and night, as though somehow a part of Cocheta was always there.

Joe thought he could never love a woman long enough to stay. And that had been true for years. But Cocheta twisted his heart around until it was open and exposed, raw to a feeling that he'd never experienced before. Why it took him so long to figure it out, he didn't know. Cantankerous, maybe. Selfish even. But now that he'd made up his mind, he didn't plan to leave Breyer without her. No matter what it took, he was taking Cocheta home with him to Wyoming. He loved her. It was as simple as that. He could only hope she felt the same.

A slight whisper through the waving grass, and a dark silhouette appeared against the backdrop of a starlit night. Joe's heart raced. It was Cocheta. He could tell by the way she swayed to the rhythm of the wind. He stepped from behind the tree and approached her.

"Cocheta," he said quietly.

The figure stopped short, then walked slowly toward him. He waited, holding his hand out for her. She did not take it, but approached him warily, the way a wounded animal might. He knew she carried a knife, and he prayed he'd never feel the cut of her disdain. He'd rather she twist her blade into him than not to love him in return.

She stood silently before him, the scent of her encircling him until he thought he might swoon with emotion. This time, when he reached for her hand, she let him take it.

Exhaling in relief, he stepped even closer and whispered into her ebony hair.

"Cocheta, I have so much to say, but I fear we'll be caught out here. I've been a complete fool. I should have never left Breyer without you. Every single day since then I've thought of you and can't get you out of my mind."

She remained silent. He squeezed her hand.

"I love you and want to marry you. I swear to God above that I will never leave you again."

Now he swallowed hard, knowing what he would say next was the most important thing. He prayed she might understand.

"I know it ain't easy for you to trust anybody, particularly a man. But I am asking you... no, I am begging you to trust me, to hold tight to my hand here, and leave Breyer right now tonight with me. I know it's asking a lot, but we can't stand here in the darkness for hours and talk about it. It's too risky. Leave The

Crow Fly. Leave Confort. Come with me and make a new life. Marry me. Please." He glanced around nervously. "I wish I could give you more time, but you need to decide now."

Up near the house, Cocheta heard a noise. A rustling sound. Maybe the dog. Maybe Confort. Or just the sound an old house makes when the wind rubs against it. She shivered.

She peered up at Joe. His face was barely visible in the meager light from the slice of moon. His eyes glinted in the darkness. His voice rumbled in his chest, and she longed to put her head on it and hear more.

Another noise, this time a shutter knocked on the siding of the house as though asking to come in. The sound rang out like a shot, and they both jumped.

"Please," he said, grasping her wrist, pulling her toward him. "Please."

The wind stopped. Suddenly every noise, every breath, was noticeable. It was as though Breyer was listening to their beating hearts and heard the sound of her indecision.

As she stood in the orchard, Cocheta remembered her pony, Twig, and how they raced through the desert together when she was young and carefree. She remembered jumping over a small arroyo, the horse beneath her legs and the sensation of flying, if only for a moment, until they touched down to earth again. She recalled how she trusted they would land on the other side safely, and the joy she felt when the pony regained her footing and together, they thundered across the valley floor. It was a bright moment from long ago, and a reminder of the faith she once had that day.

Faith. How do you find faith when it had been taken from me again and again? she thought.

Then she realized this question framed the true meaning of faith. To trust when there is no answer. To hope when there is no reason to hope. And to believe that when you jumped over an arroyo, you would land safely on the other side.

"Yes," she said. The word was simply said but drawn from a lifetime of pain and wariness. She clasped Joe's hand. He drew her close to him and touched her cheek with a trembling finger. Then he put his arm around her waist and guided her through the darkness and on to a lifetime together.

SCORCH THE EARTH

THE FIRST THING LYLE CONFORT was aware of was the sun pouring through the windows. He'd shut them last night against the whistling wind, but now it was stifling in the bedroom. A bee batted at the glass, trying to get in, then flew away. Confort threw back the covers and stretched.

The next thing he noticed was Cocheta wasn't lying by his side. He had slept overlong. Perhaps she tired of the bed and wanted to wander through the orchard or sit on the swing with Zeus.

He yanked up the window and stuck his head out, aiming his voice toward the trees.

"Cocheta!"

There was no answer. He hollered a couple more times. A door swung open below, and Christiana stuck her head through and peered up.

"What do you need, boss?"

"Cocheta. Is she down there with you?"

"No, sir."

"Have you seen her?"

"No. I just arrived. Had to stop and pick up fresh eggs for breakfast."

Confort cursed in frustration and pulled on the clothes he wore last night. They were tired and wrinkled. He frowned. They needed a good pressing was all, and maybe a stain or two removed. Lyle looked crumpled wearing them. He remembered last night's overindulgence with the wine. There was no time to waste. It would have to do for now. He wanted to find Cocheta.

He stepped into the upstairs hall and called her name again. Nothing. Was she in the other room, taking a bath in the copper tub? His loins tightened at the thought. He wasn't able to have sex with her last night because he fell asleep, but now his desire was full-blown. He eagerly walked down the hall, only to find an empty tub.

"Damn it!" He knew she was around here somewhere. He would not let her go back to The Crow Fly for a few more days.

Walking down the stairs, he noted that Main Street was particularly busy for a Wednesday morning. The sun was already high. He'd slept longer than he thought he had. It must be close to noon.

Confort opened the back door and shouted. "Cocheta, where are you?"

Still no answer.

He lumbered into the parlor and stopped short. "What the hell?"

There, on the wingback chair, was the beautiful burgundy velvet dress, splayed out just so, as though Cocheta had been wearing it, and then evaporated, leaving only a husk behind. On the floor were matching velvet shoes, and next to it a lovely bracelet Lyle had given her.

Grabbing his hat and walking stick, he stalked toward the door and yanked it open.

"That whore went back to The Crow Fly without my permission," he said, stepping into the heat of the day.

But maybe not. Maybe she went somewhere else. Maybe she was gone. His fists clenched in fury and sweat dampened his already rumpled collar. Slamming the front door, he hastened to town, and The Crow Fly.

It startled Peg when Confort burst through the swinging doors, knocking the chain right off its hinges. It clattered on the floor like a string of bells, ringing in the empty saloon.

"Where is she?" Confort asked, gasping for breath.

"Where's who?"

"Don't give me that, you sorry whore! You know perfectly well who. Where's Cocheta?"

"I haven't seen her. I thought she was up at the house with you."

Beet red, Confort swung around, using his walking stick like a compass, searching each corner of the saloon with bulging eyes.

"Cocheta!"

Kate Dawson came out from the office, a worried look on her face.

"What's wrong, Lyle?"

"Cocheta's gone. What did you do with her?"

"Me?"

"Yes, you! You were the last person she saw. I demand an answer, and I want it now!"

Peg stepped forward. "Now, Lyle, calm down. You'll give yourself a heart attack. We don't know where Cocheta is. Why don't you go home and wait for her? Maybe she's over at Buttons and Bows, or just took a walk."

"You're joking, right? The bitch took off and I'm going to find her if it's the last thing I do!"

He lumbered toward the stairs. "Are you hiding her up there? Huh?"

Peg touched his shoulder. "You can't just go up there. It's private."

Furious, he turned and swung his stick. Peg's arm cracked from the blow. She doubled over in pain.

Confort took the stairs two at a time, his cheeks billowing

like bellows. Flecks of saliva flew from his mouth. At the top of the stairs, he whirled and opened one door, then another. They were vacant. He stood in the hallway and glared down at the two women over the railing.

"Tell me where she is now, or I will destroy you!"

Kate hissed, "We don't know!"

The enraged man howled like a wolf, then screamed and swung his stick upward and knocked a kerosene sconce off the wall. It shattered. Hungry flames sprang up from the carpet and made their way swiftly up the wall. But Confort didn't seem to notice. He flailed and struck at another sconce, then another, oblivious to the smoke and fire.

Peg screamed. "The Crow Fly's on fire! Help!" She looked around frantically for Bob or Shorty but they were nowhere to be seen.

"Kate, we have to get out of here!" They burst through the swinging doors and out into the Texas heat.

"Fire! Fire!" Peg hollered for help, then grabbed a bucket, dipped it in the horse trough, and ran back inside. Kate followed her.

People heard the screams and raced toward The Crow Fly, including Jed Thornton.

"Get buckets! Fill them with water from the troughs! Now!" Thornton said, then ran toward the saloon.

It was astonishing how fast The Crow Fly became engulfed in flames. The fire raced down the carpeted stairway and ate into the wooden banister. One by one, the kerosene sconces crackled, then exploded, sending embers and sparks everywhere.

Kate and Peg staggered outside, coughing, their faces darkened with soot.

"Is anybody else in there?" Thornton yelled as he grabbed a pail of water.

"Lyle Confort!" Peg shouted back, rubbing her arm. "He's

upstairs. He started the whole thing!" Despite the heat, she shivered.

Jed lunged toward the swinging doors. Kate grabbed his sleeve.

"You can't go in there! You'll die! Maybe he made it out the back way!"

"I have to go in. Let go!"

Thornton shook her off and ran into the burning building. He looked around. The second floor was engulfed in flames, the stairs crumbling beneath the fire.

"Lyle! Lyle! Are you in here?" Jed spun in circles, the smoke searing his throat, cutting off his breath. He put one foot on the stairs but jumped back as sparks caught on his shirt. He frantically swiped at them, searing pain pouncing on his arms and back. The smoke was so thick he couldn't see the doorway. Jed couldn't breathe. Confused, he turned in circles, trying to get his bearings. Short of breath and lungs burning, he drifted toward the floor.

An arm encircled his shoulders and dragged him through the smoke and into daylight. Shorty pulled him to safety and tossed water onto his burning clothes. Then they both collapsed in the middle of Main Street and watched The Crow Fly explode into a fiery ball that shook the whole town.

ASHES TO ASHES

OC WINTERS KNEELED IN THE street and examined Jed.

"You're lucky, son. Your burns aren't too bad. You'll have scars on your arms and back, but not on your pretty face," he joked. Then he sobered. "But all that smoke you drank in is still rumbling in your chest and it ain't good for your lungs at all. Dangerous, Jed. You need to go straight home and into bed and let Lara take care of you for a few days."

"Doc, I can't," Jed said, then coughed so hard he had to lie down. He moaned and grimaced as the pain from the burns raced along his arms and shoulders. The smell of singed hair permeated his nostrils. Never had he felt so tired, struggling with every breath. *Is this how I'm gonna die?* he thought.

"Jed, there's no choice. I'm gonna have Shorty help you get home. Lara's right here. She'll help, too, won't you, dear?"

Lara nodded. She longed to reach out and hold her husband, but knew he was in pain. Her heart trembled as she thought of him in The Crow Fly and how he could have so easily been killed by the fire.

"Thank God you're alive. Thank God, Jed," was all she could

say, tears of gratitude on her cheeks. Their girls ran up and clung to Lara's skirt.

"Is Daddy okay?" they asked.

"He will be, sweethearts, if he goes home with you and your mother and spends a few days in bed. I'm sure of it." Doc patted the girls on the head and then turned somber eyes to Jed. "You go on now, Jed. There ain't nothing you can do here right now, anyway. Everybody's accounted for except Confort, and he likely died upstairs where he started the fire. When the ashes have cooled, we'll look around for his body and bury what's left of him properly up on the hill. There ain't no hurry now for anything. Go on home now."

Thornton nodded and staggered to his feet. He stumbled toward home with Shorty cradling him around his waist and Lara and the girls encircling him.

Peg and Kate sat in the dirt and clung to each other. Almost everything they owned was in The Crow Fly. Clothes, books, things that meant something to them. Not to mention The Crow Fly itself.

Kate brushed a strand of hair from Peg's face. "Now what?" she asked, her voice weary and thin.

Peg swiped at her grimy face with a sleeve. "I have no idea."

Emily approached them. "I know what to do right now. You two will stay with me until you figure something out. I have a spare bed, and you can stay as long as you need. I won't take no for an answer, so don't waste your breath."

Emily looked around at the townspeople who clustered in the street. Lifting her chin, she spoke.

"These two women just lost everything. They will stay with me. If you could spare some clothes or food, it would be greatly appreciated."

Several of the town ladies pursed their lips, but didn't dare say anything. A few folks nodded.

Marian Humphrey piped up. "We just slaughtered our pig.

There's plenty of bacon I can spare, and some eggs too. And vegetables from my garden. I'll bring them over this afternoon."

Another woman offered blankets, while yet another said she had some clothes to donate. One by one, the citizens of Breyer stepped forward to offer help.

"Much obliged," Emily said, then turned toward Peg and Kate. "Come on now, let's get you home and into some fresh clothes and brew a nice cup of tea."

The crowd parted to let Emily usher the women down Main Street toward her home.

There was an eerie silence in Breyer after the sun went down. Several men stood around The Crow Fly with buckets of water to make sure no sparks drifted to any of the other buildings during the night while the saloon burned itself out. They had little to say to each other as the warm breeze swept through town, then carried the smoke with it as a hazy goodbye.

It could have been worse. Much worse, they all agreed. But Breyer now wore the remains of The Crow Fly like a black eye, sullen and tired.

The restless soul of Lyle Confort already seemed to haunt the town, leaving in its wake uneasiness and distrust. First Big Andy, now Lyle Confort left their bodies behind at The Crow Fly, as though the once flourishing saloon was now a graveyard.

ALL THE TEA IN CHINA

EMILY, KATE, AND PEG SAT around the table after dinner, sipping on black tea in fine china cups. On a plate were cookies that Marian Humphrey brought over, along with a slab of bacon and a dozen fresh eggs in a basket.

Kate was barefoot, stretching her long legs out under the table and cupping the tea with both hands. Peg slumped over in her chair, as though her head were too heavy to hold up. Kate wore men's clothing—an old shirt and pants. Peg looked lost in a bleached-out dress three sizes too big. Emily told them she would look around Buttons and Bows in the morning for more suitable attire.

Emily cleared her throat. Peg opened her eyes. It was only seven o'clock in the evening, but it felt like days had gone by since the fire that afternoon. The probable death of Lyle Confort weighed heavily on her mind. Thinking about the man, Peg rubbed her sore arm. Doc Winters said it hadn't been broken, but it hurt like the devil and already had erupted in bruises—deep purple and yellow slashes from her shoulder to her elbow. All she wanted to do was curl up somewhere and go to sleep.

As if reading her mind, Emily set her cup in the saucer and

spoke. "Let's not go to bed just yet. Today has been a nightmare and I don't mean to figure out everybody's life before morning, but I had some ideas and was wondering if either of you wanted to talk about it."

Kate nodded, wiping at her face with a napkin. She set the teacup in the saucer and straightened her shoulders.

"What do you have in mind?"

Emily turned to Peg. "I don't know if you've been aware of this, but Kate and I have been talking—in loose terms, mind you—of opening a dress shop somewhere outside of Breyer as partners. I do well here with Buttons and Bows, but Kate and I are working on designs that are far more, shall we say, sophisticated, than what a Texas rancher's wife might use."

Peg shook her head. "I didn't know."

"Well, it's only been talk until now. Kate designs beautiful frocks, and I love to sew. We've bantered about with the idea, haven't we, Kate?"

Kate nodded. "Of course, now everything seems to be ruined. I'm so sad that I can't even begin to dream any further than the soot and ashes down the street."

"Thank God you left most of the beautiful bolts of fabric you've invested in over at the dress shop. Between your fabric and the inventory I have, I believe it's enough to start a fine little shop in a more developed city."

"But what about the shop? What about the money to open up a new place, to actually move? Seems like it would be impossible."

"Not impossible, but it will be a lot of work. I don't own the building. As you know, Lyle owned it and we aren't sure if he's dead or alive. I would assume he perished in the fire, since he was last seen upstairs. So, we can simply ship all the goods to another town, another shop. Say, someplace like St. Louis."

"St. Louis? Why that's a lifetime away, Emily! It would cost a lot of money to put all the contents of the shop on a train. My word!"

"I would consider it an investment. Yes, we might be in debt for a while, but I have faith in our designs and workmanship that eventually we can make a profit." Here, Emily's voice filled with emotion. "An old friend of mine from childhood lives in St. Louis. We have written to each other back and forth over the years. I am certain she could help us find a small shop in the clothing district and perhaps locate a boardinghouse for us until we can become established. It's exciting."

Emily waved her hand around the room. "I own this house. Lyle Confort does not, and never would. It's mine to keep or to sell. The money I get from the sale would more than pay for the shipments, and a bit of a start."

Kate brightened. "I don't have much money, but I never kept it at The Crow Fly. Some of those men would have stolen the clothes right off my back if they could. So, I opened up an account down at the bank. It isn't a lot, but it's handsome enough, and it's intact." She stood up and paced the room. "Why, it could be a fresh start! And we have such ideas together! I think it's a grand idea! It's time I left Breyer."

"Me too," said Emily. "So, it's a deal then?"

"Deal!" Kate grinned and twirled across the room, reaching for a cookie. Then she sobered. "But how soon could we do it? How fast can you sell this house, do you think?"

"Well, that's the thing. Just the other day, Lillian White was admiring it. You know, she and her husband have a pretty prosperous business running the hotel and restaurant. Confort didn't own the building, and they refused to sell to him. She asked recently if I ever thought of selling my house." She looked at Kate. "I'm sorry I didn't mention this sooner. But now, with The Crow Fly in tatters, it's time. I could certainly talk to Lillian and see if it was something they still might want."

Kate reached for another cookie. "That's great! I love the idea. But, aren't you fairly content here in Breyer, with your shop and beautiful home?"

Emily shrugged. "Life is supposed to be an adventure. Moving to Breyer was one of those adventures. But now it's time to start anew and leave the dust of Texas behind on my bootheels."

Peg smiled. "I am so happy for you two. It sounds like a fresh start, and I know you'll do well." She ran her fingers along her exhausted cheek. "I think I need to go to bed and sleep this off. It's been one helluva day."

"Wait, Peg," said Emily. "I know you lost it all over there at the saloon. I'm sure Kate would agree that you are welcome to join us in St. Louis. You can find work there of some sort, I'm sure, and we can all stay together and split expenses."

Kate put her arm around Peg's shoulder. "Come with us. It will be fun! We can reinvent ourselves and live a better life than the one here in this dusty excuse for a town."

Peg teared up, wiping at her eye with the napkin. "That's mighty kind of you two, and I admit it's something I might like to do. But, well, I am wondering what Shorty might be thinking, now that his job is also over at The Crow Fly." She looked wistfully at her friends. "I'm hoping maybe he might want to include me in his life. We've never gotten around to talking about anything like that, mind you, but we've grown close over the past several months."

"Of course, of course," Emily said. "We'll start with our plans. Just let us know if you want to come along or not. Either way is just fine with us. No pressure at all. Now, let's all get to sleep. It's been a very hard day."

Kate cupped Emily's delicate china between her hands. "You two go on ahead. I think I want another cup of tea, maybe ten cups. Who knows! Maybe all the tea in China! I'm too wound up to go to sleep just yet."

After Emily and Peg went to bed, Kate sat, gazing out the window toward Main Street. It was quiet now. The town had turned in, except for the few men watching the remnants of the fire.

She took another sip of tea. Now, after all this time, and after all those men, she was free. Free from her parents. Free from The Crow Fly and Breyer. And free to have her own thoughts. Funny, she mused. After all these years, she finally had come to grips with her hard-nosed family and their values, and recognized that maybe, just maybe, God had a plan for her.

For the first time in decades, Kate bowed her head in prayer.

SHORTY AND PEG

IT WAS LATE THE NEXT morning when Shorty knocked softly on Emily's door. He took a step back, his battered Stetson in one hand. With the other, he smoothed his hair, then cleared his throat.

Kate answered the door with a kind smile.

"Why, Shorty! How goes it? Here you are, a real hero! Jed Thornton might have died if it hadn't been for you. The whole town's grateful."

Shorty ducked his mammoth head and fussed with his hat. "It was nothing. I was glad to help out."

"Well, I for one will always be grateful to you for yesterday and for all the other nice ways you treated us at The Crow Fly." She said, "Peg, too, I'm sure. I imagine you've come here to talk with her?"

"If she's around, that would be nice."

"Come on in." Kate opened the door wider.

"I ain't fixin' to bother you all," Shorty said. "Miss Emily has a bench out behind the house near the cottonwood tree. I'll just wait there for Peg, if you'd care to tell her I'm out back."

"Of course. I'll let her know you're here." Shorty turned toward the back of the house as Kate shut the door and went to find Peg.

PEG BRUSHED HER HAIR AND pinched her cheeks. She smoothed the bodice of the simple dress a rancher's wife had left for the poor in the church vestibule. The dress hung on her but was clean and had no rips or stains. Peeking through the curtains, she saw Shorty sitting on a bench in the yard.

She stifled a laugh. The man resembled a buffalo. He sat with his legs outstretched, his dark curly hair dancing in the breeze. Shorty took up the entire bench in a commanding way, his chin jutting out as he surveyed the property. He could be a frightening sight for people, but Peg knew how tender he was beneath his enormous exterior. Her heart tripped. She hoped Shorty wasn't coming by to say farewell on his way to another town without her.

He rose when she stepped out the door and into his arms. To Peg, it felt like a lifetime since she'd seen him last. She needed him, and that scared her.

The sun beat through the slight breeze, leaving a sheen of sweat on Shorty's forehead. He tightened his grip on her arms.

"Come sit, Peggy," he said, using his name for her. When he said it, Peg felt like a young schoolgirl. She sat on the bench, moving over for Shorty. He shook his head. "Gonna stand. I have things to say to you today and it ain't respectful to sit at a time like this."

Peg caught her breath and nodded. She crossed her ankles and folded her hands as though sitting in a pew in church. She smiled up at Shorty, who blocked the sun, sending shadows across her face.

"Well, that was quite the day yesterday," Peg said. "You saved Jed Thornton. You could have been killed, Shorty, but you put him before yourself. Where did you come from, anyway? I looked all around for you. I was so worried."

Shorty cleared his throat. The taste of smoke lingered in his mouth, and it was painful to speak. "I ran in through the back door, thinkin' you were in the saloon. I ain't no hero. Just happened to be there when Jed needed me. But truth be told, I was lookin' for you."

Peg nodded, her eyes wide. "I called out for you and didn't know where you were. I'm just so grateful everybody made it out alive. Except for Lyle Confort, of course. I suppose he died. What a shame. What a cruel man to burn down The Crow Fly."

Shorty flinched at the sound of Confort's name. He bent down and picked up a cottonwood twig and sent it sailing across the yard. It landed near an old speckled hen, who glared at him and ruffled her feathers.

"Look, Peggy, I ain't here to talk about Lyle or Jed or anybody else. I'm here to talk about us before I run out of voice altogether. You know I don't talk much, and that fire seared my throat." He twisted his hat in his hands, bending the brim. "I just want to ask you to listen to me."

"Of course," Peg said. She noticed he was wearing a fresh shirt, deep green with shell buttons. There was soot under his fingernails, but he had scrubbed himself clean. Next to his foot on the ground was a small deerskin pouch.

"I came to tell you I'm mighty glad you weren't hurt in that fire. I know that neither one of us has a job now, with The Crow Fly in ashes down the street. Do you have any plans?"

"Kate and Emily invited me to join them. They're moving to St. Louis to open a dress shop," she replied.

"St. Louis, you say?" Shorty scuffed at the ground with his boot. "That's a far piece from Breyer. How would we keep in touch? I ain't much of a letter writer, but I can try. Are you yearning to go with 'em?"

Peg shrugged. "I don't know. I suppose I could. At least we

three would be together. But, well, I was hoping maybe you and I could talk about it first."

"Me too."

Shorty took a step closer. Peg slid over and gestured for him to sit.

"Please, Shorty. I'm craning my neck to see ya."

He perched on the edge of the bench and leaned in toward her. A hummingbird hovered near them and they smiled. In the distance, the train whistle announced its arrival in Breyer. Shorty shifted his weight on the bench, then turned to Peg.

"I may not have told you, but I grew up on a small farm in Nebraska. We had cattle. Not a lot, but enough to live on for our meat, and we sold some too. My family grew vegetables and even had an apple tree or two. Farmed enough to get by. My ma and pa were born and raised in Nebraska. They had three children. Me, my sister Martha, and sister Tansy. Tansy died, and Martha is living far away in Vermont."

"I didn't know that," Peg said. "I would have never pegged you as a farm boy."

"Well, that's the problem, in a way. I didn't want to live on the farm all my life. My daddy wanted me to stay. He was mighty angry when I decided to seek my fortune elsewhere. For me, that was California, looking for gold. A fool's dream, really, and I left California after only a year. I should have gone back to the farm then, only I didn't. I was young and foolish and there was a whole world out there between the ocean and Nebraska, and I explored it."

He chuckled. "How I ended up in Breyer, I will never know. The whole town looks like it needs a shave. I didn't plan to stay for long. But then, well, I met up with you.

"That farm is still standing, and although my father was fit to be tied when I wouldn't stay, he and Momma left it to me. Martha is long married with a big family and wants nothing to do with the place. Pa died almost seven years ago now. I traveled back to the farm once a year to see Ma and stay a month or two so I could help out with things that needed to be done."

Shorty chewed on his lip, as though holding back the words might be easier than saying what he needed to say. But he continued.

"My mother died three years ago. I didn't even hear about it until six months after she was gone, then I rode to Nebraska to see what's what. The farm's empty as a tomb. There ain't no cattle or vegetables, but the house is fit as a fiddle." He glanced at Peg. "You'd like it. It's pretty as a picture and not too far from town for supplies.

"Anyway, I guess I am talking around the subject too much, but I am not sure how I want to say it." He took Peg's hand and rubbed her wrist with his thumb.

"What I'm trying to say is, I would like it very much if you would marry me and move to the farm. It's nothing fancy, but I think we could make a good life together in Nebraska. Nobody in town needs to know about our past. They can watch us carve out a sweet future."

Peg started to talk, but Shorty interrupted her. "I ain't finished yet. Then you can say your piece. My tongue's loosened up now, and that ain't easy for a man like me. Please listen to me the rest of the way." He put his finger in his collar and tugged at it. Sweat trickled down his face, and he wiped it with his sleeve.

"Now, I have no idea the grief you've felt since your husband and son were murdered on that train. Every person walks with their own brand of sorrow, and you've had more than your share."

Peg looked away from him and watched as a hawk flew in lazy circles, dipping its wings in and out of the breeze. She seldom discussed losing Samuel and Jody. Nonetheless, the whole town of Breyer knew about it. She saw the pity on their faces sometimes. Hearing their names from other folks' lips made her uneasy and out of sorts.

Shorty moved a little closer and put his arm around Peg's shoulders, drawing her close.

"Now, I know Nebraska holds some mighty bad memories for you. I know you suffered such a huge loss there, so far from home. There don't seem to be much sense in life, but sometimes things are meant for a reason, like me coming home to the farm." He hesitated, then spoke again. "Last year, remember when I was gone for a while? I went back to the farm to see it again. And then I took a trip to find the town where you ended up after the train robbery. I have something here for you."

He reached down and took the deerskin pouch off the ground and set it gently in her lap.

"Open it."

Peg untied the rawhide and reached into the pouch. She brought up two slivers of weathered wood, each one about an inch or two long. She looked up, bewildered.

Shorty tightened his hold on her, keeping her close to his chest.

"I found their graves, Peggy. Samuel's. And little Jody's. I bowed my head and prayed for them. Then I took my knife and carved out these two small pieces from their crosses. I figured they might not mind, and I hope you don't either."

"You see, honey, there's a little knoll not far from my farmhouse with two of the prettiest trees you'd ever want to see. They turn gold in the autumn. A true gold. Not the gold I went chasin' after in California, but the real gold that means family.

"I thought we could bury these two slivers up there in a metal box, and put up new, nice crosses with their names on it. You can go up there every day and talk to them. And when it's our time to die, we can be buried up there too. You right next to little Jody, and I guess my ghost will shake hands with Samuel." He smiled at the thought, then looked at her with pleading eyes.

"Say yes. Say you'll make me the happiest man in Breyer and come with me to the farm."

There were no words. Peg could think of no words. Only feelings. The bursting joy in her heart to touch the two slivers of wood. The peace she finally had, knowing her little boy would find his way home and never leave her again. And the love she felt for the mountain of a man who held her tight.

"Oh, Shorty, yes! Yes, for the rest of our days!"

He slapped his knee and planted a kiss on her cheek. "All right, then! I'm going to wander over to the preacher and see when he can get us married." He flushed with excitement. "You might want to tell Kate and Emily. Maybe they'd want to be a part of it."

Peg kissed Shorty goodbye, then floated back into the house. For the first time in decades, she was truly happy.

WEDDING BELLS, OLD DONKEYS, AND QUESTIONS

KATE AND EMILY WORKED DAY and night to sew a dress for Peg. Made of the finest silk in spring green, it was a luxury. The dress swirled around Peg's ankles like seafoam, frothy and delicate. Emily made a deep-green belt that fastened around the waist and ended in a soft bow, trailing down the back of the dress.

"Oh my," Peg said, placing her hand on her heart. She twirled in front of the mirror and watched the silk dance in the light of an early afternoon. "It's so beautiful. It's not practical at all, but I love it."

Emily smiled. "We know. It's a keepsake. Something for you to have to remind you of this day and a gift from us with love."

"Fat chance I would ever forget you two," Peg replied. "I can't thank you enough for such a beautiful present. It's very special."

Kate brought out two more dresses from the sewing room. "These are for you too. Much more serviceable on the farm. We picked this cheerful yellow-flowered one to remind you of Breyer and its sunshine. And the blue checked one is so calm and lovely, like the first day of summer. I picture you wearing it in the garden."

Peg hugged herself with joy. "Oh, my friends, I can't tell you how happy I am. The only dark cloud in my life right now will be when I say goodbye to you. I don't think I can bear it. I will miss you so!"

Emily patted her shoulder. "We'll write from St. Louis and tell you everything we're doing. And you can write back. We promise we'll stay in touch!"

Peg looked at herself again in the mirror. "I can't believe I'm marrying my best friend."

"You're a lucky woman," Kate said. "Shorty loves you the way you deserve, and there's no doubt you will be happy."

"We best be going," Emily said, her voice brisk as she wrapped up Peg's clothes. "The wedding is in an hour, and we still have to go back to my house to fix your hair and for Kate and I to get dressed."

"Don't you mean Lillian's house now?" Kate asked.

The Whites were eager to buy Emily's house when she told them she was moving to St. Louis. It sold so fast that Emily's head spun. She wasn't sure she could get it all done—the dressmaking, Peg's wedding, and moving her things out of the house while sending bolts of fabric and spools of thread back to St. Louis to her friend's house. But the women all pitched in and did it in record time.

Back at the house, Emily surveyed the parlor. "I guess all I'll take with me is my china. The furniture was too bulky and difficult to ship to St. Louis. And expensive too."

Peg touched the delicate china with her little finger. "It's beautiful, Emily. You must ship it back East to your new home. I understand the Whites gave you a fair price on your furniture too?"

"Yes. It makes sense to sell to them, and I'll be okay. Someday I'll buy more." She hesitated. Her voice quavered. "This house was the nicest thing I ever had." Then she straightened and nodded as she looked around. "But it's time to move on. Time to start fresh."

Kate overheard them as she walked into the parlor with sunflowers from Emily's garden in a white pitcher. She set it on the table and turned the flowers toward the light pouring in through the lace curtains.

"It's all so pretty, Emily. But you'll have the chance to have nice things again. We're going to make it big in St. Louis! I just know it."

"When are you leaving?" Peg asked.

"Well, we need to get the fabrics down to the railway station to send ahead to St. Louis. Jared White said he'd meet up with us and take it down there. After your wedding, Kate and I just need to pack up our belongings and we'll leave as soon as we can. The Whites are eager to move in, so we won't tarry."

The three women stood in a circle in the sunny room. None of them spoke. The moment was too powerful. Instead, they simply hugged.

OUTSIDE, BREYER POUTED. THE TOWN seemed to slip into a depression. Tumbleweeds were no longer wrangled as they paraded down Main Street. Instead, they danced up against the storefronts and lingered by the hitching posts. Since The Crow Fly burned down, the townspeople simply walked around the charred ruins. There were no plans to clean it up, at least as far as Jed Thornton knew.

Lyle Confort apparently died in the fire. There didn't seem to be any heirs. Jed Thornton was still spending much of his time healing at home but promised to look into the matter as soon as he was up to it.

In the meantime, the corpse of the charred saloon stood out on Main Street like a missing tooth. Saturday nights were subdued. The other two saloons didn't rake in much business. Cowboys felt superstitious and out of sorts riding past the husk of The Crow Fly. It seemed as though the whole town was in mourning.

Even the crows down at the graveyard were quiet, wandering listlessly from grave to grave like old men visiting departed friends.

"Good riddance to The Crow Fly," said the preacher's wife. Some of the town ladies nodded in agreement, but truth be known, there was an aching sadness at its loss.

Kate, Peg, and Emily averted their eyes from the wreckage as they made their way to the little church. Up ahead, Peg spied Shorty standing inside the doorway, filling up the space with his broad shoulders. Her heart skipped.

"Wait!" a voice rang out. They turned to see Molly Brewster and Clarisse Snow. Clarisse held little Willie in her arms. Molly grinned at her friends and skipped ahead to hug Peg.

"Peg, I'll miss you so! You must write to us! I'll want to tell you all about Willie and how he's growing. Please promise me you will."

"Of course I will!" Peg said as she embraced Molly. The girl smelled like sweet grass and fresh linens. Clarisse walked up and stroked her arm. The baby reached out a chubby hand and grasped a lock of Peg's hair in his fingers. She leaned down to kiss the top of his downy head.

"Hello there!" Lara Thornton called merrily from across Main Street. She had her arm wrapped around Jed's. "I brought you something for your wedding day, Peg."

She grinned as she produced a beautiful bouquet from behind her back. "I thought of you this morning when I saw them."

Peg took the bouquet and buried her nose in the petals. "Oh, Lara, they're beautiful! Thank you." She turned to Jed. "How are you doing, Sheriff?"

Jed coughed into a handkerchief. "Better now. But I have to tell you, The Crow Fly laid me about as low as a man can be and still be on this side of the dirt. Doc said I can get out of bed now, but I can't do much of anything yet."

Lara winked. "I am counting the days until he can go back to work."

Pastor Green poked his head out the church door and bellowed. "You folks planning on coming in, or should I marry you right there in the road?"

Emily waved. "Sorry! Here we come!" She turned toward Lara and Jed. "Please join us for the ceremony."

"We'd love to," Lara said. "Wouldn't we, dear?"

"Of course."

Thornton gazed at the women. One of them held secrets. Secrets he needed to learn, and soon. Before long, the whores of The Crow Fly would scatter like seeds on the Texas wind. He rubbed his jaw. It was difficult, knowing he might have to put one of them behind bars. But not today. Today was Peg's wedding and he would give them all a day of peace before he ruined one of their lives.

TO HAVE AND TO HOLD

PEG STOOD NEXT TO SHORTY before the preacher, a shaft of sunlight illuminating the top of her head. Shorty towered over her, clutching her hand in his so tightly that she shifted from one foot to the other. He loosened his grip and grinned at her.

Peg shut her eyes for a moment. She wanted to remember everything about this day, but truth be told, she didn't catch a word the preacher said. Jane Green broke into her reverie when she played a wedding song on the piano, the room echoing with each note in such a way that Peg thought the whole town was wrapped in a holy embrace right at that moment.

Pastor Green gestured to Molly in the first pew.

"Molly, I believe you had something to share?"

The girl nodded and walked up to the podium. She cleared her throat, looked up toward the ceiling, and in a high, pure voice, sang an Irish song about love, family, and everlasting joy.

Kate and Emily stared at each other, shocked. They didn't know Molly possessed the voice of an angel.

Clarisse Snow hugged little Willie closer to her chest. The Irish song reminded her of home, back in County Mayo. *It's strange, what life has in store for all of us,* she thought. *I crossed an ocean to find love and found it with William. Then I lost Willie and thought my life was over. Now, I have a grandson. And a daughter with a voice that could make the saints cry in ecstasy.*

Molly returned to her pew. Jed shifted in his seat. The girl had finally found a home, and love. It moved him to tears. Tears because of his own love for Lara and the girls. Tears because of these women, who survived and flourished despite the lack of promise in this dusty town. And tears because he was torn with indecision about his investigation and the feelings he had. Startled by his emotion, he wiped at his eyes and peered out the window. A tumbleweed drifted by as though witnessing the wedding, and a crow landed in a tree nearby.

The preacher asked the proper questions and Shorty and Peg both said, "I do."

"Well, now it's my pleasure to introduce you to Mister and Missus... er, Shorty? Your last name?"

Everyone chuckled.

"Thompson," he said, then laughed. "And my first name is Abraham."

"Mister and Missus Abraham Thompson," the preacher announced with a flourish. His wife struck a chord, the piano trilling the wedding march as Shorty and Peg turned toward the congregation of seven. They rose and clapped as the couple strode by. Shorty pushed open the door, and he and Peg descended the steps, the others following.

"Well, congratulations!" Emily said, kissing them both on the cheek. She turned to everybody. "I would love to have you come back to the house for tea and cookies, if you'd like."

Jed opened his mouth to say no, but Lara cut him off. "We'd love to, Miss Augusta. I hear from Lillian that she already has a china cabinet, and so you might sell yours? I am in need of one and would love to see it."

"Of course," Emily said, leading the way to the small white cottage at the edge of town.

The little procession marched down Main Street and gathered in Emily's parlor. The round oak table held three varieties of cookies, a coffee cake, and sliced fruit, served on splendid china. Next to it was a floral teapot, and a small bowl of nuts. Peg thought she'd never seen anything so lovely.

Jed approached Shorty and shook his hand. "Congratulations. You have a lovely bride." He clasped the big man on his shoulder. "And I can't thank you enough for saving my life in The Crow Fly. Lara says it was an act of God that you arrived when you did. Another minute or two and I may have never made it."

Shorty cleared his throat. "It was nothin', Sheriff. No act of God, or anyone else. I just did what needed to be done." He turned toward Peg and reached for her hand.

Lara called out. "Jed, come look at this beautiful china cabinet. Emily is asking a fair price. I have a few dollars set aside and I hope you approve, as it is something I've wanted for a long time."

The cabinet stood in the shadows of the room. Jed ran his hand along the smooth wood and marveled at the grain that shimmered beneath the finish. He pulled open a drawer, which still held Emily's silverware. In the drawer's corner was a sachet. Jed knew before he drew it to his nose what it would smell like. Distinct. Something like lavender and sage—the sweet and the bitter, the purple and the green. Something he'd smelled before. On Big Andy's body. And in a packet of old letters in a shack by the arroyo.

"Excuse me," Peg's voice rang out. "This has been the best time I could have ever imagined, but Shorty tells me we have to go. He wants to reach safe shelter by tonight. I can't tell you all how much I appreciate everything you've done for us. We love all of you. I promise I'll write the moment we get to Nebraska."

There were hugs and kisses all around. Then the newlyweds opened Emily's door and walked around to the side of the house where Shorty's buckboard waited. A welcoming bray rang out as loud as a church bell.

"Old Gringo!! What on earth?" Peg stared at the sight before her. The donkey stood patiently tied to the back of the wagon. He raised his massive head and Peg swore he grinned. Tucked into his halter, behind one ear, was a cheerful sunflower.

"Well," Shorty said, "I decided this donkey needed a home. I think it's beneath his dignity to come to Breyer every day and beg for food. He needs a proper place to live. So, I figured we'd bring him to Nebraska to our farm. I hope that's fine with everybody."

Kate laughed and walked over to Gringo. She scratched his neck, and he bobbed his head up and down in agreement.

Shorty handed Peg up onto the buckboard. She moved her skirt aside as her new husband settled into the seat and picked up the reins. He clucked to the horses, and they started off, Old Gringo following sedately.

Peg turned around and blew kisses at everybody, then looked forward and faced the sun.

On her way out of town, she tossed petals from the bouquet. They settled into the rutted wagon tracks of Main Street, tiny jewels in the middle of a thorny town.

For one moment, Breyer, Texas, wore a bright necklace of flowers as the afternoon sun shone on the town. Then a wagon made its way down the middle of the street and crushed the blossoms beneath its heavy wheels.

THE SCENT OF SIN

EMILY PEERED OUT THE PARLOR window and saw Jed Thornton heading her way. Kate was over at Buttons and Bows, packing up the last of the fabric to load on the train. Lara loved the china cabinet and promised that Jed would be around with the money to purchase it.

"Hi there, Jed," Emily said, opening the door. She stood aside and motioned him in. "Quite the to-do for Shorty and Peg yesterday, wouldn't you say?" She gestured with a delicate hand. "Have a seat, please."

Thornton smiled, his eyes taking in the parlor, then settled on the green sofa, ambled over, and took a seat. "Sure was. I owe Shorty my life. I'm glad those two found each other and will set up a life together."

His eyes narrowed a bit. "What about you? Are you and Kate about ready to pull out of town too?"

"Yes. I've enjoyed Breyer, and most particularly, Buttons and Bows. But I think there's more opportunity awaiting us and our talents elsewhere. If nothing else, it will be a grand adventure." She pointed to the cherry cabinet in the corner. "Are you here about this piece? It will look mighty fine in your house. I know Lara loves it."

He laughed. "I can't say no to Lara. I brought the money and will send some help to haul it up to the house later this afternoon."

He pulled several dollars out of his back pocket and set it on the table. "Is this right?"

Emily nodded. "Much obliged, Jed. That will go a long way toward our train tickets, and I can't think of a finer couple to own the cabinet than you and Lara."

She stood by the door with her hands clasped in front of her, but Jed did not rise from the sofa. He leaned back, his chiseled face deep in concentration.

"Breyer will miss you and Kate. You sure had a following of ladies for Buttons and Bows, including my Lara."

He picked up a small crystal bell from a table next to the sofa and rang it. Its sweet sound resonated throughout the room. He set it back and drummed a finger on the tabletop.

Jed cleared his throat. "So, I was thinking. Now that The Crow Fly has burned to the ground, I might spend more time investigating Big Andy's murder. It's wrong that it happened over two years ago and still hasn't been solved. Now I'm wondering if I followed all the proper clues. Maybe there was something I missed. Something right there in front of my nose. It's a real puzzle. Seems like somebody should know something, wouldn't you think?"

"Well, Jed, I imagine the killer got clean away that night. Most likely it was a cowboy, a stranger who came to town and got himself in trouble at the saloon."

Thornton nodded and stroked his mustache. "That makes sense. But I've stumbled upon some clues that point to the murderer being a person Andy knew, and knew well."

Emily opened a window. A slight breeze danced past the curtains. "Andy Connor knew a lot of folks here in town, and many of them disliked him. Just like Lyle Confort. I'm sure Lyle had a lot of enemies as well."

"You're probably right. Andy had no shortage of people who didn't like him. Or maybe, the killer shot him in self-defense. Big Andy was a brute. Maybe someone felt threatened?"

"I don't know why you're running all of this past me, Sheriff." Emily tipped up her chin, her eyes cold and distant. "I want to forget all about it. It was terrible to find the man out behind The Crow Fly that Sunday morning. I prefer not to dwell on such ugliness." She pulled a handkerchief out of her pocket and dabbed at her nose with it.

Thornton shifted in his seat. "What do you think I should do with the killer, if I find him or her? What if I think the killer had been threatened or blackmailed? Should I make an arrest? Let the murderer go? It might even be somebody I know and have grown fond of here in Breyer. Maybe that person needs a fresh start, and not have their future ruined. I'm tellin' you, Emily, it's been a tough investigation. It weighs on my conscience."

He rose and walked over to the china cabinet. He patted the satiny surface. "Lara will love this cabinet. We appreciate you selling it to us."

Emily nodded, then walked to the sofa and traced the fabric with her finger. She spoke with her back to Thornton. "You asked what I would do in your place, Jed? Well, I think you have to weigh what's right and what's wrong, and how sometimes wrongs happen for reasons that you may never know. Then take into consideration the killer's age, how long they would last in prison under harsh circumstances, and if you think they learned their lesson."

She turned toward Thornton and cocked her head. "I also think you don't have enough evidence to prove anything, or you would have placed that person under arrest months ago."

The two looked at each other. Neither broke the stare. In

the parlor, Emily's clock ticked away the seconds. Outside, a dog barked over near the Humphrey house, breaking the silence.

Jed talked first. "Well, I reckon you might be right. I'll take all of it into consideration. Much obliged to you about the cabinet. I wish you and Kate only the best. I hope your life in St. Louis is a success."

He opened the door, then turned back. "I forgot to tell you the funniest thing, though. When I examined Big Andy, his body had the strangest odor. Like lavender and sage blended together. A very distinct aroma. I've come across it a few times lately. Isn't that unusual? I can't quite pinpoint that aroma, or exactly where I've smelled it in the past several days."

He looked her straight in the eye. "Rest assured, Emily, I know who the killer is. I doubt I could prove it in a court of law, though. How can you pin a crime on somebody just because of an odor?"

Jed tipped his hat and stepped off the porch.

Emily closed the door quietly on her past and leaned against it. Then she sighed and sank to the floor, her scented handkerchief pressed to her heart.

KATE AND EMILY

"I GUESS THAT'S IT," EMILY SAID, wiping her hands on her apron. "I think we're ready for our new adventure."

The two women surveyed Emily's house. They'd stacked boxes and satchels by the front door. Lillian did not need all of Emily's furnishings, so bit by bit the folks in Breyer purchased them, including the beautiful cabinet that Lara Thornton bought.

The house appeared solemn and empty. Where the cabinet once stood, a small reddish stain bloomed on the floral wallpaper. Emily had kept it hidden under a painting.

"I never noticed that mark before," Kate said. "Maybe some vinegar will clean it off the wallpaper?"

Emily peered at the stain and swiped at it with her finger. A shiver ran up her spine.

"Well, I don't know if it will clean up. I guess Lillian will have to decide what to do." Then she brightened, a touch of relief in her voice. "Actually, I think I have a small amount of wallpaper left over. Maybe we should patch it?"

"Oh, I wouldn't bother, Emily," Kate said. "What's done is done. Leave it for Lillian to patch, or not. Let her decide what to do. We're running out of time."

Emily shrugged. "If you say so." She pulled her shawl around her shoulders and tended to the boxes, printing her name on them in wide, dark strokes.

EMILY'S HOUSE HAD BEEN SOLD, and Buttons and Bows stood empty on Main Street. The women had shipped several cartons of fabric to St. Louis. All that was left to do was board the train.

Kate shifted nervously. "I think we need to go. I know the train doesn't come for a couple more hours, but I would just as soon get there and talk to Gus rather than stay here."

Emily put a few things in her trunk and locked it. "Of course. Marian's husband will pick us up in his wagon when we're ready. Do you want to run down to the bank and tell him we're locking up?"

Kate nodded and pulled the door closed behind her. Emily walked through the house one last time. She ran her fingers along the walls, walls that kept her company for years. Walls that often hugged her in moments of contentment. Walls that were stained with secrets.

It was time to leave. Time to start a new life in St. Louis. Time to reinvent herself yet again. She wouldn't miss Texas. Breyer was a pouting child of a town. Its sullen character seemed caked with obstinance and trouble. She'd tried to make something pretty out of it, and in some ways, it helped. Many ladies wore her dresses, and it improved the looks of Main Street on a Sunday morning. Emily was proud as she watched them walk into church, dressed in something she had designed and sewn.

She looked forward to the cool green glades of Missouri and the finer culture of the folks there. Her clothing business would be welcomed. Kate was a suitable partner and asset. Her designs were excellent, and she was willing to work hard in order to get out from under the life she had been living at The Crow Fly.

Mr. Humphrey helped the women load their things and drove Kate on to the depot. Emily said she'd catch up with them and locked the door for the final time. She stood on the front porch and surveyed the town. It struggled on a Tuesday morning, limping through the hot sun, which promised to become even hotter. She swore she still smelled the aftermath of the fire, a perfume that Breyer now wore and would for a long time.

As she walked down Main Street to the station, Emily stifled a sigh of relief. Her china had been carefully boxed and would accompany her to St. Louis. Already she looked forward to sipping tea in her new home.

She tripped over a rut in the street and fell onto one knee. A flash of pain shot through her ankle. Straightening, Emily held her head high as she passed the fine folks of Breyer on her way to a new beginning.

TRAIN OF THOUGHT

NOBODY CAME TO WISH KATE and Emily farewell. After all those years, there was still a line between decency and sin. Kate was tainted and always would be in Breyer. The two women looked at each other as the train approached the station. They did not need to explain their feelings. The cinders from the track sparked, reminding Kate of The Crow Fly, now in ruins. She was eager to leave town.

A man rode by with a sense of purpose on his way to the bank. Kate recognized him as one of her customers. A quiet man, he often sought comfort with her on a Friday night. She knew he was married with three children. He spoke of them to her, his voice filled with pride. But, should she see him on the street, he walked right past. Once he even jostled her elbow in his haste to place distance between them, and didn't even say he was sorry.

Kate was determined to make a better life in St. Louis. She hoped someday she would walk down the street and feel like she belonged.

She didn't shed a tear as Gus helped her up into the train and handed her a worn leather valise.

"Godspeed, Kate and Emily," the old man said. "I hope your trip to St. Louis is safe and sound."

It seemed like Breyer itself pushed the train out of the station in one last burst of indifference. The lurch forward from the mighty engine felt like a nudge from the past. Within moments, the town distanced itself and looked as closed up as a spinster's mouth.

Kate leaned her head against the window and shut her eyes. She hoped to open them far away from Breyer, Texas.

Emily sat with hands clasped and felt the tug of the rails as it jostled her in the seat. Kate already had slumped against the window. In the morning light, she looked serene and unfettered. Emily might have preferred a different partner, but in the end, it was a good fit for both of them, and they had become friends.

Friends. Emily snorted. Did she ever really have any friends? It seemed as though everyone in her life had let her down at some point. The train neared the edge of Breyer, and she craned her neck for one last look. She saw her house in the distance. It already looked different, as though it had shifted shape in the Texas dirt. If she were to be honest, the house itself was the only true friend she ever had. It never betrayed her. It was welcoming and beautiful and calm, just the way Emily liked things. And now it belonged to somebody else, and the echoes in the walls would eventually sing another song.

Emily looked away. It was hard to bid the house goodbye, but easy to leave Breyer behind. Breyer was an afterthought. Its ugliness repulsed her. Her house was all she wished she could take with her.

She shifted in her seat and brought the scented handkerchief up to her nose. What had once been a welcoming scent now was a bearer of bad news, fear, and vigilance.

The conductor came through the car and she handed him her ticket, as well as Kate's. Kate didn't stir. The train settled into a constant rumble, traversing the tracks in a steady rhythm that left Emily oddly comforted. It was the first time since The Crow Fly burned that she allowed herself to fully relax. She had just left Breyer, and Jed Thornton didn't follow. It must have cost him many a night's sleep to bid her goodbye and walk away. Closing her eyes, she thought back to the day, over two years ago, when life as she knew it swiveled on its axis and the taint of blood overrode the scent of sage and lavender on her lace handkerchief. Resting her head on the back of the seat, she remembered....

THE MURDER OF BIG ANDY

SEVERAL PEOPLE STEPPED DOWN FROM the wheezing train that pulled into Breyer's dusty station one hot July morning. One of them was Big Andy Connor. Miss Emily Augusta was another.

Big Andy had been run out of Chicago for cheating at cards in his saloon near the stockyards. He didn't care. Heck, he was planning to leave the city, anyway. He'd made enough money off the rubes and gamblers to start a new business all the way out in Texas, where there were even more easy marks.

He took his money and his favorite whore with him and never looked back.

Andy set Emily up with her own dress shop as an investment, then built a cottage at the edge of town and deeded it to her in return for her favors. They kept their secret all these years. Nobody in Breyer ever connected the two together. The pair ignored each other on the street and never spoke. But on Saturday nights, Andy crept in the darkness to Emily's house and sneaked in through the back door.

Emily did not want the townspeople to know about them, and Andy agreed. He was fond of her and didn't mind the shadowy way their romance developed. To him, it was exciting. To her, it was necessary.

Andy reaped success at The Crow Fly, and Emily felt fulfilled running the dress shop. For the first time in her life, she was proud she had achieved something, even if the benefactor who launched her was a scruffy liar and cheat. The partnership worked for years.

Things had been going well between the two of them until Andy took to drinking more heavily than usual. He'd started in lately with surly talk when he'd come to visit Emily for a little poke every Saturday night.

One night, Andy arrived with a bottle of whiskey in his hand on unsteady feet. Emily could tell he'd already been drinking by his foul breath when he bent down to kiss her. Resisting the urge to wipe her mouth against her sleeve, she turned instead toward the parlor and beckoned him in.

But Andy wanted to go straight to bed, stopping only to grab a glass from the kitchen, then shuffled into the frilly bedroom. He looked around and snorted. The place looked like the inside of a castle in Europe, he thought, not a simple town in Texas. It stood out like a sore thumb. Ridiculous looking! Emily had placed frothy curtains on the window and matched them with an equally dressy bedspread. He stumbled, spilling a drop of liquor on the dainty bed.

Emily grimaced. "Could you be more careful, Andy? This stain will be hard to get out. Here, hand me that bottle and I'll put it on the nightstand."

Andy tossed her a dirty look and held the bottle tighter in his fist.

"Seems like you're forgetting who gave you a new life here. If I spill a drop or two, it's only my sweat from working hard so you can have the finer things you always craved."

Weaving, he undid his pants and let them pool around his boots. He squinted at her, then sat down heavily on the bed. Emily stood in the corner with her hands on her hips.

"Please, Andy. I'm just asking you to calm down and give me that bottle."

"I'll give you the bottle if and when I feel like it! In the meantime, come over here and help me out of my boots."

Emily hesitated. She did not want to kneel before this man. This man, who had been her benefactor for years, and yet extracted more than his share by using her body every weekend as though she were one of his whores at The Crow Fly.

Andy noticed her reluctance and waved his finger at her. "So, it's like that, huh? You put on airs, sashaying all over town in them fancy dresses, and then use your share of the profits from the shop to buy all this useless stuff, like china and silverware." He pointed through the doorway. "And that silly wallpaper in the parlor. Why, Emily Augusta, you think I'm beneath you now, don't you?"

Andy yanked off his boots and threw them across the room, then rose from the bed like a large, angry bull. He shouldered his way into her parlor and slammed the bottle down on the round oak table.

"Never forget where you came from, Emily!" he said. "I can break you just as easily as I made you. You owe me everything!"

He pulled back a meaty arm and threw one of her precious china cups against the wall. It shattered into a hundred pieces, just like Emily's reputation would shatter from Big Andy's loud mouth. Everything she had worked for, everything that mattered to her, seemed as fragile as that teacup. She trembled with rage.

"How dare you! How dare you come into my house and threaten me!"

"Your house? Don't forget who built it for you, my dear," he sneered, and purposefully shattered another teacup, then lurched toward Emily in a menacing way.

Frightened and angry, she ran into the bedroom and pulled a pistol out from the top drawer of her dresser. Trembling, she stalked back into the parlor and aimed it at Andy.

"Stop right now! Take a seat and calm down. Stop, or I swear, I'll shoot!"

Andy reeled in surprise when he saw the gun, then lunged. "Give me that, you bitch!"

Emily's hand trembled as she pulled the trigger. Andy's eyes widened as the bullet hit his chest. He looked down at the bloom of blood on his shirt, then stumbled toward her. She shot him again. This time he went down, drifting to the floor, sprawling on his back upon her lovely braided rug, blood seeping into the cotton loops, staining it forever.

Emily dropped the pistol and covered her mouth in horror.

"Andy? Andy?"

She approached him slowly, like one might approach a rattlesnake, poised to jump out of the way in case it coiled. Andy was dead. She could tell. His chest wasn't moving. His eyes were vacant. Blood seeped from his mouth. She refrained from touching him.

"Oh God, what have I done?"

Panicking, she paced back and forth past his body. Walking to her bedroom, she stripped the sheet off the bed and tossed it over him, hiding her sin until she could think straight.

Emily sank to the sofa and tried to sort things out. Andy had gone too far. He'd been taunting her for weeks, his drinking worsening and his attitude right behind it. There was simply no love between them, if there ever was. Andy had turned into a large problem, constantly berating and mistreating her when he visited.

She had endured him for years. Years! And now the ungrateful sod lay belly up in her parlor with two bullets in him.

Serves him right, she thought, then cringed at her own coldness.

Emily didn't know what to do. She knew she wanted her life

back. Back the way it was before Andy elbowed his way into her house with his damned bottle of whiskey. Back to the pleasant afternoon she enjoyed earlier in her parlor before he sullied it with his rank behavior. What on earth was going to happen now? Why, Jed Thornton might have heard the shots and be heading down to see what was going on.

Trembling, Emily quickly extinguished the kerosene lamps and blew out the candle in the bedroom until the only light in the house was from the full moon as it streamed in through the windows. Andy looked ghostly under the sheet. If she closed one eye, she could make him disappear from sight. Then the parlor looked the same before she shot him. Oh, how she wished it was the same. Her throat tightened.

She needed Rick. Rick would know what to do. He was still playing the piano at The Crow Fly. She heard the music faintly in the distance. But would he help her?

Emily had taken Rick as her lover three years ago. He, too, crept to her tiny white cottage on the edge of town each week. He, too, kept their secret from everybody.

Rick James had longed for Emily from the moment he saw her on the street as she locked up Buttons and Bows one evening. He never knew the link that existed between Emily and Andy. He only knew she was a woman he wanted to get to know better. After asking around, he discovered she was a single lady. Nobody knew much about her, but they assured him Emily was a spinster. And a harsh one at that.

There was something about her that drew him in. Rick was mesmerized by her cool exterior, as though her heart were made of marble. The way she walked, gliding along Main Street in dainty shoes instead of slogging through the dirt and grime like a farmer's wife intrigued him. Her impeccable speech and formal manners touched his imagination. It was enough to drive a man crazy. Rick wanted to have her, the way some folks want to reach out and touch the moon. He wanted to press his lips against hers until the coldness warmed beneath him, then kiss her breasts until they were rosy. He wanted her to weep with passion, and he wanted to break through the crust that surrounded Emily Augusta until he could find the soft part and revel in it.

Over time, Rick touched her and kissed her but never found the soft part. He knew she had a heart because he heard it when he placed his head on her chest, but it was the closest he ever got to it.

THAT NIGHT, EMILY SENT A cowboy into The Crow Fly with a note, then waited along the side of the building in the darkness. The man leaned down and handed the note to Rick, who read it then thrust it in his pocket. Rick strode to the swinging doors and peered around. Emily stepped out of the shadows. Rick nodded once, then disappeared back into the saloon. A moment later, he struck a lively chord on the piano. Emily stepped across the street and into Buttons and Bows, made her way through the shop in the dark, and out the back door. She crept behind the buildings, then down the road to her cottage.

It was well after two in the morning before Rick knocked softly on Emily's back door. Even so, he'd left The Crow Fly early. A few cowboys still whooped it up, and Peg and the girls continued to wander around the floor when he stole out the back and disappeared.

Emily opened the door and grasped his arm. "Oh Rick," she whispered and sobbed as she pulled him forward.

"What's wrong, sweetheart?" he asked. He'd never seen Emily so out of sorts. Even in the darkness, he saw silvery tracks of tears on her face, and she trembled like a leaf.

"In there." She pointed toward the parlor.

"Could we have some light?" he asked, trying to find his way through the house.

"No."

The moonlight through the window outlined something large on the parlor floor. Rick froze. He took a few steps forward. It was a body under a sheet.

"What the hell?" He nudged it with his foot. It didn't move. Kneeling down, he lifted the sheet and recoiled.

He shouted and fell backward on his haunches. "Andy! What?" Emily broke into sobs.

"Emily, what the hell? Andy? What happened?"

"I shot him," she said. "I didn't mean to, Rick, I swear. It just happened."

"Just happened? What was Andy doing here? What's going on?"

"Well, it was a bit like self-defense," Emily said. She wiped her nose on a scented handkerchief she held over her mouth.

Rick walked over and put an arm around her. He guided her into the bedroom and sat her down on the mattress.

"Tell me what happened here."

Emily wiped her nose again and steadied her breath. "Andy threatened me, and I guess I got scared and shot him."

Rick's mind reeled in confusion. His hand trembled as he took hers. "I don't understand. I didn't even think you knew Andy."

Emily straightened her back and took a breath. "You might say we were business partners for a long time and Andy abused the agreements we had."

"Now I'm really confused." Rick walked over to open the window. He tripped over Andy's boots on the bedroom floor and saw the glass of whiskey on the bedside table. Startled, he slowly put it all together.

"You were sleeping with him! And sleeping with me too?"

Emily said nothing. She hung her head and sobbed into her hands.

Rick walked toward the door. "I'm getting the sheriff."

"No! No, please! Jed will arrest me and ask questions later. I swear to you it was self- defense."

"Emily, I want no part of this."

"Please! Help me! We have to get Andy out of here. I... I can't do it on my own. I need you."

Rick tugged at his hair in despair and walked in a circle, his chest heaving.

"It's all wrong. Let the sheriff help you, Emily."

"No!" she said, then pulled on his sleeve. "I'll go to the gallows for this. I swear, if you help me, I won't say a word to anybody. I promise."

Emily leaned against the wall. She looked ready to collapse in the thin light in the bedroom. Rick saw the whites of her eyes. She looked like a monster. He shuddered.

"What do you want me to do?" he asked

"Go get your horse and buggy. We'll put Andy in the buggy and then come around to the back of The Crow Fly when everybody's asleep. We'll leave him back there. The sheriff will think it was a robbery or something."

"Somebody might see us, for Christ's sake!"

"Maybe. But it's the only thing we can do. Either that or drive him clear out of town and there's a better chance of somebody seeing us doing that than just going behind the building down the street."

Rick rubbed his chin. "Maybe so, but then what? I'm supposed to just go back to the boardinghouse for the night and pretend nothing happened?"

He peered around the corner into the parlor. Andy was still there. Still dead.

"You help me with this, and then do whatever you want," Emily said. "Just help me get him over there. I'll do the rest."

"Em, I never want to see you again after this. Never. We're finished. Do you understand?"

"I do. But I swear to you, if you keep my secret, I'll keep yours.

After all, if we say anything, why, Jed might think you helped me kill Andy."

Rick lowered his head in shock. He didn't know what to think. Was Andy blackmailing Emily, or the other way around? Did she spring a trap on Andy, like she apparently just did on him? He'd never know. But Jed Thornton might think he'd killed Andy. After all, he worked for the man. With every breath, Rick felt a noose tighten around his neck. He longed to rid himself of the pressure.

"Okay," he said. Then he slipped out the back door to get the buggy.

MISS EMILY AUGUSTA CUT BEHIND The Crow Fly on her way to church the next morning, Bible in hand. She had spent the past several hours cleaning up the mess in her house, disposing of the bloody sheet and rug by cutting them into pieces, then burying them in her small flower garden.

A half an hour before church, she carefully dressed in her Sunday finest, then let herself out the front door and trudged toward the back of the saloon.

It was not too hard for her to scream at the top of her lungs when she came upon Andy's body. Old Gringo stood by the deceased near a cottonwood tree and snorted, his ears flattened by the shrill sound.

The memory of the night before gave her wings to fly past the body and out into the street. As she screamed, she felt as though she were releasing her sin into the sky. As every second ticked by, she was sure of one thing. Big Andy was dead. Emily Augusta killed him. And now it was time for her to survive. No matter what.

Sometimes it is best to flee a situation. Sometimes, it's best to stay where you are. Emily and Rick stayed in Breyer. By remaining motionless, she figured it wouldn't draw Jed's attention as much as if they bolted, and it hadn't. That is, until the sheriff came across the scent of lavender and sage and put it all together. He must have talked to Rick recently. Rick was smart to leave when he did. She should have run, perhaps, too. But as it was, Jed let her go.

EMILY STIRRED FROM HER REVERIE and looked across at Kate, who was still sleeping, her head nodding to the rhythm of the train. Kate trusted Emily. Trusted in their future in St. Louis. Believed they would put their past behind them.

"If you only knew, Kate," she said under her breath.

Kate eyes fluttered open. She turned toward Emily. "Did you say something?"

"No." Emily straightened in her seat and crossed her ankles. She peered out the window as Texas bid a last goodbye.

"No, Kate. I didn't say a thing."

DERAILING

JED THORNTON HEARD THE LONELY whistle as the engine pulled out of Breyer. It was a mournful reminder that Emily and Kate were on that train, heading for a new life in St. Louis.

Thornton rubbed his forehead with a weary hand. Emily had gotten away with murder. And now the taint of sin was on Jed's conscience. As the train gathered speed down the tracks, it took her farther away from any recourse and set him firmly in front of God.

Never in his life had Jed not done the right thing. He didn't like liars. Or cheaters. Card sharks or thieves. And yet, after a fistful of sleepless nights, he purposefully let Emily Augusta waltz out of town, knowing full well she carried the crime with her.

Emily was right, of course. Trying to prove murder would be difficult. Yes, he had letters between her and Big Andy, and yes, the letters and Andy's body smelled like the sage and lavender scent Emily favored. But that was hardly grounds for arrest for murder.

Why a prim woman like Miss Emily Augusta would be tied up with a sow's ear such as Andy was a mystery. Maybe he was blackmailing her. Or, Jed thought, his heart quickening, maybe she was blackmailing him. Underneath her cool exterior beat a stubborn heart, he thought. A heart capable of murder. He'd never know the whole truth. Only that he was as sure as the sun would rise tomorrow over Breyer, Emily Augusta had shot Andy. Maybe in self-defense. But why didn't she come to him if Andy had threatened her? Why did she keep the secret to herself?

He was sure, too, that Rick had something to do with the murder. He had fled so fast and so far, it would take Jed a lifetime to find him. More than likely he headed to Mexico or even back East, to hide in dusky corners of a big city like a snake under a rock, never to be found again.

Jed glanced out the window at the swollen pile of boards that had once been The Crow Fly. Men were still peeling the wood away, piece by piece, searching for the remains of perhaps more than one person. A lonely cowboy could have perished in that burned down saloon. A wrangler nobody knew might have been upstairs that day. Somebody who would never be missed in Breyer but was now lost in the fire. He shuddered. Every inch of the saloon needed to be examined.

Thornton jammed his hat on his head and locked the door behind him. He thought it best he check in on the workers and offer encouragement and warnings. After all, they might miss something important. Gritting his teeth, he knew with a flash of resentment that he'd be spending more time than he wanted at the rotting corpse of The Crow Fly.

A wrangler rode by from the Five Bar Ranch, loose in the saddle, his pants filthy and hat dusty. Down the road, two girls pushed and shoved at each other under the eaves of the dry goods store. Jed watched them hug, then dance in circles. Sisters, no doubt, weary of each other, but together always, just like his girls.

Jed looked down at his dirty boots. They were impossible to keep clean. Maybe tonight he'd brush and polish them, using an old military bristled brush that had seen better days. Straightening, he took a hard look around town.

Breyer hadn't cleaned up well. It bore the scars of many events and wore them listlessly. Children still played on Main Street with the broken hoop. The tumbleweeds conquered the town now, without the efficient demands of Miss Emily. They rolled along in an arrogant fashion, right up the street and into the graveyard, and then rested at the door of the church until a loyal parishioner swatted them away each Sunday morning. Crows patrolled the cemetery day and night, their relentless caws sending an eerie pall over the town. If they weren't roosting on the crosses, they were down at Cora Sanders's garden, dining, while she waited in the shadows with a broom.

His thoughts drifted back to Emily and Kate. Now, she was a nice woman, that Kate. A good person. He hoped Emily would do right by her and make her a full partner once they reached St. Louis. He wished Kate Dawson only the best.

Cocheta had run off with Breaker Joe the night before the fire. Like every man who had ever set eyes on her, Jed harbored a twinge of regret that he didn't, couldn't, love her. It was a strange ache he didn't even know he had. Staring at such beauty was like staring into the sun, burning into his soul, despite his love for Lara. Cocheta had that effect on men, it seemed. And now Breaker Joe was holding her in his arms somewhere in Wyoming, keeping her supple body warm on a cool night and thanking God above for the honor. And every other man in Texas was aching and empty and didn't know why.

JED THOUGHT OF OLD PEG and smiled. If any woman deserved to be loved and cherished, it was her. Such loss. Such redemption. And who would have ever thought she would find romance again in the company of that oak tree of a man! Shorty would cherish her forever, and he hoped Peg would find the time to write back to those left behind in Breyer and tell them all about the new life they started in Nebraska.

And then there was little Molly Brewster. Molly with the sweet smile, the auburn hair, and a voice that sounded like a harp. Already the waters of Breyer's judgment had receded, and the townsfolk spent some energy forgetting all about Molly's past and letting her rest in the bosom of the Snow family with baby Willie. Every Sunday she walked into church with Clarisse and William and met with the smiles of Breyer's respectable citizens. It did his heart good to think that Breyer had enough gumption to welcome her as one of its own. Sometimes, if you were lucky, life could work out well.

That afternoon, back in his office, Jed unlocked the safe and withdrew the letters between Andy and Emily. Then he walked over to the door and locked it. In the room's corner was an old potbelly stove with a tarnished coffeepot that produced a drink as thick as tar. Inside the stove, a few embers fought to stay alive.

Jed poured a finger's width of whiskey into a tin cup and sipped. It slid down his throat like sin and hit his belly with a vengeance. Wiping his mouth, he pulled up a chair and sat before the stove.

One by one, Thornton fed the letters into the fire, watching as the famished embers licked at the paper, then devoured each sheet as they curled into wisps and burst into flames. He poked at the smoldering ruins until every shred of evidence had disappeared into ash, then sat by the fire with his head down, praying for forgiveness.

RAISING CANE

PREACHER GREEN LOOKED OUT AT his congregation
and counted heads. Fifty-three souls this Sunday. Not a bad
turnout. Enthusiasm bubbled up from his ample belly and spread
across his florid face. Today he planned to shake them up with
his homily. Maybe scare them a bit. Mostly, though, he wanted
to provide them comfort. He felt strangely connected to his flock.
James Green was protective of them, and of Breyer. Sometimes
it seemed as though the whole town was dancing with the devil,
which worried him. *Good people could turn into sinners at the drop
of a hat*, he thought. *It was so easy to sin. And so hard to redeem one's
soul.*

Today, fifty-three people shifted restlessly on the hard pews.
Jed Thornton and his wife and daughters sat in the back row, as
always. The pastor watched for signs that the sheriff was nodding
off. It irked him that Jed napped each Sunday. He raised his voice
sharply, and Thornton's eyes popped open. Green enjoyed a
tingle of satisfaction.

Several people gazed out the window with interest. A few
poked at each other and pointed. One little boy left his mother's

side and walked over to the windowsill and pressed his nose to the glass.

The sky to the east was darkening. Clouds rode a brisk wind across the blue canvas, slashing across the usual calm and dependable sunshine, threatening rain. The pastor figured it would likely rain out where it was, carrying only a stiff breeze with fresh scents into town, and hopefully, washing clean the souls of his congregation. He stood tall at the podium, and in his finest voice, preached to the fine folks of Breyer.

The crows lifted as one from the cemetery and flew into a large cottonwood tree, roosting in the middle of the morning as though it were night.

Jed Thornton stretched his aching legs out in front of him. Preacher Green was in fine form. It didn't sound like he was going to wind down anytime soon. People wiggled in their seats and children whined. His own family was fidgety. Thornton was glad they always sat in the last pew. Even though Jed had come today to pray for his mistakes, his mind danced from one thought to another like sand drifts in the desert.

Finally, the service ended. The congregation rose and headed for the door and freedom. By now, the clouds looked ominous. The ranchers' families didn't linger to talk but scrambled into their buggies and left for home.

The Thorntons were halfway down Main Street when Doc Winters called out.

"Jed! A moment here?"

Jed waved at the doctor. "How are things this morning, Doc?"

The little man scurried up to the Thorntons. He nodded at Lara and the girls.

"If we can talk for a moment? I need to speak to you about The Crow Fly. I'm afraid we found some remains."

Lara drew her breath in sharply and gathered her daughters close.

Jed kissed her on the forehead.

"Run along, darlin'," he said. "I won't be here but a few minutes. Then I'll join you and the girls for dinner."

Lara nodded and walked across the rutted road with Nan and Beth toward home. Jed longed to go with her. It was a perfect day for resting. The saloons weren't open and the dreary sky cloyed at his brain, sapping him of energy.

Sighing, Jed turned to the doctor. "So, you finally found a body. Was it Confort?"

The doctor nodded, his gray eyes solemn. He adjusted his glasses. Jed thought he looked like an old bobcat, small and quick moving, with tufts of hair coming out of his ears. "Yep, the body was upstairs, right where Peg last saw him that night. There aren't a lot of remains. Bits of clothing, bones, and his skull. Enough to identify him." He picked at his thumb, then drew a pen knife out of his pocket and cleaned his fingernail. "Until next of kin are located, we placed the charred remains in a small pine box and we'll bury it in the graveyard. The smithy will make a cross with his name on it. It's the least we can do."

"Mighty nice of you," Jed said. "Now that I know that he's truly deceased, I'll go up to his house and poke around. Maybe there's some information up there. I think his cook is still around, and the groom at the stables." He frowned. "It appears the others left as soon as Confort went missing. Guess they figured they needed to find work elsewhere."

He turned toward home when Doc spoke again, freezing Jed in his tracks.

"I have to tell you more bad news. It was Confort all right. Even though most of his clothes were in ashes, his gold pocket watch was still intact in a charred waistcoat." The doctor shuddered. "It must have been a very painful death." Then he touched Thornton's shoulder.

"But, there's more. The thing is, Confort likely didn't die by fire."

"What are you saying, Doc?"

"There's no soft way to say this. Someone bashed his skull in. I suspect from his walking stick. The cane was a foot or so away. Most of it's gone, burned up, but the silver head remained. The size of it matches the break in his skull. He was no doubt murdered. He sure didn't do it to himself."

Thornton closed his eyes. Another murder. That changed everything. *What gets into people?* he thought. What makes somebody so angry they'd kill another? No matter how long he worked as a lawman, he'd never understand the criminal mind, though he understood rage and passion, and he supposed that supplied a lot of motives for folks. Feelings could bubble up and simply boil over. First Big Andy, now Confort. Someone boiled over. Now he needed to find the heat source.

"Thanks, Doc. I'll come along shortly after supper and look at the remains before you bury them. Come to think of it, not sure you should even put 'em in the ground. I guess I'll take custody of them instead, as they are now part of an investigation. I'll fetch them later this afternoon."

The men shook hands and Doc walked over to the hotel for lunch. Jed turned toward home. He felt older than his years, a weariness that threatened to weigh him down and tether him to this brash and barren town. He looked up at the swollen sky, darkness swirling through the clouds and blocking the sun.

The Crow Fly was gone. So was Lyle Confort.

And, somewhere out there, was the killer.

THE WINDS OF CHANGE

IT WAS A RARE STORM that hit Breyer that afternoon. Petulant clouds fought their way across the vast flatness of Texas and rained on Breyer in a way the town had never seen before. It pummeled the houses and screamed down the chimneys. The train tracks were slick with mud, and old Gus wondered if the mighty engine would derail as it made its way into town. When it slid into the station, two men got off and scurried into the depot, wet to the bone. The train pulled out again in a hurry, chugging away from the storm.

Animals huddled under bushes, and birds fought their way into tree branches, where they fluffed their feathers and tucked beaks under wings.

The arroyos filled with water that sluiced past town on its way to somewhere better.

Main Street flooded with rivulets of water and mud. A few rattlesnakes swam by, pulled out of their holes by the river of rain. Tumbleweeds brushed up against storefronts, broken and sodden, no longer making their merry way through town.

In the graveyard near the edge of town, a few crosses shifted in the wet earth and fell over.

The vacant space where The Crow Fly once stood filled with water, washing away any clues about the murder of Lyle Confort.

When the wind whistled through the scorched and rotting boards, some folks swore they heard the tinny echo of a piano and phantom voices. Maybe the voices were ghosts, they said. Someone moaning to be free. Someone lookin' for his soul, only it had washed away with the rain.

Breyer held it all in its sleepy arms throughout the night, then went about the business of drying itself off.

By the next day, the sun was out, drying the earth until it cracked in exasperation. People swept away the tumbleweeds and debris and tried to set the town straight.

But something had shifted, just like the soil. Breyer slumped in the harsh light of day, struggling to regain her balance.

Jed Thornton sat with his hands clasped on the desk in his office. *This time,* he thought, *this time I'll do it right.*

The sheriff tossed a list into the wastebasket, straightened, and walked over to the door. He buckled his pistols around his hips and yanked his Stetson off a hook.

"I know you're out there," he said to the unknown killer. "You murdered Lyle Confort. He probably deserved it. But it wasn't your privilege to take the law into your own hands. Rest assured, I'm going to find you. And this time I ain't letting you go. No matter who you are."

In the graveyard, the crows cackled among themselves. A light breeze ruffled their feathers as they hopped from one grave to another. Then they flapped their wings and rose into the lonesome Texas sky.

Another day in Breyer had begun.

THE END

ABOUT THE AUTHOR

Award winning author Sharon Frame Gay grew up a child of the highway, playing by the side of the road. Her work has been internationally published in over two hundred literary journals, magazines, and anthologies, and has won awards and recognition in several genres. She is the recipient of The Will Rogers Medallion in 2021 for Western short fiction.

Collections of her short stories, "Song of the Highway", "The Nomad Diner", and "The Wrong End of a Bullet" are available on Amazon.

Sharon lives between the mountains and the sea with her dog, Henry Goodheart.